*He felt so close to her, as if the two of them were the only people who mattered in the entire world.*

He tried to tell himself that this was just because of their isolation, because of what they'd shared over the past two days, but this didn't make sense or feel like the truth. There was more to it than that.

She was such a maddening woman, and her own worst enemy, asking herself all those complicated, angst-ridden, unnecessary questions about her life because for some reason the simple, necessary questions just scared her too much. He found it a compelling quality. It made him want to laugh at her and rescue her from herself at the same time.

*Shay, sweetheart, you don't have to live your life this way.*

And it reminded him of someone.

It reminded him of...himself.

Shoot!

Dear Reader,

All three of the heroes in my WANTED: OUTBACK
WIVES trilogy essentially have their own kingdom.
Callan's in *The Runaway and the Cattleman* is the most
rugged and spectacular. Brant's in *Princess in Disguise*
is probably the most lush and beautiful to the eyes of
a European-bred woman such as Princess Misha. But
Roscommon Downs, Dusty's kingdom in *Outback Baby,*
is the biggest and the richest. On paper, he's worth
millions of dollars but all his assets are tied up in his
land, his cattle, his machinery and the people who
work for him.

When wealth comes in the form of such a huge tract of
land, it's a responsibility more than an easy ride, and
it's not the kind of heritage he could easily turn his back
on. Does Shay Russell want him to? Could she possibly
embrace a lifestyle so totally different from the one she
grew up with? These are not easy questions for her to
answer. I hope you enjoy the multilayered journey that
she and Dusty make together, as well as a final glimpse
of Callan and Jacinda, and Misha and Brant.

Lilian Darcy

# OUTBACK BABY

## *LILIAN DARCY*

Silhouette®

SPECIAL EDITION®

Published by Silhouette Books

America's Publisher of Contemporary Romance

 **SILHOUETTE BOOKS**

ISBN-13: 978-0-373-24774-5
ISBN-10:   0-373-24774-5

OUTBACK BABY

Visit Silhouette Books at www.eHarlequin.com

**Printed in U.S.A.**

## Chapter One

The best way to get work done on an airplane was not to look out the window.

As always, Shay Russell had a ton of work to do, so she didn't look out the window once in three flights. Taking off from Sydney airport, she opened her laptop the moment the flight attendants announced that it was permitted, and barely took her eyes from the screen long enough to ask for coffee.

It came lukewarm, and was accompanied by the cookies she'd by this time learned to call *biscuits* when talking to Australians.

She was from New York.

She was busy.

She wished she didn't have to adapt her vocabulary to Australian conditions, even though she'd been here for a year. Half the TV here came direct from the U.S. Australians knew what the word *cookie* meant. Culturally, her

New York–based boss at *Today's Woman* magazine considered Australia to be the fifty-first state. He was wrong, as it happened, but she wished Australia would listen to him. It would make her job a lot easier.

Between Brisbane and a dot on the map called Charleville, she stayed focused on laptop, electronic organizer and handwritten notes. And on the mail plane's final hop to Roscommon Downs, she thought solely about her magazine's circulation figures until she felt the final dip of the descent.

The wheels had just touched down when she finally looked up to see the sun glinting on a wide stretch of silvery lake lapping almost to the edge of the airstrip.

Pretty.

Birds wheeled in a blue sky. Other birds splashed lacy arcs of water into the air as they landed on the lake and folded their wings. Some dark reddish brown cattle grazed on the thin stretch of grass between the airstrip and the water.

Very pretty.

She would take some photos of it, with the hopefully photogenic Dustin Tanner and his new fiancée, Mandy, smiling in the foreground. It might even make a good enough cover shot for the magazine. She was pushing the "Wanted: Outback Wives" campaign as hard as she could, but the shot would need to be pretty special.

As soon as the plane came to a halt, she hopped up out of her seat, impatient for the pilot to open the door and let her out. She was the only passenger, and hers was the only suitcase he had to unload. It was the small, efficient, wheeled kind, and she grabbed it from him saying a quick, "Thank you," and began to trundle it along the hard, damp clay of the airstrip toward the four-wheel-drive vehicle awaiting her.

"No worries, love," the pilot said in reply, apparently in as much of a hurry as she was.

Looking at the pretty lake—the pretty *big* lake—he pulled a couple of boxes from the bowels of the aircraft. He put them on the ground, waved at the man standing beside the vehicle, wrenched the cargo hatch closed and leaped straight back into his tiny cockpit.

While walking toward the waiting vehicle, Shay remembered a research detail she needed from her assistant for next week, and flipped her electronic organizer out of her jacket pocket to note it down in cryptic shorthand, keyed in with one hand. She'd gotten very good at that. Her stride stayed exactly the same.

Somebody passed her. A woman, heading for the plane. "Have fun," the short brunette said, but didn't stop.

"You, too," answered Shay, equally brief. She was still looking at the tiny screen in her hand.

Behind her, the airplane engines began to rise to a screaming state of readiness for takeoff. Ahead, a man in sunglasses, a gray polo shirt and jeans waited beside the four-wheel drive, as motionless as the trunk of a tree. It might be Dustin Tanner, but she wasn't sure because they'd only met once, months ago. She vaguely thought he'd had a couple of friends who'd also submitted their details for the "Wanted: Outback Wives" campaign. A guy with blue eyes, from South Australia? Callum? No, Callan. Or was she confusing both men with other people?

They'd had such a huge response from single farmers all over Australia, it was hardly surprising that she couldn't keep track. Even though Dustin had been pictured in the magazine at the beginning of the year, she'd retained no visual memory of him at all.

Reaching the solitary figure, she hedged her bets and simply stuck out her hand. "Shay Russell."

"Shay…" He muttered something under his breath. Then he swore. "The magazine!"

"That's right." She smiled. "We—"

"Met in Sydney, at the magazine cocktail party," he finished, to her relief. He flipped his sunglasses up and wiped his fingers across his eyes before dropping the dark lenses back into place. "That's a while ago."

"Yes. Yes, it is," she agreed.

So this tall, dark, strongly built stranger was indeed Dustin. Good. There need be no more fear of awkward misunderstandings if he had turned out to be a ranch hand, or whatever they called them out here.

Shay switched at once into professional-gush mode, at the same time remembering with the unused portion of her brain that there was something else she needed Sonya to research for her in Sydney. Would she be able to e-mail or phone from here?

"Thanks so much for agreeing to a follow-up story, Dustin."

"Call me Dusty, but the thing is—"

"Dusty. We are so excited about the whole thing. An engagement, with the wedding date already set! It's wonderful. It will thrill our readers, to find out that our campaign has had some success stories so quickly." She hated gushing. He didn't seem too impressed by it, either, so she stopped and switched tack. "Um, can I put my bag in the back or something?"

Fifty yards away, she heard the plane begin to taxi along the red dirt runway. The engine speed seemed particularly high and the noise made talking difficult.

"I'm sorry?" His strongly drawn face wore a blank expression.

"Put—my—bag—in—the—back," she yelled.

"But…didn't you see her?" He still looked blank. His not-too-full, not-too-thin bottom lip dropped open, showing even white teeth.

"No, I said—" she began, even louder.

He cut her off. "I'm talking about the engagement. It's off. It's only just happened." He wiped his eyes with his fingers again, this time barely troubling to push the sunglasses out of the way. "That's her. You spoke. Didn't she say?" He pointed over her shoulder.

Shay turned, followed his gesturing arm and saw the plane's wheels just leaving the ground. The airstrip shimmered with what looked like a desert mirage. Dusty swore again.

*"Her?"* she echoed. "Mandy? Your fiancée? In the plane? As in…leaving?"

"Right. Ex-fiancée. It's over. She's not coming back."

Shay looked helplessly at her surroundings—at the damp airstrip, at the flat horizon, at that really quite enormous lake. It appeared to spread around to the opposite side of the airstrip as well, which made the airstrip's location an odd choice. It was more like an island than an airfield.

"The engagement is over?" she clarified to Dusty, just in case she'd still gotten it wrong, because—because—

Oh, hell!

"Yes," he said, and walked past her to pick up the boxes that the pilot had left on the ground.

As he came back in her direction a few moments later, carrying the boxes, she looked at him more closely.

Hmm.

She wasn't surprised that Mandy had gone.

Or maybe he only looked like this *because* Mandy had gone. He was rigid with suppressed emotion, and there were lines of stress folded into deep grooves at the corners of his nicely shaped mouth.

He had an ancient felt hat wadded into one hand, and hair that could do with a good brush. His polo shirt was untucked on one side, but he'd pushed it too tight into the waistband of his jeans on the other. She had an out-of-character maternal impulse to fix his clothing.

Was it maternal? There was a sudden kick of awareness inside her that in better circumstances he might actually be a very good-looking man, the kind to appeal to a very different set of female instincts. He had a great facial bone structure, an impressively tight, hard stomach and not an ounce of fat on his entire frame, but, maternal impulse or not, she'd have to tactfully persuade him to tidy up a little before—

Before the photos for the magazine story?

Shoot!

Triple shoot!

The realization ambushed her again. Her story was dead.

She had personally introduced this couple, Dustin and Mandy, at the cocktail party in February that had launched phase two of *Today's Woman* magazine's "Wanted: Outback Wives" campaign. They had apparently hit it off at once. They'd spent most of the evening together, and had started e-mailing and calling each other as soon as Dustin had returned to Roscommon Downs.

He had come down to Sydney to see Mandy and she had come up here to see him. They had fallen in love with satisfying speed. Dustin had proposed. Mandy had accepted and had called Shay, all tearful and excited, to announce the news and ask if Shay wanted to do a follow-up story. The woman had displayed a naked hunger for the publicity, but Shay wanted the story anyhow.

And now Mandy had called off the whole thing.

It hit Shay like a blow to the stomach.

She'd come all this way…time out of her schedule… forcible separation from her office space…extra expenses to justify…for nothing. Her hair was already turning to frizz in the lake-induced humidity. And for some incomprehensible reason, neither Dusty nor Mandy had managed to tell her not to come before she'd gotten here.

She opened her mouth and took a big breath, ready to cut her losses and launch into some rapid-fire questions about getting away again—ASAP. The plane with Mandy in it had already taken off, which was an incredible nuisance. When was the next mail flight? Shay had been scheduled to leave tomorrow afternoon, but if she could go very first thing in the morning instead, she wouldn't have wasted a totally timetable-crippling, career-scuttling, nervous breakdown–inducing amount of time on this fiasco of a romance.

But then something stopped her from speaking—a sudden rush of intuition and understanding that was the equivalent of someone clapping their hand across her mouth to prevent her foot from shoving itself in.

*Dusty is feeling really bad about this,* she realized.

*Gutted,* as Australians said. That was why he had failed to clarify the situation in time.

Shay would have to possess the hide of a rhino and the tact of a flea to pester him about flight schedules right now.

"I'm sorry, this is bad timing, isn't it?" she said. He'd put the boxes in the back of the four-wheel drive and pushed his sunglasses up again. He had incredible eyes, the color of deep pools of warm brandy, and his eyes were suffering. His mouth said he was trying not to let it show, but the eyes were winning. "To have me show up like this? I'm sure you'd rather be alone."

"Uh, yeah. It's okay." His mouth barely moved as he spoke. His square jaw looked as if someone had wired it shut.

"Well, no. It's not okay. I've been there. I know." It was the same for everyone, wasn't it? "You want to lick your wounds and eat junk food."

"Junk food?"

"Yeah, fat, salt and chocolate. A broken heart is *the* best flavor enhancer."

He didn't smile. They were strangers, and he wasn't ready. She thought she could see a chink of vulnerability inside him like hot lava behind the cracking seam in a rock. He was deeply uncomfortable about it, too. He wore the vulnerability like boots that didn't fit.

Meanwhile, she'd triggered too many of her own bad memories.

She remembered the weight she'd put on two years ago, and only just managed to lose again, after her most recent, should-have-been-perfect-for-her art museum curator boyfriend Adam had intellectualized his way out of their relationship. He'd fed her all this stuff about "meetings of the mind" and "fractured perceptions" that she'd tried so hard to understand, but no longer bought for a second.

Her discovery two weeks later that he had already been sleeping with someone else had something to do with her change in attitude. She'd been so hurt, and then so angry. She'd buried herself in work even more than usual because success was definitely the best path to recovery. She hadn't been out with anyone since, and that was just fine.

Once bitten, twice shy.

Or in her case, three times bitten, shy until further notice.

"Don't worry about the story for a minute," she said to him. "I'm really sorry. You said it only just happened?"

She wanted to touch him, give a sympathetic pat to his shoulder or arm—both body parts were so sturdy and well muscled—but managed not to. His body language screamed at her not to get that close, not to break down his rock-hard defenses with too much feminine understanding.

What did outback cattlemen do in this situation? They

couldn't stay up half the night crying over chocolate with their women friends, and wondering out loud and in great detail what they'd done wrong. They had to suffer in silence.

"She came out of the bedroom with her bags packed twenty minutes ago," he said. "I thought she was happy. I thought we both wanted the same things."

"So you haven't even been able to talk to each other about it?"

"There was nothing to say. This place *wasn't what she'd been expecting*, apparently." His tone placed bitter quotation marks around the words. "Once she'd said that, there was really nothing left to talk about." And he didn't look as if he wanted to talk about it now. His voice was rough and every word abrupt. It occurred to her that maybe he was always like this. "Look, we'd better head back to the house. And don't worry, I'll live."

He picked up her suitcase, heaved it in beside the boxes, closed the rear door, then came round to her side. He held the passenger door at a courteous angle, inviting her to slide into the high seat. She did so and, as she passed him, she became aware once again of what an impressive physique he had. The way he held himself, his whole body looked like carved sandstone.

"I won't trespass on your privacy any longer than I have to," she said.

She understood that she must be the last person Dustin Tanner wanted to be with because she could only remind him of Mandy and the way the two of them had met. And she was no less anxious to get out of here than he was to get rid of her. It gave them one thing in common, at least.

He came around to the driver's side, climbed in and started the engine.

"When's the next flight?" she asked.

"That's an interesting question," he growled. The vehicle idled as he looked sideways at her. There was an extra light of suffering emotion in the brandy-brown eyes. Impatience stretched to breaking point, she realized. "Notice the floodwater?"

The question brought her up short and she forgot about his broken heart. "The—? You mean the lake? Is it higher than—?"

He barked out a laugh. "This?" He gestured at the silvery expanse. "It's not a lake! It's Cooper's Creek, flooded nearly a hundred miles wide, and it's still rising. We've been pretty dry here, but they had several inches of rain in the headwaters of the Thomson River and the Barcoo. There've been flood warnings on the weather report for the Channel Country for days."

"Uh, right, but I tend to focus on the weather a little closer to where I live."

Like, the small amount of weather she could see from her apartment's bedroom window in Sydney. Even then she usually found it irrelevant. She spent most of her time in a high-rise office. There, the air was dry and the temperature stayed at around seventy degrees Fahrenheit all year round.

"And Grant didn't tell you?"

"Grant?"

"The pilot."

"We didn't talk much." Certainly not about weather. "I was working on my laptop."

"You must have seen how much of a hurry he was in to get out of here?"

"Well, yes, but…" She trailed off, feeling dumb and out of touch. For a journalist, she had failed to ask any of the right questions. "So—so the next flight might not be until…" She hazarded a guess. "…The day after tomorrow?"

The vehicle started moving. Dusty looped it in an arc so he could head back the way he'd come. He pointed across Shay's line of sight, to the far end of the airstrip, above which the airplane taking Mandy away was still visible, hanging like a baby's crib mobile in the yawning blue sky. "See that?" He wasn't pointing at the plane.

"Oh—my—lord," she whispered. What she'd seen in the distance as the plane had taken off had not been a desert mirage. She could see it much more clearly now. The lake had invaded a third of the airstrip in a silent silver tide, visibly higher than it had been when the plane had first landed.

"The flood peak is still to come. The water's rising fast. The airstrip could be out of action for as long as three weeks."

"Three *weeks?*"

"Even when the water goes down, it's hard to take off if your wheels are stuck in thirty centimeters of mud. It'll need regrading before it's any use."

"So—so I'd have to take a bus?" Surely the public roads would be better maintained and more sensibly located than this ill-thought private airstrip.

"You think there's a bus out here?" A smile flickered and died on his face.

She knew he was feeling bad, that he had a broken heart and needed kid-glove treatment, but this time the words came anyway. "Okay. There's no plane. There's no bus. I get that. And I don't suppose there's a boat." Her voice rose to a frustrated yell. "So will you just damn well stop making me feel like an idiot and tell me how I am going to get out of here?"

She wasn't.

Unbelievable.

Short of chartering a helicopter, which Dusty mentioned but she knew would run to, probably, a thousand dollars an hour, it appeared she was stuck. Roads were awash, low bridges were under two meters of water, cattle were being moved urgently to higher ground.

According to Dusty—his name should have been Muddy—people were stranded in way less comfortable circumstances than they were here at Roscommon Downs, so she had no right to complain. Even though she was only here thanks to him and Mandy in the first place, he seemed to feel that she should count herself lucky, and grateful.

"We have plenty of food and water, and plenty of room," he told her. "There's enough high ground for the stock, most have been moved already, and we have enough manpower on the ground to move the rest, so we've got no choppers coming in. No emergency service is going to make you a priority, I'm sorry, so if you want a flight out of here, yes, you'll have to hire a private one and pay for it yourself. If there's one available."

"You could have told me this before I got here! You could have told me before the damned plane left!"

"I would have thought you might see news reports on the flooding, realize it was risky and not show up. To be honest, I'd totally forgotten you were coming until you got here, and even then it didn't click until you said your name."

"But Sonya confirmed—"

"Sonya spoke to Mandy," he cut in.

"Mandy—"

"Wanted the story and her picture in the magazine, even if she didn't want the engagement. I had no idea she'd confirmed your visit. I've been pretty busy."

"Sounds like you weren't talking to each other much."

"Apparently. I didn't notice."

"You didn't *notice?*"

"I hate those kinds of games. If she had problems, she should have said something straight out, not tried to manipulate me into asking what was wrong."

Silence.

Shay didn't know what to say.

Finally, she ventured, "So it'll probably be for…?"

"A couple of weeks. It depends on whether there's any more rain. If we had a medical emergency, you might be able to hitch a ride out on a rescue helicopter. Our boreman's wife has a baby due in four weeks."

So what was he suggesting? That she give the woman curry and strong drink to bring the birth on early?

*Maybe I could find a hunting gun and shoot myself in the foot….*

For a moment, Shay almost considered the idea.

*You know, it could work….*

Just a flesh wound. Something that would require evacuation and qualified medical intervention but wouldn't threaten her life. Something that would allow her to use her laptop in the hospital and would leave her free of scars.

*Perfect. I'm contemplating a bullet to protect my career.*

Her boss would probably expect no less.

She gave a half-hysterical hiccup and tried to think about what being stuck here for two weeks would actually mean. For a start, would her boss in New York believe her, or would he think it was merely a thin cover story for a personal crisis of some kind? Tom Radcliff was notoriously unsympathetic to any senior personnel with time-consuming private lives.

The Australian edition of *Today's Woman* had launched ten months ago, and Shay had been promoted to editor-in-chief, flown to Sydney ahead of the launch and put in charge—partly because she showed no evidence of having a private life at all. So far, the promotion was not an enhancement to her résumé. Circulation figures had been disappointing. Shay had her theories about why, but Tom didn't want to hear them.

Recently, the series of articles centered around their campaign to match lonely farmers with willing women had shown the promise of paying off. The story Shay herself had tracked down and written for the June issue was particularly strong, she thought. City-bred European-American girl falls in love with good-looking Aussie sheep farmer. Brant and Michelle—"But please call me Mish"—made a gorgeous yet down-to-earth couple.

Was this kind of story strong enough? Her boss only ever revealed the hard numbers on his own timetable—one that was designed to keep his staff under maximum stress—so she couldn't know for sure.

She had pushed hard for the whole "Wanted: Outback Wives" idea, and she needed it to pay off, and soon, or Tom would pull her back to the U.S. He would put her on *Boring Hobbies Monthly* or *Make Your Own Plumbing Fixtures* or one of the other dry yet solidly successful special-interest magazines that were part of the Shieldpress Corporation's publishing stable, and her climb up the ladder would effectively end.

She'd fought hard for her career and she wanted it.

Really wanted it.

Didn't want that horrible realization she'd seen happen to other people that somehow you'd missed the boat, taken a wrong turn, been sidelined or overtaken or promoted sideways and everyone else had seen the writing on the wall before you had.

Absolutely did not want to run into Adam—or Jason, or Todd—in the lobby of Carnegie Hall and have to say to them, "Me? My career? Oh, I'm editing the women's pages of *Gun Dealer News* now."

Her hunger to feel like a success snapped at her heels like a wild dog. It woke her every morning at dawn with a sick feeling in her stomach and chased her late into the night. It had her eating take-out meals in front of her computer and yelling at dumb ideas in meetings, and only getting as much work as she did out of her staff because she herself so clearly put in way more than they did.

To sell *Today's Woman* to the Australian market, she needed top international celebrity gossip, a good astrologist for Your Stars, some lifestyle and cooking, a couple of thought-provoking articles, and heartwarming *local* human interest, and she had to get it right, which was why she'd chased this romantic outback-engagement story herself instead of leaving it in the hands of more junior staff.

Now, as well as wasting her time, she was stuck.

Through the front window, she saw water spreading across the track ahead, and asked Dusty Tanner, "Where are we headed?"

"To the main homestead."

"Will we make it? Or would we be better off in a submarine?"

"This is the last stretch of low-lying ground."

"The whole place seems like low-lying ground, to me. Why have a cattle ranch—I mean, station—" she corrected herself. *Biscuit* versus *cookie, station* versus *ranch*; why did Australians have to invent new, non-American words for everything? "On flood-prone land?"

"Because it's just about the best natural fattening country on the planet."

"When it's not flooded," she pointed out.

"You've struck it lucky. It doesn't flood this bad every season. This is the first time we've had the airstrip under water in four years."

"Well, aren't I just so fortunate?"

They didn't like each other.

The fact was suddenly apparent to both of them and magnified by the close confines of the vehicle. Something coalesced in the air like perfumed smoke and made Shay's stomach jump. She stabbed her finger on the window button and it lowered with a hum, bringing the scent of grass, mud and rain, but doing nothing for her sudden claustrophobia.

Dusty's strong arms worked the steering wheel back and forth as he avoided more water on the road. The movement brought his elbow too far into her body space. He had one of those big, manly arms that Shay had seen in gyms, and she'd never liked men who made too much of their physical strength. She liked her males civilized, intellectual and good-mannered.

Maybe Dusty would be good-mannered enough to pick up on her desire for silence and respect it.

Nope.

"You'll be okay," he said. "We'll make the best of it."

"Thanks. Do you have any evidence for those claims?"

"Maybe if I told you a bit about the place," he said.

"Sure. If you think it will help." She could see a large cluster of buildings and greenery near the top of a low rise. Behind the buildings, probably a couple of miles away, rocky cliffs rose above the flood plain, looking hardly more substantial than a garden wall.

"Well, for a start, it's big, almost half a million hectares."

"I'd like to be impressed, but you'll have to translate."

"One point two-five million acres."

"Now I'm impressed." She knew she sounded insincere. Over a million acres? Huge, but just a number, and the only number she wanted to hear right now was an accurate estimate on how many hours before she could get out of here.

"Many of these places are owned by international agribusiness," Dusty said. "They have a whole slew of properties scattered all over the country, and put in a manager on each one. But we've managed to keep Roscommon Downs in the family since my great grandfather's time. My dad's health has failed a bit, so my parents have moved to Longreach, which is our nearest decent-size town."

Shay pricked up her ears. "Oh, yes?"

Walking distance? Or better make that *wading* distance.

He must have read her mind. "Three hundred and sixty kilometers from here, a lot of it under water."

She did a quick conversion in her head. Over two hundred and twenty miles. She'd die before she got there. Literally.

"We have a good staff, eleven people not counting me," he went on, as if he hadn't just completely broken her spirit with the news about Longreach.

"That many?" This surprised her.

"We're almost a village. Twenty-five people. We have married couples, and kids, a governess running a school. She has six students this year."

A few of the shattered pieces of her spirit glued themselves back together. Kids. A school. Other women. Small mercies, maybe, but a heck of a lot better than the kind of Robinson Crusoe scenario she'd begun to picture—herself stranded on a shrinking island in the floodwaters with what was very possibly the least civilized man she'd ever met, and one who seemed totally uninterested in helping her to get out of here.

"I'll look forward to getting to know them," she said weakly, wondering if any of them had a dinghy and knew how to row.

"Mandy didn't—" He stopped. "Uh, didn't."

Was this a recommendation that Shay shouldn't get to

know the station residents either? They reached the buildings. Nobody seemed to be around, which meant that she could focus on infrastructure instead of greetings. Climbing out, she assessed everything she could see.

There were several large sheds and a cluster of neat cottages. One larger dwelling looked more like a motel, with several doors opening onto a veranda and a couple of larger rooms at one end.

Dusty had parked in front of the main house—the homestead. Shay had been in Australia long enough to recognize the architectural style, even when it was surrounded by thick green shrubbery like this place. "This is the house," he said, stating the obvious as if it hurt him to get the words out.

It was a Queenslander—a single, sprawling level of living space, made of wood painted in soft pastel shades, surrounded by shady verandas, and built high on wooden stilts. The empty space beneath the house had been enclosed by pretty wooden lattice, but the stilts would allow cool breezes to circulate beneath.

And floodwaters? Would it keep them out, too?

Looking around, she decided they were on high enough ground to stay safe, even if the immense spread of water rose several meters higher.

Dusty grabbed her compact little suitcase, snapped the pull-along handle shut, ignored the option of wheeling it, and picked it up as if it weighed less than a bag of groceries. Possibly it did. She'd packed light. One complete change of clothing and an extra set of underwear for an emergency—which this officially now was. The underwear would have been more useful if it had had jet packs attached.

Most of the contents of her luggage consisted of short-story manuscripts submitted for the magazine's Good Read section. They'd had a contest recently: "Could You Be a Writer?" Unfortunately, about three hundred of the submissions had come from people who absolutely and utterly *couldn't*, but the stories in her suitcase belonged to the short list of thirty, which she and two junior editors would cull to five finalists before the winner was judged by a panel of professionals.

On the plus side, with all that reading she'd have something to do while she was here. On the minus side, she'd need to alternate her two outfits and wash one of them every night, and she'd left her styling wand and blow-dryer at home. By bedtime, she was going to look like Shirley Temple with her finger in a lightbulb socket.

"I could put you in the single men's quarters," Dusty told her with no hint of sarcasm, "but you'd probably be happier here."

They went up the half flight of wooden steps together, and Shay held her breath.

To her surprise, the place was beautiful. More lattice-work enclosed the veranda almost to waist height, making it feel like an airy extension of the house itself. The old wooden floorboards were stained a dark teak color and gleamed with varnish. The furnishings, both on the veranda and inside the house, had an Asian feel with big blue-and-white planter pots, and a couple of exquisite inlaid wooden cabinets, as well as regency-striped couches in dusty blue and cream that somehow matched the cool, clean atmosphere while almost begging Shay to sit down.

Following Dusty, she resisted the temptation. She'd have plenty of time to turn catatonic later on.

Passing the dining room, she saw a breakfront filled with Asian china and Italian glass, and on the walls there was a mixture of framed art that ranged from kids' draw-

ings dedicated in wobbly print *To Grandma* through to
what looked like original modern landscapes in oils.

Strangely enough, the effect was very appealing, and
she realized how cleverly the colors and themes of each
picture had been balanced. Whoever had decorated this
place—*Grandma* maybe?—had a great eye.

"But this is just lovely!" she exclaimed, sounding way
too surprised about it.

"Yeah, even though my mother took the best stuff with
her and Dad to Longreach," Dusty drawled, throwing Shay
a look that said he knew exactly what she'd pictured instead—corrugated iron walls flapping in the breeze, and
six-week-old dishes in the sink.

He led her to a bedroom that opened via French doors
onto the veranda and had a similar atmosphere of dark
wood and blue-and-white coloring. It was cool and quiet
and restful; it had a bathroom just across the corridor; it
had books, a ceiling fan and a rocking chair, and Shay
knew that as soon as Dusty told her where to plug in her
phone recharger and her laptop, she would feel about sixty
percent more fine about this whole thing than she'd believed possible ten minutes ago.

Except that she didn't.

She felt four hundred percent worse.

Because when she had her overnight bag on the bed and
her portable office up and running and Dusty had left her
alone, she discovered an urgent e-mail from Sonya, sent
about half an hour ago, just seconds after the final time
she'd checked her system on the plane.

*Crisis, Shay! Abort outback engagement story mission,
stat! Tom wants you in New York tomorrow!*

## Chapter Two

Dusty's unwanted guest stayed in her room for much longer than he'd expected.

He wasn't sure what to do about it.

It was a nuisance.

He had expected her to appear again, and he would have offered her tea or coffee and something to eat. He would have given her a towel and explained that the shower water would be hard to keep at the right temperature today because Wayne needed to bleed the air out of the pump. He would have said to make herself at home, and told her what time to show up in the dining room of the single men's quarters for the evening meal.

It was largely his fault that she hadn't gone straight back on the plane and saved them both this unwanted complication, but that didn't make him feel any more warmly toward her.

Now, thinking that she could appear at any moment, he

hung around, on edge. There were a hundred other things he could be doing, but he couldn't just leave the house. She was a guest, and around here you looked after your guests. Should he knock on her door? Write her a note?

He didn't want her here, didn't want to have to consider an impatient city-bred workaholic stranger's needs. The breakup with Mandy had been a gut-wrenching mess, and Shay-from-the-magazine's presence only reminded him about all the mistakes he'd made in the relationship from the very beginning. His whole system felt sour whenever he thought about it.

Hell, he was usually so sensible, so down-to-earth, but could he pick the right woman? Clearly not.

How could he have been so blinded by Mandy's apparent eagerness?

It wasn't even as if the chemistry between them had been that hot. This was one of the things he'd told himself in the moments when he'd allowed himself to have doubts. "I'm not rushing into this. I can tell, because it's not about lust." He knew a thing or two about lust. "And that's so often what makes people jump in too fast. This is solid. It's friendship and partnership and shared goals, and it's going to work."

He felt like an idiot. He knew that he had earned the respect of everyone who worked here for reasons that ran deeper than his degree of success with women, but all the same he didn't want Dave and Jane, or Prim and Letty, or Luke and Andy and Wayne talking about him and Mandy behind his back.

He wasn't hurt. He'd already discovered that, with a sort of numb surprise. But he felt empty, increasingly angry with himself, and deeply disappointed.

Putting the electric jug on to boil for a cup of coffee he didn't really want, he ran through the past four months again, and the mistakes remained on display in just the same unflattering light. He'd heard too much of what he'd wanted to hear from Mandy's lips. He'd seen too much of what he'd wanted to see in the way she'd behaved. He'd missed so many clues. Would he ever find a woman who played things straight?

"I *have* to get out of here!" said an American voice behind him. He hadn't heard her arrive in the kitchen doorway because of the rising noise of the water for his coffee coming to the boil.

He turned around, surprised at the intensity in her tone, to discover that her lips had gone white and she looked as if she might collapse onto the floor. "Are you okay?" he asked.

"I'm fine. Totally fine. I just have to get out of here," she repeated. "Tonight. I have to be on a flight out of Brisbane in the morning. I have to get to a critical meeting in New York."

"I thought we talked this through on the way here."

"Yes, but the situation's changed." She clenched her fists. Somehow, she must have found time to do something to her hair. It fluffed out around her face in bouncy corkscrews, and suited her better than the sleek dark chestnut curtain that he'd seen blowing in the breeze out at the airstrip.

"The floodwaters haven't," he pointed out to her. "Except that they're probably higher." The electric jug reached a final crescendo of bubbling and clicked off, adding emphasis to his statement.

"You said I could charter a helicopter."

"I said if there's one available. And do you know how much it would cost?"

"Yes. The earth. I'll just have to wear it."

She closed her eyes, as if embarking on a minute's silence in memory of her deceased bank account. Then she opened them again and he noticed their color for the first time—an electric jade that was too intense for his taste, even though it went very nicely with her creamy skin and that hair—almost the same color as his cattle. She was the kind of woman who didn't know when to stop, never looked back to see who she'd trampled on, and had no idea of the way life worked in a place like this.

"Tell me who to call," she commanded him.

"It's four in the afternoon," he pointed out.

"I know. That's why I'm giving out this slight sense of urgency, Dusty." The sarcasm cut like a blunt bread knife. They didn't like each other much. She thought he was an insensitive brute, and he *knew* she was a power-hungry careerist with tunnel vision and no life. "You said you use helicopters for mustering."

"The company we use is based two hours' flying time away."

"But they'd take on private charters, surely. Where would they fly me to?" She took an agitated step toward him, glaring her impatience for his answers. She was pretty tall. Had to be around five-ten, which meant that even though he was over six feet on the old scale, she could look him almost straight in the eye.

"Depends where your flight to Brisbane leaves from. Longreach or Charleville," he said.

"I haven't made a reservation, yet. Longreach or Charleville? I'll get on the phone now." She'd already begun to move.

"There won't be any flights leaving late enough for you to get to Brisbane today." He shouldn't be enjoying this, but a part of him was—the same part of him that was still angry about Mandy, and the part of him that suddenly felt very sorry for anyone who had to work for Shay Russell.

She was so melodramatic, so clueless, so alien to the pace of life out here. Her eyes had narrowed, reducing the bright jade color to two thin chips, and if, out at the airstrip, she had seemed to have at least some idea of what a tough day this had been for him, she'd clearly forgotten about it now. "I *have* to—"

"Look," he told her patiently, "even if you can get a hired chopper to leave the ground at its home base in the next half hour, which is unlikely, you can't possibly get to Longreach or Charleville before nine tonight, and there are no flights at that hour."

"The chopper can take me all the way to Brisbane."

"Yeah? It's over eight hundred miles. At least eight hours, even in a fast machine like a Robinson R22, plus refueling. And it leaves out the issue of night flying, and the fact that every available pilot's going to be booked solid, locating herds and pushing them to higher ground. What time's your flight out of Brisbane tomorrow?"

"I haven't booked that yet, either."

"O-kay." It was like talking to a spoiled child. Any minute she'd start stomping her feet.

In the back of his mind niggled the thought that he might have a better chance of getting her out of here in a chopper than she would if she simply called charter companies cold. He had favors he could call in, and everyone knew the Tanner family.

He weighed his options. It was no contest, really. Getting thousands of cattle to safety, versus getting a workaholic American magazine journalist to some meeting in New York. In the past he'd seen the bloated carcasses of cattle who'd died in floods. The cattle had to come first.

"That flying doctor service you talked about…" she began, her desperation like a magnetic field.

This time, he just looked at her.

"So I'm going to lose my job," she muttered, her shoulders sagging and her lips numb as well as white.

"If your job requires meeting impossible expectations like getting from here to New York in twenty-four hours, personally, I'd have ditched it long ago."

At this point, she lost it. Color flooded into her face in two bright pink blobs. Her eyes darkened. She was shaking.

"What qualifies you to say that?" Her voice rose, tight and strident. "You have no right to make judgments about my life. I shouldn't be here at all! If you didn't know this time a week ago that your relationship with Mandy was in trouble, then what the hell is wrong with you?"

He flinched. "You're right. I should have known about Mandy. Believe me, though, if I could get rid of you, I would."

"Do you have any idea how much trouble you'd have saved me if you'd had an atom of perception about how your supposed fiancée was feeling—"

Yes. He did. He'd have saved himself just a bit of it, also.

"—before she had to spell it out in words of one syllable?"

He flinched again. She'd made him feel like a fool, despite the good brain he knew he possessed. "Look, do we have to talk about it?"

"We have to work out how I'm going to get out of this place!" she yelled. "It is absolutely critical that I am not stuck here for two weeks! Or even for two *days!* And I really do not think it is too much to ask for a little help from you, a local, in working out how I'm going to achieve that! Do you understand, or do I have to say it all over again?"

She put her shaking hand up to her throat, as if she'd strained her vocal cords. To give her the benefit of the doubt, maybe she didn't yell at people like this every day.

Still, Dusty had had enough.

"You've said all you need to say," he told her quietly, already on his way out the door. "Help yourself to anything in the kitchen. We have cattle to take care of. I need to talk to my head stockman, my grader operator, my boreman and my cook." He mentioned the erratic hot water delivery in the shower. "And dinner's at seven, in the single men's quarters. I'll see you then, and you can tell me what you've arranged."

"If I've—"

He cut her off to drawl, "I'll be on the edge of my seat about it, let me tell you, because I can already feel the spin of the earth slowing down without you there in the center of it all, turning the handle."

"Tell Tom I can't," Shay e-mailed Sonya, feeling sick. "It'll be two days at the earliest."

And that would only happen if she spent around twelve thousand dollars of her own money on helicopter hire, which was more than likely not available given the flood situation, then hit up her expense account at the magazine for a first-class ticket between Brisbane and New York, and flew via Tokyo.

Her head ached and her cheeks burned. So did the spot in her spine that always began to sting when she'd spent too long in front of a computer screen or hunched over a laptop. She'd yelled at a near stranger, and they'd both been pretty damned rude to each other. The fresh memories disturbed her, and she faced the prospect of dealing with him again very soon.

Dealing with him, maybe, for weeks.

She thought about putting a positive spin on the delay, and typed, *I am chasing a great outback human-interest story.* She looked at the words on the screen for about twelve seconds and then deleted them. They sounded lame and deluded.

Tom was testing her. Or maybe it was a power game, something that rode right over everyone else's interests. Either way, she could have found a story that involved a two-year-old saving his mother's life by riding three hundred miles on the back of the family dog and getting rescued by a Hollywood movie star on the way, and Tom wouldn't care.

Okay, no, with the Hollywood movie star he'd care, but if it was just the family dog and the three hundred miles, forget it.

She briefly wished that she worked for the kind of magazine where you just made stuff up, and the more sensational the better. But no, typically, she had somehow saddled herself with standards. How sad.

She actually believed in the value of what she did. She wanted to give the readership of *Today's Woman* an uplifting, well-researched, entertaining, *true* story. She loved the idea that lonely outback farmers might find lasting love because they'd had the courage to put their faces and their stories in a national magazine. Blue-eyed widower Callan, Luke with his award-winning Tasmanian cheeses, good-looking Brant, shy Dale from Victoria, who rose every morning at four to milk his dairy herd. They'd all put themselves and their hearts on the line.

She wanted to make a difference in people's lives, even if it was only to have them think, *Hey, maybe something like that could happen to me, if I just made a couple of changes.*

*Get back to me TODAY if Tom still wants me to come,* she finished to her assistant, then hit Send.

Plotting the time difference, she realized that there was no way Sonya would get an answer from Tom today. It was getting on for seven in the evening, which meant nearly five in the morning in New York. Tom was a night owl. He must have been working into the early hours to have summoned her for the alleged crisis meeting three and a half hours ago, but even he wouldn't still be at his desk making dictatorial phone calls at this hour. Neither would Sonya, in Sydney.

She slumped her forehead onto the laptop keyboard, lifting it after several seconds to discover five lines of the letter *U,* keyed in by her right eyebrow. She'd have to call Tom at home, drag him out of sleep and say to him point-blank, "This is what I'd have to do to get to New York— in fact, to get out of here at all. Do you want me to do it?"

Sick to her stomach, she went to the phone in the kitchen that she'd already used to call airline companies. It was Dusty's private landline. There was no cell-phone service out here.

Her boss picked up on the third ring, sounding scratchy and half-asleep. It wasn't a long call. He wanted her in New York, without excuses. She then called every helicopter company she could identify within a radius of several hundred miles and heard all their answering machine messages. All over southwest Queensland, stranded motorists were being rescued, stock were being moved to higher ground, and busy helicopter pilots weren't picking up their phones.

Dusty was right.

She appeared to be stuck.

Leaning against the kitchen wall next to the phone, sipping some tap water, she felt light-headed, drained and empty inside, the whole meaning of her life reduced to two questions. How possible was it for her to get out of here? And as Dusty had so sarcastically suggested, what, exactly, would grind to a halt in the universe if she didn't?

Shay had no idea how to answer either of them.

"Dinner's on," the man himself said from the kitchen doorway.

"I'm not hungry," she told him automatically, wanting

to take as little from him as she possibly could. Truth be told, she was a little embarrassed that she'd lost her cool with him so thoroughly, earlier.

She straightened, tried to give a polite smile, and fought a sensation that the room was spinning. Her head was really burning now. All she'd eaten today were those cookies on the plane, and all she'd drunk was the coffee.

But she was used to that kind of thing.

Her body could take it.

Normally.

A couple of headache pills would help.

"How about if I arrange to have it delivered to your desk on a wheeled trolley with pre-warmed plates and covers on all the dishes?" Dusty suggested.

"Oh, you could—?" she began eagerly, then stopped.

Do that for me?

No.

He was teasing her.

If a dig so pointed and angry could be called a tease.

"I'll come over later, if I need to," she said coolly. "You go ahead." *Because then I won't have to walk across with you.*

He was clever, though, she had to admit. She hadn't seen it at first, but she could now. He didn't merely put her down; he trampled on her entire mind-set with every well-chosen word. She didn't like him, but she could still appreciate his brain.

He had stayed in the doorway, and she realized he was waiting for her, silently refusing to take no for an answer. Possibly because he'd seen that her knees were shaking. Maybe she was hungry, after all.

"I'll be there in a minute," she said, oddly grateful for his silent stubbornness. "I promise," she added.

"No, you'll be there with me. Take a minute if you

want, but I'll wait." He leaned his big shoulder against the doorjamb, to prove it.

"Why are you pushing this?"

"Because you look like you're going to pass out cold. And I'm not calling the flying doctor if you hit your head on the way down."

"I'll cross that strategy off my list, then."

"Yeah, it was pretty transparent."

"My choices are limited in that area."

"Sheesh, we're a crabby pair, aren't we?"

"Well, yes, since you're saying it without smiling."

"And I'm not going to apologize for it, either."

"What's for dinner?"

"I believe it's fillet steak with garlic sauce." He held his thumb and forefinger about an inch and a half apart to indicate the thickness of the steak. The odd feeling in her stomach was definitely a rumble. Her taste buds began to sing. She discovered she was starving. Was that a twinkle in his eye? Could he tell what the words *steak* and *garlic sauce* did to her? "Accompanied by Danish fried potatoes, seasonal vegetables, and peach cobbler and ice cream for dessert."

"I'd like to meet the other people on the station," she said.

"Yeah, they're not as crabby as me."

"But you're honest, I'll give you that."

"Point of pride."

"Honesty is good, but you want to be careful with pride. It's powerful stuff."

"You're right." He frowned, and she thought he was probably thinking about Mandy. Wretched woman.

"If you happened to have a headache pill or two, it might help."

"In the bathroom. Hang on a sec."

He came right back, holding out the two white pills. She'd already poured a glass of the tinny tap water she'd tried a short while ago. He watched her while she downed the pills in several gulps, then asked, "Going to be okay?"

"Hope so."

"That's what happens when you yell. And when you're the unfortunate mug who got saddled with being at the center of the known universe. Raises your blood pressure. Puts extra stress on the blood vessels in your skull."

"Thanks for that insight." There was no point in protesting that she considered herself quite a distance from the center of the universe already, and was desperately afraid that she'd one day end up in outer darkness. "I'll take it on board."

"My pleasure."

Without another word, he ushered her out of the kitchen, standing back to let her go ahead of him through the doorway, across the back veranda and down the steps. At the bottom, she tripped. The clumsiness was a combination of fatigue, poor vision in the sudden darkness, inappropriate shoes and her habitual impatience, and she wished it hadn't happened because he lunged up behind her and grabbed her elbow, throwing himself a little off balance as he did so.

For a moment, they clung together. His breathing went in and out with a slight rustling sound, as if he had his teeth clenched. He smelled as if he'd showered recently, although she hadn't heard him in the bathroom. It was a really good smell. Simple. Clean skin, damp hair, shampoo or some unusually nice kind of shaving cream.

"I'm fine," she insisted, before it was true. The ground seemed to tilt under her feet, even when her eyes said it was straight. "Really, I'm okay now." His grip hurt until she steadied herself further and the ground leveled again.

The air space between their bodies felt too warm. Finally, he let her go.

"Believe it or not, I actually do want you to get out of here alive, even if it's not today," he said.

"I'll look forward to proof of that claim."

"And I would like to continue this insightful conversation, but we're no longer alone."

Shay saw a male silhouette come through one of the motel-style doors in the building she and Dusty were heading toward. The large space at the end of the building was lit up and she could see some other figures moving around.

"What's the setup, can you tell me?" she asked. Her voice sounded wobbly. It was the headache. It had begun to shift into nausea, on top of the pain, and she hoped she'd taken the headache pills in time. She'd been having trouble with stress headaches lately, and if she got to the point where she threw up…she hated that. "You mentioned a cook."

She needed food.

Now.

"The families eat on their own, in their own places. Singles, living in the single staff quarters, get their meals cooked for them. At the moment that includes our pair of stockhands who got married to each other last year, as well as our bore-runner, gardener, governess and a couple of other stockmen. And Prim herself, of course."

"Prim?"

"Primrose McLintock. Our cook."

Two minutes later, Shay concluded that she'd never met a woman less like a Primrose in her life. No wonder everybody called her Prim, although this didn't suit her much better. She was about forty-five years old, round-bodied and red-faced, heavy-footed and hearty, and, if Shay's sense of smell could be trusted, she cooked like a dream.

She was also a voracious reader, it turned out. "Did my

new books show up?" she barked at Dusty. She served the meal cafeteria-style, with people lining up for their helpings then going to find a space at the big table.

"Already delivered," Dusty told her.

Instantly, he seemed different to the way he'd been with Shay in their interactions so far. This probably shouldn't have surprised her, but still it did. He held his body more easily. She was just as aware of its fitness and power, but it seemed more relaxed—a tool for hard work not intimidation. He greeted people with a word or a nod and, even though the atmosphere was casual, you would have known the moment you walked into the room that he was the boss.

"You weren't around," he went on to Prim, "so I shoved them inside the door. Give her a big helping," he added, thumbing in Shay's direction.

The food appeared on the plate, slap, splodge, splash, before Shay could protest and get the portions downsized to fit a sedentary urban lifestyle. Just the smell of it helped her stomach to settle, and if she could only get some of it into her in the next minute, she might just be okay.

Next to her, a wiry man named Andy said, "I finished that fine balance thing you lent me, Prim."

"Oh, you did?" The cook's face lit up. "Wasn't it amazing?" In an aside to Shay, she explained, "*A Fine Balance* by Rohinton Mistry. Fabulous book."

"The most depressing thing I've ever read in my life," Andy said.

"And yet, fabulous. Such a statement about hope." She filled Andy's plate generously.

"You know what, yeah, I could sort of see that. I didn't think I was ever going to get into it, but once I did, yeah, could hardly put it down, and you don't forget it. You should read it, Simone," he said to the young woman next in line.

She snorted. "I'm not a reader." Prim filled her plate.

"Prim'll get you in the end. She'll start you off easy with something light and funny, like those Bridget Jones books they made into movies, and she'll suck you in, and this time next year you'll be dragging your way through four hundred pages of poverty in India and thinking it's amazing."

"So shall we discuss it in reading group?" Prim said.

This time Andy did the snorting. "You are not getting me along to that damn women's group of yours, Prim."

"It's not a women's group. It's a reading group. We read books and we talk about them and gender is not an issue."

"It's a women's group. You and Letty and Jane and Marg and Bronwyn talk about the book for three minutes, then you get into the white wine and dessert, and talk about women's stuff."

"Get that plate a bit closer, Letty," Prim said to the next in line.

"Smaller piece of steak, Prim, thanks."

"Rubbish. You've been teaching all day, and then didn't I see you going for a ride? You need it."

Shay was seated opposite Dusty at the table by this time, holding her head together and her stomach in one place through sheer will. When Letty was satisfied with the size of her serving, she came to join them, with a hello and a smile. From Prim's comment about teaching, Shay guessed she was the governess. She looked to be about Shay's own age, give or take, and she had…oh, interesting detail…an artificial lower half to her left arm. Unselfconscious about it, she put down her plate, picked up her silverware and began to eat.

"Oh gosh, that's good," she said with her mouth full.

She spoke with an English accent, and had English-rose coloring—cornflower-blue eyes, delicate pink-and-white skin, and the shiny remnants of sunscreen slathered across her cheeks and nose. She started talking to Andy about the book he and Prim had discussed a minute ago, and Shay realized appreciatively that the governess was subtly drawing the young stockman into exactly the sort of book-group discussion he'd been so scathing about. She was probably an excellent teacher.

Shay's first thought about Letty was *Human-interest story potential*. Her second thought was *Escape ally*. And her third thought, quickly overtaking the other two and surprising her so much that she forgot to chew was *Friend*.

Friend?

Aware of Dusty's steady gaze angling in her direction every now and then, she considered the word and soon dismissed it.

She had all the friends she needed in New York. Good friends, and most of them in the same situation as she was. Busy. Ambitious. Ladders to climb. Glass ceilings to shatter. Career women's health problems to suffer in many cases, also. Stress-related stomach trouble, migraine headaches, debilitating menstrual cycles. Shay had been diagnosed with endometriosis a few years ago, and when she'd told Alicia, who traveled constantly as part of her work in international banking, Alicia had said, "Welcome to the club."

None of them had enough time for each other, so the friendship really existed between various cell-phone message systems, e-mail accounts and answering machines rather than between actual people. They had sporadic crisis meetings, rather than actually hanging out. Even her best friend, Sarah, who'd always cared about different things, was hard to pin down for some quality time now that she was a mom.

But they all moaned about it and laughed about it and it kept them in the same boat, so they had a lot in common, and Shay planned to pick up with her friends exactly as before when she got back to New York a couple of years from now. There was no reason to look for anything like that here at Roscommon Downs.

"I'm Shay," she said to Letty, and went back to the human-interest story potential. "Tell me what an English rose is doing in a place like this."

The meal lasted for three quarters of an hour and, by the end of it, Shay's headache and nausea had sneaked away without her noticing. Her stomach felt pleasantly full and the salty taste of the garlic sauce still lingered in her mouth. She felt different, and a heck of a lot better.

People had talked cattle business, told exaggerated anecdotes about previous flood experience on other properties, exchanged tips on which volume from Prim's extensive private library to try next. When Andy realized he'd been conned into having a book-group discussion, and that he had even nodded knowledgeably at the word *metaphor,* he scowled at Letty and Prim for a minute, then decided to laugh about it instead.

"You're gonna have me writing flippin' eight-page discussion papers next, Prim!"

Egos had to be both tough and relaxed around here, Shay guessed.

Everyone had reached the tea and coffee stage when she and Dusty left. He'd quietly asked her if she'd like to head back to the main house, and she was ready to go by this time, despite how much—and how unexpectedly—she'd enjoyed the meal.

She'd seen the respect he drew from his employees, and she'd noticed the way her gaze kept getting caught by his. They were too curious about each other and, if anything, the curiosity was heightened rather than lessened by the moments of open hostility between them earlier on. It felt weird.

"We've got coffee and tea in the kitchen," he told her. "Breakfast things, too, in the morning, although Prim does a great hot breakfast, if you want one. It's up to you."

Walking across the damp red earth between the two buildings, Shay took a deep breath and said to him, "Can we start again, do you think?"

"Start again?"

"I need to thank you."

"For dinner?" He glanced at her, and she wished she could see what his eyes were doing. Narrowing because he didn't trust her sincerity, probably. She couldn't blame him for that.

"For putting up with me. I've been incredibly rude today."

"So have I," he answered, blunt and easy.

She liked his voice, she realized—its pitch and its tone and its lazy speed. Her own was just a little softer and it hurt less in her throat when she told him, "But you had better reasons to be."

"Not sure about that. You were right, I should have jumped on Grant and got him to hold the plane five minutes for you. I should have thought straight away that you'd want to head back, once you'd heard the situation. I dropped the ball about that, and now you're stuck. I apologize."

"I'm calling helicopter charters again in the morning," she said, not sure if it was true.

How much was Tom Radcliff just yanking her chain? Did he really need her in New York for a meeting? Or was he only trying to remind her that she belonged to the magazine, and that her future was on the block? If circulation fell like a slicing guillotine, she was the one whose head would roll.

She could see her immediate future dividing into two distinct options, right in front of her. Respond to Tom's pressure and stay stressed and bad-tempered and antsy for as long as it took to make her expensive escape bid from Roscommon Downs? Or accept that she had little chance of getting out of here until the floodwaters receded and use the opportunity to—

Aack!

What was this emotional cliff she'd suddenly come to the edge of?

What was this can of worms sitting in front of her, with the opener already slicing into the lid?

Mentally, she veered away from it, slotting a quick, automatic and familiar pep talk into place.

*I am not over stretched. I know what I want. I can do everything I have to do. There will be time later. I like my life. I am a success. The right things will happen. Everyone feels alone sometimes. This is what I have chosen. I am nothing like my parents. I mean, they disapprove of me so much, how could I be? Dr. Chin was presenting a worst-case scenario. I've got time for a child in a few years, if I want one, and I don't even know if I do. I'm fine.*

Dusty stayed silent in response to her line about calling charter companies. She could tell he didn't think she'd find anyone to take her. She was glad he'd refrained from making a comment about it.

Grateful, in fact.

To be honest, she must be such an easy target.

They reached the steps up to the house and he stood aside to let her go first. She heard him coming up behind her, his work boots heavy and mellow on the old wood.

"Well, you're welcome here as long as you have to stay," he said, just as she reached the door.

"Yes. Thank you for that."

Because she could tell it was true. She'd seen it over dinner, in the way people talked to her, and in the way Dusty himself sat back and listened to what they all said.

In hindsight, she could even see it in the way he'd been so blunt with her about her chances of getting out of here.

She was a nuisance and she didn't belong, but she was welcome.

She hadn't done a single thing to deserve it, so help her, but she was welcome here all the same.

She didn't understand it at all.

## Chapter Three

"You'll have some coffee, or something?" Dusty asked once they were inside the house.

"Herbal tea?" Shay hated the stuff—chamomile, peppermint, whichever kind she tried—but drank it regularly most nights, as a concession to the fact that her stress levels were too high and that she'd been told by more than one medical professional to do something about it.

"Sorry," Dusty said. "I don't have herbal. I only keep the basic kind."

It was preferable to coffee, so she said yes, then watched him casually get out an antique china teapot from the thirties or forties in the most gorgeous blue with a gold trim, warm it with boiling water and make the tea with real tea leaves scooped from an antique tin canister.

He had no idea he was doing anything special.

Suddenly, she wanted to meet his mother.

"Cup or mug?"

She almost asked for a cup, to see if this would be an antique, also, but bone-china cups and saucers were finicky and the idea of wrapping her hands around the hot sides of a big thick mug was too tempting.

They sat in the living room, each on their own puffy, squishy, regency-striped couch, each with their own big thick mug, and she said, "Tell me more about your family." She was a journalist; she was used to asking questions, picking apart what people said and learning who they were, looking for an unexpected story. If she and Dusty were drinking tea together, ahead of her enforced stay on his property, she could at least treat it as research.

"I have a younger brother who's working on a breeding property on the Darling Downs, but he'll probably come back here eventually when he's had more experience, and I have a sister who married a cane farmer."

Something in the way he said this last bit led her to tease him. "Sugarcane? Please! Like that's farming!"

He gave a grin of surprise that did something unexpected to his face. "Nah, it's just that my parents wish she was closer." The grin dropped away and Shay wanted to make it come back because she was still analyzing the unexpectedness.

The whole room seemed to get brighter when he smiled. Something shone right out from the heart of him, as warm as an open fire, as true as a compass pointing north.

But that was ridiculous.

"And your parents?" she asked.

"Think I told you, they're in Longreach." He gulped some tea. "Dad's stubborn, he should probably move somewhere bigger. From Longreach he has to travel too far for some of his medical stuff. But he's spent his whole life in this part of the country and he gets jittery anywhere else."

"And your mother, did she grow up around here, too?"

"Adelaide. Dad was sent there to school, and that's where they met. She's adaptable, my mother. She gets on with people, and she finds the best in them."

"And she loves beautiful things." She kicked off her shoes and curled her feet up on the couch, pivoting around so she could see him at a better angle.

"She does," he agreed. "What about your parents? From New York, like you?"

She nodded.

"What're they like?"

Time to put on her act.

"Oh, my parents are great!" she gushed at once, her voice automatically climbing half an octave to the level she kept for talking about things like family. "Successful, intelligent. They always wanted the best for us—my younger sister and me. We had an idyllic childhood." She drank some tea.

"Lucky," he commented.

"Oh, yes, I have been. Incredibly lucky."

There was a beat of silence. "Do you know something?" Dusty said.

"What?" His tone alarmed her a little.

"I think I like you better when you're being rude than when your voice goes up and gets all sticky like that."

*"Sticky?"*

"You did it when you first landed, too, talking about… yeah…how thrilled the magazine was about the engagement. I'm sorry, you really put me off with that. Like syrup. *My parents are great! They're ax murderers,*" he mimicked with razor-sharp accuracy. *"They eat small children."* He even got the American accent down right, with the tiny lick of New York that occasionally crept into it, despite the rigorous accent sanitization of her New England schooling.

She swore lightly, before she could stop herself. She fooled most people with the gush, even people she knew quite well. "How did you see that, when you don't know me?" she blurted out.

"I just like honesty better," he said.

"Uh, okay. Noted. And Mandy wasn't honest?"

"No. Sore point."

"Once bitten, twice shy?"

"Something like that."

It resembled her own state of mind. Shay could tell he'd kept something back, but she let it go.

"So tell me what your parents are really like, Shay," he said next.

Honesty.

Nice idea.

A million miles from nowhere, stranded with a difficult man and a hot mug of tea, why not?

"Well, you basically had it with the small children thing," she told him. "Lightly sautéed and served in a white-wine sauce. They're very civilized."

"Yeah?"

She added bluntly, "They're cold. And I never realized some parents were different, until I went home with a friend—my best friend—" Sarah still was her best friend, even though she had to maintain a marriage, her iffy asthmatic health, a new pregnancy and twins, so typically they never saw each other "—and met her family, and discovered…" Warmth and fun and honest yelling. Pizza in front of TV. Toys on the coffee table. Hugs for no reason. How did you summarize all of that? "That it could be different," she finished, unable to put it into better words.

Dusty finished his tea and put his mug down on the coffee table, then leaned back with his arm stretched across the top of the couch. A clock ticked on top of the dark teak sideboard and, from somewhere outside, Shay heard the lowing of cattle. Everything else was so quiet. She guessed the people on Dusty's station went to bed pretty early.

"But they must be proud of your success," he suggested.

"Success? Journalism? Ha! Please! Just maybe, if I was the political correspondent for *The Washington Post*, or something. But women's magazines? And by the way, where's my multimillionaire husband? Where's my fashion sense and charity profile and summer home?"

"So they were brought up to that lifestyle, I'm guessing."

She sighed because it was way more complicated than that. "Do you want to know which famous person I was named after?"

"Uh…" She could see him trying to think of any Hollywood actresses or Nobel Prize winners or ancient queens named Shay. He failed.

So she helped him out. "Che Guevara."

"The— No! The South American communist revolutionary from the sixties?"

"That's the one."

"Is that how it's spelled?"

"No, it's spelled how you'd think." She said it for him. *S-h-a-y.* "They changed it when I was four, just in time for me to get into the right kindergarten."

"Handy."

"Yep." She made the word come out flippant, so he'd understand that the childhood-revelation segment of the evening was over.

It didn't work.

"No, Shay," he said, "you can't stop there." His eyes didn't move from her face. In the soft glow of ceiling lights, they looked like brandy again—a big glass of it that you stared into, contemplating your life. "You have to tell me the whole story."

"Short version?"

"Okay, the short version. Another day, you can stretch it out."

She let that one slide.

"They both come from nice Protestant middle-class educated backgrounds," she told him. "My dad's family was wealthier than my mom's, pretty comfortable. He had a trust fund—he still does. But in their early twenties they went through a hippie phase, and lived in some weird community for quite a while. They had me, then rejected the hippie phase a few years later. Turned their backs on it about as much as humanly possible, in fact."

"And then?"

"They got married, had my sister—whose name is Jacqueline, and it's never, ever shortened to Jackie. Something about the whole alternative-lifestyle episode really scared them in the end. The possibility that they might have been fooled, I think. I actually think they're still scared."

She stopped, knowing she'd said too much.

"Yeah?"

She waved at him. "Just a theory. But, yes, I was named after a communist revolutionary."

"That's amazing."

"Bizarre, you mean."

"No, just interesting. Want to know which famous person I was named after?"

She laughed. "Oh, you were saddled with that, too? Dustin Hoffman, I'm guessing."

"No, Slim Dusty, the Australian country-music singer. Dad's idea. Mum humored him, but did insist that it was officially Dustin, in case I wanted to become prime minister, or something."

Shay laughed again.

"Do you remember the hippie community at all?" he asked her after a moment.

"Not really. Odd details. A meal I hated—something green—and my mother having this tense, grim little verbal tussle with one of the community heavyweights over whether I had to eat it or not. I don't remember who won. It's strange what sticks in kids' heads, isn't it?"

"And your parents didn't retain any good stuff from that time?"

"You mean the free love?" People had asked her this kind of question before.

"I mean…no, not free love. Just love," he said simply. "Hugs and mess and warmth."

The things she'd learned about from Sarah's family.

He'd expressed it in almost the same words.

She shook her head. "No, they didn't. I don't think they were ever very huggy. Maybe that was one of the things that drew them to the hippie lifestyle when they were young and more open. The promise of learning to hug." She flapped her hands. It sounded silly. But Dusty nodded anyway, so she kept going. "But, yeah, it scared them— or other things scared them—and they backed off and ran as fast as they could in the opposite direction."

"Sounds like you've thought about it a lot."

"I come back to it. Sometimes I don't think about my childhood at all."

"Wouldn't want me to think you were obsessed, or any-thing. Don't worry. I don't. But we get some interesting people out here. Interesting histories. It's one of the things I like about my life. I hear stories more complicated than you'd expect."

"Like Letty's?"

"You saw her arm."

"And there was something different about her left eye, too."

"Yes. It's made of glass. She was in an accident a few years ago, before she left England. I'll let her tell you about it."

The words implied that she'd have plenty of time to learn the full story because she was going to be here for days…because she was stuck with no way out…because he hadn't been on the ball enough to send her back with Grant in the departing plane this afternoon.

"If we're being honest, Dusty," she blurted out, "tell me what happened with you and Mandy and why you couldn't see it coming. It's isolated out here. I would have thought there'd be nowhere for her to hide, emotionally speaking."

He'd seemed perceptive just now. A good listener. Not nearly that blind.

Although maybe she'd been too honest. He was frowning.

She jumped in again. "I'm sorry. That's too personal, isn't it? Just because I chose to spill all that stuff about my parents, it doesn't oblige you to do the same."

"It's okay."

"Doesn't look as if it is."

"Well, I'm angry with myself, and you're reminding me of it."

"I'm a journalist. I'm trained to confront people with searching questions."

"I'll answer if you want. If I can." He frowned. "I usually pride myself on being…straight, you know? Seeing what I want, going for it, getting it right, not taking any bull, not making mistakes. But with women it hasn't worked. Can I get back to you when I've had more time to think about why?"

She groaned. "No, you can't! Stop doing that!"

"Doing what?"

"Saying things like you'll get back to me, that Letty can tell me her own story. Thus reminding me of how long I'm probably going to be here."

"You've seemed a little more relaxed about the fact since dinner. I didn't think it was a banned subject anymore."

"Did you give me tranquilizers instead of headache pills? I'm starting to suspect you did. No, seriously." Her turn to frown this time. "Relaxed, no. Lulled by my sheer powerlessness, maybe? Or in denial?"

She started thinking about it again—helicopter companies, airline schedules, the expense, what Tom might want, the relentless imperative of her career—and discovered that denial was a pretty good place to be.

"I—I think I'd better get to my room." She could start reading those story competition entries, kid herself that she was at least getting work done, and fall asleep over a pile of papers at around midnight the way she usually did. "Thanks for the tea."

"No worries."

She levered herself off the couch. "Why do Australians *say* that? *No worries*, instead of *you're welcome*. It makes no sense! It drives me nuts!"

"We're a nation of philosophers." He stood up, also, and picked up their empty mugs. "We like to remind each other, in daily speech, about our powerlessness to control the universe. I mean, apart from you, of course, because as we discussed earlier, you're turning the handle. But for most Australians, *no worries* is a statement of belief about their relaxed position in the cosmic hierarchy."

"You're making that up."

"Yep."

"And if you're trying to prove that you went to a decent

school and know a few long words, it's okay, I'm convinced." She paused as she reached the corridor that led
to her room. "You're quite a bright guy."

"Thanks. I get by."

He dangled their empty mugs by the handles, one in
each hand, and for a moment they both stood uncertainly
where they were. Shay was glad about the mugs. No awkwardness over whether they should shake hands or do any
hippie hugging good-night.

Two single, consenting adults, alone in a house—it
could have gotten awkward. Dustin Tanner—*not* named
for the movie star—wouldn't be the first man to want to
heal his broken heart with a one-night stand.

"Is there a time I should wake you in the morning?" he
finally asked.

"Uh, I'll be up, I should think." She never slept in.
"Good night, Dusty."

"Good night, Shay. Sleep well."

"Hey, you never know, miracles can happen…." She
smiled at him, then went along to her room.

Maybe it was the tea, maybe it was more denial. The
miracle did happen, and Shay slept like a log.

When Dusty rapped politely on her door at just after
eight, she was still in a doze, and she was shocked to see
the time on the bedside clock when she opened one eye.
She'd fallen asleep over the sixth of the short-story entries
and, even though she'd managed to turn off the light before
finding oblivion, the two piles of manuscripts resting on
the covers slid to the floor when she sat up.

"Just a minute," she called out.

"No hurry," Dusty called back. "But I've got some news
you'll want to hear when you're up and dressed."

Following a statement like this, she was dressed in
two minutes, and was practically breathless by the time

she'd followed the smell of coffee and arrived in the kitchen.

"Tell me, Dusty!"

"There's a chopper going to pick you up sometime this morning and it'll get you to Longreach by the end of the day. I pulled a couple of strings."

He made it sound like no big deal, didn't go into detail and didn't make any reference to how difficult she'd been on the issue yesterday, but she had an inkling that she really owed him for what he'd done.

"I have to warn you, though, it's not going to be your standard charter flight," he went on. "The guy's mustering on the next property. It's owned by one of the big agribusinesses, and they have their own helicopter division. The pilot's going to fit you in when he can, because the cattle have to take priority, so you might have to experience a bit of mustering on the way, and you might not get to Longreach until dark."

"Thank you! *Thank you!* That is so great! I am so grateful!"

"No worries," he said.

"No worries, Dusty," she echoed, and closed her eyes in sheer relief. "I think I'm starting to get it, now. No worries..."

It sounded good.

Opening her eyes again, she found Dusty grinning at her, and even though she'd by this time decided—When? During her sleep?—that it was one of the best grins she'd ever seen, the thought of saying a permanent goodbye to the grin and Dusty himself didn't weigh her down for a moment.

*I have my career back!*

*I'm not going to end up on* Boring Hobbies Monthly.

*I can get to New York!*

She might even be on a plane across the Pacific today.

If she widened her search for available flights and checked the ones out of Sydney as well…

She ate breakfast over at the single men's quarters, had her bag packed and waiting on the veranda, had Sonya alerted to her imminent escape and was rechecking international flights on the Internet when the air filled with the vibrating sound of chopper blades at twenty after nine.

Dusty had gone somewhere with the grader driver, so she scribbled him a note. *Thanks for everything. Sorry we didn't get a chance to say goodbye. Shay.*

He'd touched her life….Yes, a little, getting her to talk about her parents the way she had, showing her some unexpected facets to his own existence…but he was out of it, now, and she was back on the Shieldpress corporate ladder, where she belonged.

Okay, gathering her thoughts, starting to feel that she was back in control. On the way to Brisbane, she needed to list everything Sonya had to take care of while she was in New York, and she needed to marshal her arguments about the Australian content of the magazine because surely this was what Tom wanted to hear from her. She needed—

"You're the one trying to get to Longreach?" yelled the chopper pilot, coming toward her across the red ground with his blades still slowing down behind him.

"Or Charleville," she yelled back generously. "I'm not fussy."

"I'm not going to Charleville."

"Longreach, then. Longreach is fine."

"Have to find a few cattle first."

"I know. That's fine, too." Everything was fine. She was going to get out of here and that was all that mattered.

Shay felt giddy with relief as they left the ground. A few

minutes later, she felt just plain giddy. Half an hour after that, absolutely bleeping terrified. This was nothing like an airplane ride. The chopper pilot cruised over the flat, flooded terrain, buzzing dark strings of moving cattle as if he were a fighter pilot and the beasts were enemy tanks.

He didn't seem to fly in the same direction or at the same height for more than a few seconds at a stretch, and if Shay had had any idea of which direction Longreach lay in when they'd taken off, she'd lost all sense of it now. The option of walking there seemed easier. Why had she pushed Dusty so hard about getting out of here?

"Can we fly a bit more gently?" she tried to say, but the pilot didn't hear.

He yelled something at her—something helpful and explanatory that she couldn't make out a word of. She hoped it had been, *I'll have you on the ground in five minutes,* because any longer than that and she would die.

Or throw up.

Probably both.

The chopper slid sideways and her stomach rolled. Some of the cattle were being stubborn. Was that the problem? The pilot—she hadn't asked his name—flew lower and slower and she didn't understand what kept them off the ground. It only looked to be a few yards below her. The cattle began to move toward an open gate. The pilot swore and yelled. Something about the rotor RPM.

They were going to crash.

She knew it only seconds before it happened.

The pilot yelled again.

The motor screamed, sputtered and died.

Cattle galloped ahead, splashing in tea-colored water up to their red-brown bony knees.

The chopper slammed crookedly and violently onto a piece of soft ground surrounded by flooding and no bigger than a suburban front yard. The jarring impact was like nothing Shay had ever felt before. Her vision boiled with wild color and then went black, just as her stomach came barging up into her throat.

## *Chapter Four*

Thanks to several terse two-way radio conversations with the people from Williamson International Pastoral Holdings, Dusty knew exactly where to find the downed chopper. He also knew what to bring with him, and that both Shay and Jake the pilot were basically okay. He'd also been able to reach Shay's assistant in Sydney to give her the bare bones about the crash and the consequent delay.

Taking two horses—the only mode of ground transportation that could reach the place through the floodwaters—and filling their saddlebags with equipment, he left the homestead before lunch. By mid-afternoon, he knew he must be getting close because he'd left his own land an hour ago and was now riding a winding route across WIPH's massive and extensively flooded acreage, known as Wilandra Creek.

He'd bargained to secure Shay's evacuation on the WIPH chopper by giving Wilandra Creek's manager permission to open a gate between the two properties and heli-

muster several thousand Wilandra Creek cattle onto the
nearby piece of higher ground that was part of Roscommon Downs, but he hadn't expected his deal-brokering
efforts to end like this.

The head of the pastoral company's helicopter division
was pretty ticked off, too, and the words *pilot error* had
been spoken. The man had made it quite clear that Jake
had to stay with the chopper until the company could send
a mechanic with some equipment, tools and parts to check
out the degree of damage and fix it on site if possible. The
way Dusty understood the situation, Jake might need to
settle in for a wait of a couple of days.

Shay would be luckier.

Dusty had come to her rescue, like a knight on horseback in shining bloody armor, and she'd better damn well
appreciate the fact.

Ahead, he saw something glinting, and realized it was
the sun reflecting off the chopper's bubble-like cabin, par-
tially obscured by a screen of thin vegetation. The two
horses made some final splashes through shallow water,
then came to the patch of higher ground. He saw the two
lonely human figures spring to their feet in a forlorn piece
of shade as they heard his approach, and in another minute
he had almost reached them.

Pelicans, cockatoos and other birdlife filled the air with
bursts of noise as he neared, and the sky was a soaring and
slightly humid-hazed blue—idyllic in a photograph but he
had to admit that Shay and Jake created a desolate image
in the reality of the vast landscape.

Shay stood with her shoulders hunched and shudder-
ing, biting on her knuckle and, for the first time since
Dusty had heard the news, he had time to think about how
terrified she must have been. She looked a mess, and this
was hardly a surprise.

There would have been noise, violent motion, Jake's desperate reaction and the jarring impact, all of it in the middle of nowhere. Both pilot and passenger were lucky not to have been badly hurt, lucky that the radio was still working and lucky that Dusty had been able to reach them relatively easily.

Then had come the hours of waiting, in weather that managed to be hot and unusually humid because of all the water lying around, even though this was the middle of the Australian winter in the cooler regions farther south. Had Shay had any faith that Dusty would show up for her?

He thought about worst-case scenarios and his gut soured suddenly. If the helicopter had crashed even just a few meters higher than it had, or if the pilot's radio had broken on impact, the outcome might have been very different. If she'd been seriously injured he never would have forgiven himself for yesterday's thoughtlessness in not holding back the mail flight.

He didn't usually get caught up in fretting over what might have been. What was wrong with him? He pulled Beau up and shook off the morbid speculation.

Sliding efficiently from the saddle, he walked up to Shay, with Beau's reins and those of Sally, the horse he'd been leading, still looped in his hand. His pulse was jumping strangely and his breathing wasn't quite steady. He really wanted Shay to be okay, but didn't want her to see his level of concern. He couldn't believe he felt this degree of responsibility for her.

"Hello, stranger." Suddenly, he found himself grinning, partly with relief that she seemed to be basically all right and he'd reached her in good time, and partly because, seriously, could you doubt that the universe had a warped sense of humor when something like this happened, after they'd both been so desperate for her to get away?

"Oh, Dusty," she sobbed. "Thank God you're here! Thank you, God! Oh, Dusty." She launched herself toward him, stumbling.

"Hey…What's all this about?" Her vulnerability arrowed right to his heart. "Hey, it's okay…."

"I know. I know, but let me cry anyhow."

Shay had never been so happy to see any human being in her life. She wrapped her jarred, aching arms around Dusty's neck and held him like a long-lost brother, or like her best friend. He smelled of sunscreen, shampoo, eucalyptus-flavored laundry detergent and male skin; his navy-trimmed white polo shirt was soft against her cheek, and he was big and strong and fabulous.

She had not one second's doubt that she was safe now because, if there was one thing to be said for rough physical specimens like this one, they knew how to find their way around a desert in flood, and she couldn't imagine that they ever got lost.

"Oh, Dusty," she sobbed again, and only managed to prise herself out of his deliciously capable embrace when the horse nudging his shoulder reminded her that they weren't alone.

"Are you going to accept it now?" he said.

"Accept what?"

"That the universe has promoted you sideways. Someone else is turning the handle from now on."

"Well, as long as it's you…" she said.

"Me?" He opened his hands in a gesture that said *huh?*

"Doesn't matter. Bad joke. You turning the handle instead, I meant. But it's not important. Just—just get me home safe to your place? Please?"

"No worries, okay? Don't sweat it," he crooned to her, giving her wrenched shoulders a gentle rub. "That's why I'm here."

"Mate…" said Jake, and came forward to shake Dusty's hand.

Shay hadn't really warmed to Jake during the hours of their stranded solitude. He'd been fairly obsessed with his crippled machine, sweating about his future with the company after such an expensive mistake, upset about the prospect of waiting for a mechanic, loudly profane about all of it, and completely uninterested in any of her comparable problems.

"Brought you some emergency supplies," Dusty told him.

"Like what?"

"Food, matches, clean water."

"A tent? A sleeping bag?"

Dusty glanced wryly over his shoulder at the two horses. "Sorry. I had load limitations. You'll have to sleep in the chopper." He looked at the whirlybird, with its runners dug crookedly into the damp earth. "Or maybe under it."

Jake swore again. "They're saying it's my fault."

Dusty didn't enter the debate as to whether this was true—wise of him, Shay considered. "Then this is your penance, I guess," he said. "Listen, I'm going to unpack your gear, and then we'll head back. The water's still rising and there's a crossing that was already getting deep on the way here. We're going to have to take the long way around."

Shay's sense of utter safety in Dusty's presence wobbled and cracked. "The horse you were leading…" she said.

"That's right," he told her cheerfully. "It's for you."

"But—but I don't ride. I've never been on a horse in my life."

There was a moment of painful silence as he absorbed this news, then he drawled,

"Well, I guess today's going to be a great time to start."

"I—I—" She stopped.

There really wasn't a thing she could usefully say.

Dusty unbuckled one of the saddlebags from the horse he'd been riding, and the animal pawed the earth a couple of times, flicking its tail and its ears when flies came too close. The glossy brown creature seemed enormous, powerful and as impossible to understand or control as a tornado…or outback Australia in flood.

Handing the saddlebag to Jake, Dusty told him, "You should be able to find enough dry wood for a fire around here. Pull off the dead branches on the bushes. There are tea bags, a bit of sugar and long-life milk, bread, cans of soup, I can't remember what else. My cook put it together and she doesn't often forget the essentials."

"Beer?" Jake inquired in a pessimistic tone.

Without a word, Dusty flipped open a side pocket in the saddlebag and pulled out two cans, with a blue-tinted ice pack softening between them. He tossed them to Jake like grenades, one at a time, and put the ice pack back in the bag.

"You mean it's even *cold?*" Jake said as his fingers closed around the cans. "In that case, who needs a sleeping bag?"

Dusty turned to Shay. "Ready?" He handed her a wide-brimmed felt hat that looked as if it had been used as a cleaning rag more often than as a shield against the sun. She put it on anyhow. The entire rest of her life was going to be a bad hair day and she didn't even care.

Then she looked at the horses again. "Ready as I'll ever be. Um, Jake? Thanks for…"

"Crashing you?" He made a wry face. "No worries. Anytime."

"Well, for trying to get me to Longreach, even if we fell about three hundred kilometers short."

"Right," said Dusty. "Let's get you onto that horse."

Shay was determined not to complain. Thinking of everything Dusty probably should be doing on the property instead of riding to her rescue like this, she'd already vowed not to earn any more seething reluctance from him than she'd already earned last night.

As a goal, it stretched her from the very beginning, however.

Dusty had brought her some old riding boots. He consigned her grossly inappropriate heels to her overnight bag, which he decreed must be left with the chopper, along with her laptop. "Unless your bag has some survival gear in it that you haven't told me about?"

"There are a couple of things I'd like to grab." Like the underwear she'd fortunately washed by hand last night and hung in her room to dry. "But it's mainly short-story manuscripts," she said.

"There you go, Jake," Dusty said cheerfully. "Something to help start your campfire."

*Button your lips, Shay,* she coached herself. *Don't let out that moan.* "Do I really have to leave my laptop?" she couldn't help asking.

"Do you want it to work, next time you switch it on? It's going to get jolted around. We'll be wading in some places. It could get wet. And I really don't want any more baggage than necessary. I think it's safer staying with the chopper, Shay."

"Okay." She closed her eyes and gave a short nod, then put on the boots. "I'm ready. I think."

Dusty made his hands into a stirrup shape. "Knee up," he said.

"Sorry?" Thank heavens she was at least wearing yesterday's black trousers, rather than the pleated silk skirt she'd optimistically packed in Sydney for the homeward journey.

"Put your knee in my hands and I'll boost you up. You're riding Sally. I'm taking Beau, here." He indicated the big, brown, tail-flicking one whom he'd been riding before, and Shay felt some momentary relief. Sally, the black-maned gray, looked friendlier.

Standing beside the pretty mare, she put her knee in Dusty's hands. The impact of the helicopter had jarred every muscle, bone and tendon in her body, however, and the hours of inactivity as she'd scanned the water-logged horizon for signs of his approach had stiffened her even further. Just the simple action of boosting herself up with his powerful assistance burned her shoulders and her back. She gasped as she landed in the saddle.

"She's quiet," Dusty said, clearly thinking that she was afraid. "You'll be fine."

"Yes," Shay managed to say, without complaint. "She seems lovely."

"Okay, now, thirty-second riding lesson. Feet in the stirrups. Heels down. Grip with your knees but don't get tense about it. Reins…Well, you can hold them cowboy style in one hand, or classic dressage style, in two." He demonstrated both options.

"Two," Shay decided out loud because it sounded as if she'd have more control this way.

And a degree of redundancy if one arm suddenly fell off from the pain in her shoulders.

"Everything all right?" he said after he'd shown her.

"You mean that's it? That's how to ride? Don't I have to…um…kick? Or steer?"

"I'll go ahead on Beau. Sally thinks he's her boyfriend. She adores him, so she'll follow. You shouldn't need to give her much guidance."

"And doesn't *he* think he's her boyfriend?" Shay instantly empathized. The rat! Poor Sally! Beau was Adam and Jason and Todd, all over again. Men were the same the world over, even when they were horses.

"Well, he sort of is her boyfriend. He totally agrees with Sally about it. The thing is, he's been gelded, but we don't tell him that. So when I say *boyfriend*, think preschoolers holding hands, not a model, a rock star and black satin sheets."

Shay snorted out a laugh. "That is so cute!"

She was glad about the undignified snort because it disguised the fact that the laugh instantly turned into a groan. The slightest movement made her shoulders ache and her back spasm with pain.

Dusty pulled himself into Beau's saddle with one heave of his thighs and arms. He slid the scuffed toes of his boots into the stirrups, and his legs and butt seemed almost to graft themselves to the horse. He clicked his tongue, nudged the horse's sides with his heels and he and Beau were off. As he'd predicted, Sally immediately took off after them, at the same steady gait.

"You're still in radio contact with your boss, aren't you, Jake?" Dusty said to the pilot as he circled around the stricken chopper.

"When he can be bothered," he confirmed. "It's going to be a bloody boring wait."

"See you later then, mate. Keep smiling."

"Yeah, you, too."

"Will Jake really be okay?" Shay asked after the first fifty yards or so of agonizing movement on the rickety horse. She wasn't convinced that *she* would be okay, but didn't dare to ask how long it would take them to ride to the homestead, in case it sounded like an over-entitled, career-obsessed New Yorker's whiny complaint.

"He should be," Dusty answered. "They're punishing him a little bit, but they'll get to him as soon as they can."

"It seems harsh."

"Life out here is harsh, sometimes."

"I guess it would be."

"There's no point in a station owner or manager having a high tolerance for mistakes, when the land itself has no tolerance at all. That's the way I operate, anyhow."

"According to rules? That rigid?" The questions distracted her from the pain in her back.

"It's not rigid. I don't think it's rigid. I ask a lot from my people, the way WIPH asks a lot from its pilots, but we don't ask for anything that we couldn't or wouldn't give ourselves."

"Okay." She looked at him ahead of her, straight-backed, relaxed, confident, strong in his body and in his convictions.

He was different to most of the men she'd known. Different from Adam, for example. Adam's logic and his ideas seemed so slippery, in hindsight, compared to Dusty's. Had there been any steady sense of right and wrong in Adam's world, or only a shifting landscape of wants and desires?

"Would you rather have stayed with him and taken your chances on an air rescue?" Dusty asked, cutting across her train of thought before she'd reached a conclusion.

"Are you kidding me? I am *never* going in one of those things again!"

"The mustering was pretty scenic, then? You saw the outback from seventeen different angles and altitudes at once?"

"Something like that. I felt so sick to my stomach I thought I was going to die. And then Jake lost control, the rotor speed dropped too low, or something, and I *really* thought I was going to die."

She shuddered, remembering the fear, the pain and the

way she'd been shaking so hard that it had taken her ten minutes to unbend from her seat and climb to the ground after the ugly whine of the chopper's blades and motor had died away.

At which point she'd lost her breakfast.

"It was…" She trailed off. *Don't complain, Shay!* "…Yeah." She brightened her tone. "Great research."

He laughed, but didn't comment.

The knife play in Shay's back and shoulders continued, and her thighs and butt began to burn, also, from the unaccustomed straddle position. The black trousers were comfortable in an executive office, but as riding gear they chafed her skin badly. It was a testament to the degree of pain in her back that the chafing barely seemed to matter.

The landscape around them was incredible, but again her enjoyment of it was filtered through her pain. In the distance—to the west, she thought—she could see what looked like sand dunes the rusty orange color of cayenne pepper. They were dotted with clumps of gray-green grass, as well as dapplings of color from wildflowers in bright yellows and pinks.

Around what she guessed was a major river channel, she saw black swans, pelicans and other birds that she couldn't identify, stalking on stilt-like legs. She caught a brief glimpse of something that looked like a huge eagle, but then it soared higher and she would have had to turn in the saddle to track its powerful trajectory through the sky.

Turning, right now, was not an option. She knew it would hurt too much.

"How far have we come?" she asked brightly, after what felt like an hour.

"A couple of kilometers, probably. Not quite a mile and a half."

No! Not possible!

She pressed her lips together for a moment, then asked, "And how far is it altogether?"

"Longer than my outward journey. There's a detour we'll have to make this time, because the water is still rising and the crossing was already pretty iffy when I came through." He looked at her stiff, ungainly position on Sally's back. "You probably wouldn't be too comfortable with swimming the horses. So it's going to be over twenty miles."

Shay wondered how she'd survive.

The pain got worse. Since Sally just kept walking in Beau's tracks without guidance, as Dusty had promised she would, Shay tried slumping in the saddle, loosening her grip on the reins and letting her feet out of the stirrups. It didn't help. Every rock of the horse's gait made her spine shift, and every shift brought a fresh stab of agony.

They had to have been riding for well over an hour—a real hour, this time, not a mental anguish hour that was actually only twenty minutes—when she admitted defeat and knew she had to say something to Dusty. They'd splashed through stretches of water that came to the horses knees and her trousers were soaked and stained and stuck to her legs, chafing her worse than ever, but this was nothing compared to the pain in her back.

"I don't think I can do this anymore," she gasped out to him.

He twisted in the saddle, frowning. "You're doing fine."

"No. I'm not. My back got jarred in the crash, I think. And my shoulders. I've tried all sorts of positions. I'm sorry. It's getting worse and worse. The shoulders are bearable, but the back...really isn't."

Dusty dammed back a curse word, brought Beau to a halt and took a good look at his traveling companion, expecting to see symptoms of spoiled New Yorker throwing a tantrum about nothing.

The reality was different.

The color had drained from Shay's face, leaving her like a ghost, and her lips were dry. She had pink sunburn flaring on her neck, although her face was protected by the hat he'd given her. He should have asked her about sunscreen, back at the chopper. He should have stopped for a water break before this. There was nothing he could do about the water dripping from her boots and the hems of her trousers, but he knew it couldn't be comfortable because his own boots and jeans were in the same state.

And he should have seen that she was in this level of pain because, now that he'd looked at her properly, he couldn't doubt it. "Why didn't you say something?"

"Because I've given you so much grief already. And because what's our choice?"

Good point.

He considered it.

The sun had dropped toward the horizon. Darkness would soon fall, which meant they'd have needed to stop anyway, within the next half hour. Anticipating a night en route, he'd asked Prim to pack two sleeping bags and a billycan for cooking and heating water over an open fire—the same fire that would dry out the soaking lower half of her trousers and his jeans, he hoped, because wet fabric chafed more than dry.

There were no luxuries, though. No tent. No air mattress. They'd be lying on the bare earth.

He dismounted and went to her, realizing that she would need help in getting to the ground. Seeing how stiffly and carefully she moved as she attempted to ease her sodden leg over the horse's back, he suspected they might be camping out tomorrow night, as well.

"I can't get off," she gasped. "I'm stuck. It hurts too much."

"Take your feet out of the stirrups, lean on the horse's neck. Try kind of rolling off. I'll catch you."

"You'd better."

"I promise."

She yelped and groaned and hissed with pain, although he could tell she was trying as hard as she could, and then she rolled into his arms with a dry sob and he lowered her gently to the ground, feeling her unsuitable silk top slip against his skin. It, too, had been splattered with muddy water, and would probably be useless after this. If she'd had any doubts about leaving her laptop behind, she'd most likely rethought her objections by now.

As if the silk and the laptop mattered. The pain in her back was the critical thing.

"Gee, how high was that chopper when it came down?" he asked her softly, still holding her because she felt as if her legs might give way beneath her if he didn't.

She felt good in his arms—tall and willowy and soft.

Very different from Mandy.

Better.

He shook off the thought and felt her steady herself and take a determined breath. She pushed him gently away, saying, "It seemed like fifty feet. It *wasn't* that high. But it came down so hard, so fast, and I had no idea how to brace, or—— And then maybe if I'd, oh, done some stretches or walked around a lot once we were on the ground, but I was so shocked, I just sat and everything stiffened up."

"You're burned, too."

"There wasn't much shade."

"Have you been drinking enough fluids?"

"Jake had water. We'd almost finished it when you arrived, so it's good that you had more for him." She was right to assume that the floodwater that surrounded them would not be particularly safe to drink without boiling. "I'd like some now, if that's okay. I'm thirsty."

He got it out of a saddlebag for her and she drank gratefully, steadier on her feet by this time. "What are we going to do, Dusty?" she asked when she'd finished her drink, and there was an almost childlike note of trust in her voice, as if she had absolute faith in his answers.

He felt comfortable with the responsibility—after all, he knew the country, knew how to survive—and oddly touched at the same time. "Walk a little bit," he answered. "Just take it easy. Help you loosen up. There's a place I'd like to get to about another kilometer ahead. Can you manage that on foot? Half a mile or so? Some of it will be through water."

"I'll have to manage, won't I?"

"If you can't, you have to tell me."

"I'll manage. And then?"

"We'll set up camp."

She nodded. She'd obviously realized that with twenty miles of trackless and flooded ground to cover, they weren't going to make it back to the homestead tonight. "Dare I ask? You had no tent for Jake. Is that because you were saving it for us?"

He shook his head. "But the place I'm hoping to get to has an overhang."

"A cave?"

"Calling it a cave would be a stretch."

He waited for a litany of questions about what the hell she was expected to do with something that didn't even qualify as a cave, and about what he had or didn't have in the crammed saddlebags, but she stayed silent for a good thirty seconds, then simply said, "So we should get walking," and started off. A moment later, she stopped. "Should I lead Sally?"

"Do you want to?"

She flexed a couple of muscles experimentally. "Maybe I'll just walk."

And she did, without a word, through wildflowers and mud and thigh-deep water, until they reached the place he'd had in mind.

## Chapter Five

The hour of walking had to qualify as one of the best performances of her life, Shay decided.

She wanted to yell, moan, sink to the ground and sob, pray for death, and beg Dusty, "Ca-a-rry me!" like Sarah's three-year-old twins did. Her wet trousers dragged and chafed, and every time she thought the late sun might dry out the fabric, they came to another place where they had to wade and the trousers got even wetter.

But she kept her mouth shut and just put one foot in front of the other beside Dusty and the horses, over and over again, until she heard him say, "Here we are."

"This is the overhang."

"Yes."

"It's…pretty." There was a line of big river trees not far off, and the dying sun made rich, gorgeous colors in the sky that reflected off the sea of slowly drifting water.

Nonetheless, its scenic attractions would not have featured in a more honest reaction.

She saw the way Dusty tucked in the corner of his mouth and raised his eyebrows, and added bluntly, "Okay, it's one of the loneliest places I've ever seen in my life."

Ahh, speaking the truth. It felt almost as good as stretching her stiff muscles.

He laughed. "It's shelter, and there should be some dry wood for a fire."

"I'll gather some," she announced bravely.

"It's okay. You should rest now. Prim will have packed a first-aid kit, so I can give you something for the pain. Then how about I set up the sleeping bag for you, under the overhang, and you can take off your wet things, get into the bag and have a snooze while I get us organized?"

"I'm—"

"You're not fine." His brandy-colored eyes crinkled up around the edges in a sympathetic smile as he looked her up and down, and she felt as if he understood her far too well. "You don't have to say you're fine. It'll be easier for both of us in the long run if you're honest."

"Really? You're good to me!"

"You've been in a bloody helicopter crash today, and Jake was obviously playing it down for the sake of his career, because if I'd known you'd gotten this jarred I would have tried to get hold of a medical evacuation chopper."

To her own astonishment, Shay heard herself say, "That would have been a waste of resources. There must be people who need evacuation more than I do. I was doing okay until I got on the horse. But there was something about her gait…I hope my back has settled down by tomorrow." This seemed doubtful, when she had to sleep on the ground. "If I have to walk the whole way back—"

"We'll work something out," he promised her, laying a

sheet of thin green plastic on the dry earth beneath the overhang as he spoke.

He anchored it with stones at the edges, then spread out the sleeping bag. His shoulder stretched, the fabric of his jeans tightened across an impressively firm butt. Shay watched him at work, appreciating his efficiency and confidence on a level of instinct and gut that she couldn't remember ever feeling before. How could he look so fit and supple after such a long day in the saddle?

"Now give me your wet gear and sleep, okay?" he said.

For a blessed hour and a half, she did, lying inside the puffy down-filled sleeping bag beneath the eight-foot high jutting shelf of ocher-colored rock. The effect of the painkillers crept over her and she felt the agony in her back and shoulders miraculously ebb.

It wasn't just a doze, but a heavy, nourishing sleep that had her feeling groggy and disoriented when she first woke. She knew at once where she was—who could forget, even in sleep?—but what was that crackling sound? What was that smell?

She sat up, rediscovering the sunburn on her neck and the general stiffness that the medication couldn't mask. It was fully dark now, but Dusty had lit a beautiful fire within a ring of stones, several yards beyond the overhang. The flames leaped brightly, creating the crackling sounds Shay had heard while still half-asleep.

Her clothes must have dried because they sat neatly folded and within her reach on the sheet of plastic. She sat up and let the sleeping bag slither to her waist. Lifting her silk top, she discovered stains that would never come out, but put it on anyhow, and found it was still faintly warm from the fire's heat. It felt surprisingly good against her skin. The trousers were a different story. The skin on her inner thighs was tender and rough.

Approaching the fire, she discovered that the delectable smell came from slices of onion frying on a blackened sheet of corrugated metal balancing on the stones.

"I'm operating some creative cooking strategies tonight," Dusty said, seeing that she was awake. He squatted, stretched, straightened, leaned. Again, she couldn't help watching him. The man even cooked as if it were some kind of easy evening workout. "Feeling better?" he asked.

"Ask me again when I've had some more water and… um…been for a walk." She hesitated for a moment. "Dusty, if our house is a rock shelf and our cookware is an old piece of roof, can I ask about our bathroom?"

"Your choice of bush, a discreet distance away, but within sight of the fire. You don't want to get lost."

"Lost on the way to the bathroom. A new concept." She drank the water he passed to her, then went off into the darkness for a few minutes. On her way back, she discovered the horses hobbled by some kind of strap on their back legs so that they could graze and drink but couldn't wander too far, and stopped to reach up and stroke Sally on her warm, silky, aristocratic nose.

When she returned to the fire, the onions smelled even better. "And look what Prim packed," Dusty said, holding up a gracefully shaped green bottle.

"What *is* that? Not—"

"Yep." He grinned. "Champagne."

"I love her! Can I drink it direct from the bottle?" *All* of it.

"You'll have to, because she didn't pack any glasses. Or there are two slightly coffee-stained enamel mugs, if you prefer."

"I'll go with the bottle. Strictly medicinal, you realize, don't you?"

"Shay, after the day you've had, I'd authorize strictly

medicinal hundred-percent-proof vodka if we had any. There are also crackers and a can of smoked oysters, by the way, to go with the champagne. We are surviving in style, tonight."

"Have you opened it?"

"Not yet. If you're drinking from the bottle, do you want to stand close by? It's probably been pretty well shaken up this afternoon."

"Not to sound too desperate or anything, but I'll even open my mouth in advance."

It was a crazy moment. They stood together beside the fire. Dusty angled the neck of the bottle away from them, untwisted the wire and pushed on the cork with his work-hardened thumbs. It gave way with a loud pop and jetted out into the desert darkness, while foam began to flood from the bottle's opening and down over his hands.

"Help!" he said. "Even fizzier than I thought."

"Oh no, we're losing it *all!*"

She pressed her mouth to the side of the bottle just as Dusty did the same and they lapped at the cool, sticky foam like animals, with their shoulders nudging each other and their bare arms bumping. They laughed as they lapped. Shay felt the bubbles fizz on her tongue. She felt Dusty's fingers against her lips for a moment, and the slippery glass, and then their sticky wet cheeks brushed together and they laughed some more and the foam subsided, leaving a good half a bottleful still left.

She stepped away, embarrassed. Dusty had foam still fizzing on his jaw and she wanted to brush it away.

Or lick it.

"Don't tell Prim how much we wasted," she said. "Maybe I'll use a mug after all. Oh, my face is all sticky."

"I packed a towel." He gestured, and she saw that he'd hung it on something that passed for a tree—a spindly little thing that leaned gracefully toward the rock shelf.

"Thanks." She grabbed it, wet a corner of it and unstickied her face, standing on the far side of the fire from Dusty because the two of them licking champagne foam from the neck of the same bottle, just now, had felt a little too much like getting their whole relationship onto a deeper level.

When she'd finished, he wanted the towel for himself, and that felt too intimate, also, as she watched him use an adjacent dampened corner, then wipe his face and hands with the same dry section she'd just used. Why had she suddenly become so interested in watching his body in action?

"How are your thighs?" he asked.

"My—?"

"The inner skin. Sore?"

"Uh, yes, a little."

"Because Prim packed some soothing cream if you want to use it. I found it in the first-aid kit when I was looking for the painkillers."

"That would be great."

He got it out for her and then turned discreetly to stir the onions while she stripped her trousers down and rubbed the cream onto her tender skin. It felt almost as intimate as licking the champagne, even though he scrupulously avoided looking. He knew what she was doing, and she knew it wouldn't take much imagination on his part to picture it. She finished as quickly as possible and refastened her trousers, hoping the soothing effect of the cream would last.

"I'm done," she announced, and saw his shoulders relax.

The onions were cooked. Dusty slid them deftly onto slices of bread balanced on smooth rocks, then put the piece of roof back on the fire and started cooking steak.

"Want to prepare our hors d'oeuvres?" he asked. "You don't need an opener for the can. And if you're cold, Prim borrowed something for you from Letty."

Unbelievable.

A few minutes later they were both sitting there, cross-legged on the ground, with enamel mugs of champagne, eating oysters on crackers while steak sizzled and potatoes baked in their blackened jackets in the coals. In her borrowed oilskin cattleman's coat, Shay felt…content.

Strangely so.

Peacefully so.

More than content, really.

Happy, even though she didn't have the slightest idea why.

"Prim believes in serving a balanced meal," Dusty told her. "There's salad and ketchup, too."

"It having been established by the highest authorities that ketchup is a vegetable."

"Exactly."

It tasted so good. Dusty squirted ketchup on top of the onions, put the steak on top of the ketchup and another slice of bread on top of that, so they didn't need plates. They ate the salad directly from the container with two plastic forks, and with the same forks scooped the hot, soft, butter-and-salt-flavored potato out from the middle of the charcoal skins. The fire kept them company, along with the sing of water heating in what Dusty called a *billycan*.

"Do you know what? I hate herbal tea," Shay said when the tea was made and she'd started sipping.

"This isn't herbal, it's just ordinary."

"I know, and it's really good. Which is what's made me realize how much I hate herbal."

"But herbal is what you normally drink?"

She shrugged, feeling foolish. "My doctor said I had to

do something about my stress levels. You know, and on the packet it always has words like *soothing* and *restorative*."

"And you think that combatting the effect of a ninety-hour working week in a hermetically sealed high-rise office with an herbal tea bag or two counts as doing something about your stress?"

"Well," she said indignantly, "yes, something, a little bit."

He laughed long and loud.

"And I did a yoga class once," she said, more indignantly still.

"For how long? A semester?"

"Uh, no, as I said, it was once. A free come-and-try. But then I never had time to actually sign up for the whole class. Even though I did *want* to. But I still try and do some of the breathing."

"You make me laugh."

"I've noticed. It's good to feel useful. Remind me why I'm here, again? Is it because you couldn't manage to tell me I'd be trapped if I didn't get right back on that mail flight?"

"Shay, I could have left you with Jake today, don't forget."

"We were going to stop this, weren't we?"

"Arguing about whose fault it is? I think so."

"I mean, I guess we have to do something to entertain ourselves but this topic is beginning to get old."

"You're right. Do you know what?" He took a mouthful of tea. "It was Mandy's fault. There. I've said it. It's out in the open. It was one hundred percent Mandy's fault and we can leave it at that."

Even though his mention of his recently turned ex-fiancée was pretty light and flippant, it somehow dampened the atmosphere all the same.

Which was probably a good thing.

"I mean, there were some other things that weren't her fault..." Dusty muttered. "That were definitely mine."

He fell silent, took a stick from the ground, stretched forward and poked the fire with it, releasing showers of sparks into the air. Looking up at them, wondering if he wanted a response to what he'd just said, Shay saw the night sky and was astonished at the sheer weight of the stars above her head. She'd had no idea there were that many.

They encrusted the whole inky black bowl of the heavens, and when she really looked closely, she could see subtle differences in their colors. They weren't simply white, but blue-white, or pink-white, or yellow, and in a crooked band across the sky, in the places where she couldn't see individual twinkles, there was a milky, misty quality to the emptiness.

"What *is* that?" she asked Dusty, pointing at it. "That sort of paler, misty trail in the sky."

He looked up. "You don't mean the Milky Way?"

"Ohmigosh," she whispered, after a moment. "I think that is what I mean. You mean, that's our galaxy? The earth's galaxy?"

"It's not mist, you see, it's a billion stars, so many of them and so far away that they just blur together."

"That's why it's called the Milky Way, because it makes the night look milky up there? I never knew that!"

"I guess you've never been somewhere before that had so little interference from lights on the ground. You probably can't see the Milky Way in the city."

"No, you can't." Not that she'd ever thought to look, admittedly. "Wow. Ouch, this is hurting my neck, I think those pills are wearing off, but I can't stop looking. It all looks so close. And so big. Don't laugh at me."

"I'm not."

"You probably are. Secretly. But I don't care."

"I'm really not. I'm not a very secret person. If I was laughing at you, you'd know it."

"So why aren't you laughing? You should be! I'm acting like a five-year-old, here, awed by the stars!"

"That's not something to laugh at. People shouldn't ever lose the ability to act like five-year-olds."

"Yeah? Including the whiny behavior?"

"Well, no, not that."

They stopped looking at the stars, looked at each other instead, and grinned. He'd put on a long-sleeved chambray shirt over the polo shirt. The two collars got in each other's way and she wanted to straighten them so that they sat the way they were supposed to, but she knew she couldn't. What if her fingers brushed against his brown, outdoorsy, sexy neck?

Something—not the sexy idea—made her ask, "Did you bring Mandy camping under the stars?"

"No, for some reason she had a strange reluctance to experience the necessary helicopter crash, first."

"You could have just taken her camping, with an SUV and a tent and camp chairs and a camp shower."

"You think if I'd shown her the stars she might have stayed?" He shifted a little. She didn't look at him, but her whole body knew he was there, back hunched, elbows resting on knees.

"I'm just wondering if she appreciated…" How to put this? "…The things that there are to appreciate out here."

"You've decided there are things to appreciate, since yesterday?"

"Even yesterday I knew there were. Your beautiful house. Letty's courage. Prim's cooking, and her books."

"Mandy didn't really manage to get to know Letty and Prim. She always ate at the house. She had…diet ideas."

"Oh?"

"Shakes. She made a lot of shakes, in the blender."

"What kind of shakes?"

"Brewer's yeast and alfalfa and cooked liver… And, I mean, she had the right to eat what she wanted but, oh jeez, they were disgusting!"

"Did you tell her that?"

"Yeah, I did!"

"But you didn't tell her to come eat with the others, read some of Prim's books and get to know everyone."

"That was her decision, too."

"Yeah?" She looked at him, tilting her head a little. He looked steadily back at her. "Or were you just keeping her to yourself?"

"Are you psychoanalyzing the relationship?" He stirred his stick in the coals of the fire again. It was getting chillier and she was glad she wore Letty's borrowed coat.

"I seem to be, don't I?"

"You do."

"I guess you give the impression that you don't understand what went wrong, and I'm curious about it, too. I'm a journalist, I sometimes ask people interfering personal questions."

"At least you're honest."

"So what was good about Mandy? What was right about her? There must have been some things."

"There were." He thought for a moment, rubbing his jaw against his index finger. "She was a good listener. She had a pretty smile." He thought again. "That sounds shallow, but smiles are important. A pretty smile can be way more important than a pretty face."

"I'd never thought of it like that," Shay murmured, impressed by the observation. A lot of men wouldn't have thought that a woman could have a pretty smile without the face to go with it.

"And she talked about herself in this rambly, psycho-babbly way that didn't make *any* sense, and when I laughed at her about it, she always started laughing, too. I liked that. People shouldn't always take themselves too seriously."

"So what did go wrong?" She remembered how he'd phrased it beside the airstrip. "Why wasn't Roscommon Downs *what she'd been expecting?* Do you wish you'd done more to make it meet her expectations? Could you have, if you'd tried, or were her expectations just too far out of touch with reality?"

He thought about it for a moment, then said, "A bit of both. Her expectations were unrealistic. There's quite a well-known book about one of the big nineteenth-century pioneer pastoral families called *Kings in Grass Castles*. Mandy thought she was going to be the queen, but it's not like that on Roscommon Downs. From my end, I probably stepped back too far, let her have too much of her own space, expected her to make her own way, too much."

"That doesn't sound like such a bad thing. Some women do have a degree of independence, these days."

"I took it too far. There's independence, and then there's lack of support. I trusted her to fill her own needs or ask for what she wanted. But she wasn't straight about that kind of thing. She was one of those women…people…who says, 'I'm fine' about twenty times and then gets angry when you believe she means it. And since she didn't seem interested in getting to know anyone on the station, I didn't push it. I probably should have. I should have pushed her a lot harder to stop the stuff about saying she was fine when she wasn't. If she'd understood, seriously, how much I hate that… But then, with Rebecca—" He stopped.

"Aha! There's Rebecca, too."

"What do you mean, aha?"

"You expected me to assume Mandy was your first girlfriend? I don't think so! You're, what? Around thirty-four?"

"All right. Of course Mandy wasn't my first girlfriend." He reached for his stick to poke the fire again.

"So tell me about Rebecca."

"Rebecca." Another shower of sparks rocketed and spiraled in the air. "Short version. She was another one of our governesses. Really vibrant, a little bit wild, loved horses. We were involved with each other for three years."

"That's a while."

"Yeah, especially since in all that time she never told me she was still married."

"Yikes!"

"Yeah, exactly." He looked at her, then looked away. Shay found herself waiting and hoping for the next time it happened. His eyes in the firelight mesmerized her. "Anyway, we were open and flexible, honest with each other, or so I thought, and I really supported her having a social life and going to local events. Rodeos and track meetings, that kind of thing."

"Well, sure."

"I didn't expect her to go off with one of my racehorse trainer's jockeys."

"Oh."

"But at least then *he* was the one who had to deal with her half-crazy husband when he finally tracked her down."

"That sounds like fun." Shay knew it must have been anything but, and understood all the mess and hurt and anger he'd carefully not talked about.

"I think it explains Mandy a bit more, doesn't it?" he said. Another look—clash, sizzle—and another look away.

"That I went too far the other way with her? That maybe, yeah, I did want to keep her too much to myself."

"You've had about as much luck with women as I've had in getting out of here."

"Which, as we've now agreed, is Mandy's fault. And on that note…we should make an early start tomorrow, so we'd better think about getting to bed."

The word hung in the air after he'd said it. This time he didn't look anywhere near her direction, and all the ease of their conversation by the firelight suddenly disappeared like the sparks flying up into the night.

## Chapter Six

"There's only one piece of plastic," Dusty said, stating the obvious.

"But two sleeping bags."

"Yes."

"So we're not going to be idiotic about this, Dusty. We'll share the plastic. It's okay. Unless you think there's a dangerous level of chemistry between us."

A second later, Shay wished she'd left off that final sentence, and especially the last three words. An image flashed into her mind of that crazy moment before dinner when they'd both been sucking foam from the neck of the champagne bottle, laughing.

She'd licked his fingers by accident. Their cheeks had brushed together, wet and sticky and grape-scented. Even without fully touching him, she'd been aware of how strong his body was, next to hers. Their shared laughter suddenly felt as if it had been worth twenty hours of the restaurant dinner conversations, art museum visits and snatched cell-phone exchanges that had built her relationship with Adam. A little kick and twist of female need moved low in her stomach, echoing in her pulse and reflecting all those looks they'd exchanged in the firelight, while they'd been talking.

She closed her eyes and told herself to get a grip.

There was no chemistry!

Really!

They seemed to converse quite comfortably together, when they weren't seething mad at each other, but he wasn't even her type. She valued his practical cattleman's skills *intensely* in a situation like this, valued all that strangely graceful efficiency and masculinity in the way he moved, but they weren't the skills—or the grace—that she needed in the kind of man who fit with her usual existence.

Yeah, fabulous specimens of manhood like Adam and Jason and Todd, said a sneaky little voice inside her.

Opening her eyes abruptly, she waited for Dusty to reply to her line about the chemistry, but apparently he didn't plan to. He'd bent down to straighten the plastic, which had rumpled a little during her earlier nap, despite the anchoring stones. Now he was pulling the second sleeping bag from its tight nylon bag.

"I'm going to sleep by the fire," he said. "I'll keep it fueled during the night so it's still hot in the morning for coffee before we start. I want to get going as early as we can."

"Why are you saying this? Because you think there's not room on the plastic for both of us?"

Shay, you idiot, why push the subject? He's said he values honesty, but not to this extent.

"Because I'll be more comfortable on the ground, that's all," he said.

She stopped pushing.

After ten minutes of largely silent night preparations, they were both in their sleeping bags.

In the night, the ground grew harder and colder beneath her with every painful toss and turn of her stiff, sore body, and the painkillers had definitely worn off. Looking out of the shallow shelter to where the fire still glowed with orange coals inside its ring of stones several yards away, she saw the inert dark shape of Dusty's body lying close to the warmth. He was sound asleep. She could hear the unmistakable rhythm of his breathing.

The desert seemed so quiet and still. Desert? Ridiculous to call it that, when it was flooded on every inch of low-lying ground as far as the eye could see. But the water was a temporary feature, while the isolation and silence would never change.

Silence was a relative term, of course, she decided. As her ears attuned to the night, she could hear frogs fluting and croaking nearby. The birdlife was mostly asleep, but every now and then there came a muffled squawk from high in one of the huge eucalyptus trees that lined a major channel of the river nearby, or a snickering sort of sound from the water itself. She thought she heard a snort from Sally or Beau, too.

But she felt lonely. The physical cold creeping into her from the ground echoed her awareness that Dusty, asleep, and Jake, keeping his lonely vigil with the helicopter, might well be the only other human beings in a radius of ten or fifteen miles. She thought about New York, and could hardly believe the city was real.

There could be ghosts here, of course. She and Jake had flown over an abandoned rammed-earth stockman's hut this morning, and Dusty had told her that there were several early explorers who had perished in the Channel Country long ago.

What must that have been like? Traveling on horseback over those cayenne-pepper sand dunes in the scorching heat of an outback summer, with no understanding of native foods and none of the aboriginal skill at finding secret water sources. A NASA expedition to the moon would have seemed less alien.

She shivered, and told herself sternly to send her thoughts elsewhere.

But thoughts were disobedient entities. The images of ghosts and loneliness stayed.

She struggled out of her sleeping bag and into her borrowed riding boots, freezing like a statue every time her back spasmed and having to slowly shift from the frozen position into her next cautious movement. The process took a while. At least she didn't have to get dressed, since she was sleeping in her clothes. She was so horribly stiff and sore! How would she possibly cover the remaining miles back to the Roscommon Downs homestead tomorrow, whether on horseback or on foot?

It would be a tough, painful day at best.

The realization pushed her spirits lower.

Dusty was still asleep, and she didn't want to disturb him. She crept past him and out into the night, looking for the horses because she needed to make contact with a red-blooded living creature, even if it wasn't human. She found both horses standing close to each other, snoozing in the dark.

"Hi, Sally, hi, Beau," she whispered, and put her arms around Sally's neck.

The horse didn't seem to mind. Her beautifully styled long black mane tickled Shay's cheek—no frizz for this girl—and her breath and body were so warm. But the effect only lasted a short time. Shay gathered her energy and went back to her shelter.

"You all right?" said a voice as she bent awkwardly to straighten her sleeping bag.

"Oh, did I waken you?" She eased herself upright. "I'm sorry."

"It's fine. Are you okay?" he repeated. He propped himself up on his elbow and studied her. She wondered if she would ever get used to the amount of perception that seemed to fill that brandy-brown gaze.

"I was getting cold and pretty uncomfortable," she admitted. "Do you have a couple more of those tablets? Are they mild enough for me to take another dose now?"

"They're fine. Over-the-counter. I think you call it acet-amino-something in America."

"Oh, right."

"They're in the first saddlebag, there, under the overhang. Do you want me to get them?"

"No, you stay. I can do it." She found the pills, downed two of them with a mug of water, then put them back in the bag. When they got back to Roscommon Downs she was going to thank Prim about a thousand times for packing that first-aid kit.

"You'd better come by the fire," Dusty said. "Nothing's going to stop you from being sore tomorrow, but the warmth might help a little."

"I was lonely, too," she blurted out. "And scared."

"Scared? Of wild animals?"

"Of ghosts. It's so isolated. And quiet. And you told me about those dying explorers a hundred and forty years ago, whom even the aboriginal tribespeople couldn't save…"

"Come here. Bring your sleeping bag." He sat up fully, brought a bare arm and shoulder out of his own sleeping bag and beckoned her, and she just didn't have it in her to keep safely away.

She fetched her sleeping bag, while he leaned toward the pile of broken wood he'd kept handy for feeding the fire during the night. He must have taken off most of his clothing, she realized, because his back was bare. He threw on the fuel. It blazed up, and she could feel the welcome heat on her face and front as soon as she got near it again.

"Slide your legs into your bag and sit in front of me," he said.

She wriggled and shifted and winced several times as more jolts of pain ambushed her body, then lowered herself awkwardly to the ground. He circled his arms around her and she leaned against him and that strange, happy feeling flooded into her again.

Her real life and the rest of the world seemed so far away that maybe they didn't really exist anymore, and the only thing that mattered was being safe and warm right at this moment, in close contact with a fellow human being.

"Sleepy?" Dusty asked, after a silence.

"Not yet."

"Me neither."

They sat for a little while. She could feel the rhythm of his breathing in the subtle movement of his body behind her.

"My mother organized a local history of Roscommon Downs several years ago," Dusty said lazily, his voice barely more than a creak. "One of the old-timers remembered a couple who used to travel around in a wagon selling things or doing odd jobs, during the Great Depression. They slept under their wagon on the ground. Sometimes the station people would invite them to use a spare bedroom for the night but they always said no. Said they couldn't sleep indoors. It spooked them and they felt suffocated. I've sometimes thought that would be a good way to be—to need your air and your freedom so much that you couldn't sleep indoors."

"Air and freedom I can relate to," Shay said, "but mattresses are a great invention. I'm still not sleepy, though…"

"We should have brought a few of those short-story manuscripts for entertainment. Were they any good?"

"A couple of them were great. Will Jake really use them to start his fire?"

"Sorry, I shouldn't have put the idea into his head."

"Oh hell, you mean he will?"

"Short stories probably don't feature too strongly on his list of life's essentials. Don't you have copies?"

Relief flooded her. Yes, of course they had copies, back in the office. But since she was half convinced that she'd dropped into some alternate universe where the office didn't exist this week, she hadn't thought of it.

She felt his arms firm around her a little. "Shall I show you the Southern Cross? That's the constellation on the Australian flag."

"I did actually know that."

"Okay, ten points to you. Will you know how to find it, next time you want to look at stars?"

"Um, no."

"Want to?"

"Yes, please." As long as it involves this delicious, undemanding body contact.

"Up there, see those?" He pointed, his arm nudging harder against her shoulder. Despite the long, physical day, he smelled good—a mix of man and soap and the faint aroma of spilled champagne.

She saw the group of four stars. "That's the Southern Cross?"

"No, you see, people get it wrong. That's the false cross.

If you try to use that to find the South Celestial Pole, you'll be stuffed."

"So what's the South Celestial Pole, and why would I want to find it?"

"To navigate, or tell time. It's the point in the sky that all the southern stars appear to rotate around."

"Right. And I need to navigate and tell time this way because my global positioning system and diver's watch, waterproof to a depth of three hundred meters, have been…?"

"Eaten by a crocodile."

"Right," she said again, in a slightly different tone.

"Which we don't have around here, so don't tense up like that."

She relaxed her shoulders with a sincere effort, and he laughed, which made her feel funny and fluttery inside. He could feel and intepret her body language that closely? Could he tell how good she felt, encircled by his arms and aware of his strength right behind her?

"Hurry up, Dusty," she said. "Tell me how to find the South Celestial Pole, because I need to locate true north *now!*"

"That's the spirit. You're sounding like an overworked corporate executive again. Excellent, you must be feeling better. But it's south, actually."

"Sorry?"

"We're locating south."

He told her the system. Locate the Pointers, also known as Alpha and Beta Centauri. Locate the true Southern Cross. Follow the long arm of the cross four lengths, to reach the South Celestial Pole. Drop your eye to the horizon. Ta-da!

He also showed her Achemar and Canopus, and the constellation of Musca—the Fly—and might have shown her more except that her neck began to ache again. She told him this and he said, "We should try to get back to sleep, anyhow. We'll learn how to tell time another night."

He put another few pieces of wood on the fire and lay down. Shay saw that he'd used most of his clothing as a pillow, wadding it into his sleeping-bag cover. She hadn't thought of doing that.

"I'm blocking your fire heat," she told him.

"I'm warm. Stay where you are, it's fine."

Very fine.

Too close.

But if she moved she'd either have to shuffle along like a caterpillar in her sleeping bag, or get out of it again and set up a whole new sleeping place. Somehow, she'd grown attached to this particular piece of rough ground, warmed by the fire and Dusty's body.

She lay down, but was still wakeful some minutes later, and wondered how long it was until morning. If she'd learned Dusty's method of telling time by the Southern Cross, she would have known.

She laughed to herself. Who knew that such an arcane skill would have come in handy so soon?

"What's funny?" Dusty said sleepily.

"Nothing."

"Tell me in the morning."

"If I can remember." Although he wasn't quite touching her, she had a strong sense of his body behind her, a buffer against cold and danger and loneliness, somehow vigilant even in sleep, making her feel very safe...

Mmm, and sleepy.

She woke up several hours later, drenched in dew, with Dusty's arm flung around her shoulder.

Dusty knew the moment when Shay first stirred into wakefulness. He felt her body move and stretch, and then go warily still. He'd put his arm around her in his sleep, but when he'd woken ten minutes ago in predawn air that had lost the unusual humidity of the past few days, he hadn't eased away.

Instead he'd lain there trying to work out what he thought about all this. Thirty-six hours ago, he'd sincerely detested her. He'd had no time for her, and had felt the utmost difficulty in following through on the code of hospitality that had been bred in him as a child in an era before satellite communication, the Internet and tourism had lessened the isolation of Roscommon Downs.

He knew he'd let too much of his negativity show, but there'd been something refreshing in acting that way, especially when Shay Russell could clearly give as good as she got and seemed to value the upfront nature of their confrontation as much as he did.

They'd both grown kinder to each other as time went on. Prim's evening meal in the single men's quarters could take a lot of credit for the change—the good food, the friendliness, the lively nature of the conversation, which he knew full well had been pitched at a more elevated intellectual level than Shay had snobbishly expected.

Then they'd had the one-to-one over their mugs of tea. Without that, without its softening effect on both their attitudes, he might not have gone to the trouble of arranging the helicopter deal with WIPH in the morning. He could never have envisaged that it would backfire the way it had…and he certainly wouldn't have envisaged that Shay would be so courageous about it.

Courageous *and* good-humored, which was a further plus, because bravery was pretty hard to handle when it took itself too seriously.

In short, he liked her now.

Which had to count as a change for the better, but it had its downside.

Lying behind her with his arm curved over her body, he felt the chilly fall of the dew and had an instinct to protect her from it by sliding even closer and folding his whole body over hers. The instinct was about a lot more than protection, too. It was achingly, insistently physical.

Male.

Imperative.

It was about the way she smelled and the softness of her skin. It was about his need for release and for renewed proof of his manhood. It was about human connection and closeness, the desire to give and receive the sweet, beautiful blessing of making each other feel good.

Okay, be honest, it was mostly about sex.

Here.

Now.

If not on offer, then at least hanging as an unspoken possibility in the air. He knew Shay would have moved away, even in her sleep, if she'd found him repellent. He knew she'd still be back beneath the overhang if she felt as hostile toward him now as she had been at first.

He also had this—possibly primitive—belief that a healthy heterosexual man and woman could only get to a certain point with friendship and with being honest and relaxed in each other's company if they also, at some level, wanted to rip each other's clothes off.

Yep, it sounded primitive, but he believed it all the same. He thought people were kidding themselves when they said, "He's my best friend," or "She and I are just good mates," but denied any sexual-slash-romantic element to their feelings.

He simply didn't believe that he and Shay would have sat here last night, wrapped in their respective sleeping bags, with her half leaning against him and his arm pressing her shoulder as he pointed upward, looking at the stars, if there hadn't been a very definite vibe.

Whether to act on it, that was the question.

He knew he was in the wrong mental state. If you wanted to get analytical, this would have to be a rebound affair, about proving that Mandy herself was wrong, not that there was something wrong with *him*. To get even more clinical, it was about a man's response to the sudden and unexpected withdrawal of the sex on tap that he'd enjoyed for the past couple of months.

This was the point he'd reached in his thinking when he'd felt Shay's first movement.

"Your hair is soaked," he said quickly, sliding his arm from her shoulder as he spoke. Pointless. Of course she must have realized the arm was there. "It has little beads of dew all over it."

"And let me guess, it looks like an antique doll's hair, right? A million tiny little nineteenth-century corkscrews."

"Yeah." He wanted to touch it, no matter how wet or nineteenth century it was. Then he wanted to kiss her, to see how her mouth felt. The timing was wrong in every possible way, so with a wrenching effort, he let the wanting go.

"It's the moisture," she was saying. "I *hate* my hair when there's damp in the air and I can't get to a salon."

"I like it."

"Oh, you're a man, you have no hair sense."

"You'd rather I did have hair sense and hated it."

"Well, of course!" But she was smiling now. He could tell by her voice, even though he couldn't see her mouth or her eyes.

"The air's much drier today," he told her. "Will it calm down?"

"Not until it's taken its medication."

She sat up stiffly, awkward and cautious with every movement, and he thought of the twenty-five kilometers or more that they still had to travel before reaching the homestead. They didn't have enough water or food for a second night in the open. He could deal with it, their survival wasn't in doubt, but if Shay thought that last night's lifestyle options had been primitive, she would be in for a further shock today.

"Let me take a look at that fire," he said. "And we'll open out the sleeping bags and spread them on bushes to dry."

She held her hand palm up, while he slid out of his makeshift bed. "Won't they get wetter? I think the dew is still falling."

"As soon as the sun gets up, the chill will lift." He stood up and began to unzip the bag.

She looked toward the eastern sky in surprise. "You mean it's not even dawn?" At that moment, the first thin sliver of fire crested the horizon and she gasped. "Oh, wow!"

She sat there watching the changing light while he draped his sleeping bag over a scratchy piece of bush then examined the fire. It had died almost to nothing, but when he dug among the black coals and gray ash, he found a small remnant of glowing heat. Adding eucalyptus leaves one by one so as not to suffocate the coals, he saw first a tiny flame, which soon grew into a crackling blaze as he put on more leaves, then twigs and sticks, and finally pieces of broken branch as thick as his arm.

By this time, the sun had left the horizon and Shay had wriggled out of her sleeping bag and spread it on a bush just like Dusty's. Aware of the need to conserve their clean water, he measured two mugs' worth and poured them into the billy, then nudged a flat rock closer to the center of the blaze. The water in the billy soon began to sing.

Prim had included a juice box each, as well as mini boxes of cereal, UHT milk, bread and peanut butter. When he'd toasted the bread on the end of a stick, and added instant coffee grounds and milk to the billy, Dusty considered that they had a pretty fine outback breakfast.

Shay seemed to agree. "Coffee…!" she breathed, inhaling as he poured it into the mugs.

"Hey! Please! Not coffee. Latte."

"Latte." She laughed. "You are funny."

"Taste it and tell me this is not latte."

She sipped obediently. "Okay, you're right. And I sincerely appreciate the trouble you've gone to in adding preserved milk to instant granules just so a city girl can call her morning coffee by an Italian name. It's…mmm…"

She pressed her lips lightly together, closed her eyes and lifted her face. It was lucky about the closed eyes because he couldn't take his off her pretty mouth. He liked her neck, too, liked the clean, graceful line of her jaw

"…Heaven." She opened her eyes again, and he looked quickly away. "Although, if you want the truth, I would probably have sucked the dry granules off the spoon if I'd had to. Thank you, Dusty."

"Do you think you're going to be able to get on the horse today?" he asked.

She took a doubtful, shuddery breath. "I'll give it a try. And I'll put some more cream on my legs. Otherwise—?"

"Yes. We might get to do some more campfire astronomy tonight."

After they'd finished their breakfast, packing up the simple camp took only a few minutes. Dusty doused the fire with a billycan full of the clear-flowing floodwaters, despite the laughable lack of bushfire risk in current conditions. Their sleeping bags were still slightly damp, but if they did have to camp out again tonight, they could dry them by their campfire before the dew began to fall in the early hours.

The horses had had a peaceful night. Rains earlier in the season had brought good grazing, and they'd been within easy reach of the water despite being hobbled. He unstrapped their legs, took their blankets and saddles from beneath the overhang where he'd stored them, and fastened the girths.

Helping Shay onto Sally's back, he knew after only a few of the mare's paces that it was going to be too painful. Shay winced and hissed, "I'm sorry. There's just something about her gait, or my posture, or something. If there was something to brace against..."

"We'll try it."

"How?" She looked at him, immediately alarmed.

"You'll have to ride Beau, in front of me."

She nodded, and he saw a tiny flash of pink that was her tongue escaping nervously from between her lush lips.

Oh great.

Lush lips, when she'd just agreed to ride with her back against his stomach and her backside against his thighs while big, loose-limbed Beau created a rocking motion beneath them.

Lush nothing.

Lush quantities of mosquitoes, breeding in the floodwaters. Think about that, Dusty. Lush floods of sun on their unprotected skin. Lush, lewd, embarrassing and too-close-to-the-bone suggestions from Prim or Wayne or Andy about how he and Shay might have entertained themselves during the lonely desert night.

He got his equilibrium back and helped her onto the horse. "Do the stirrups help?" he said. "Because I can ride without them, if you want."

"No, you use them," she said. Then she winced and hissed with pain when he hauled himself up behind her.

The saddle didn't give them a lot of space to keep their distance, but then that was the whole point. He reached around and pulled her even closer, using the reins one-handed, keeping his free arm firmly at her waist and still somehow managing to hold Sally's lead rope. The mare would probably stick close to Beau without it, but he didn't want to take the chance that something might spook her and he'd have a runaway horse to further slow their progress home.

"Ready, steady, go?" he said to Shay.

"Ready as I'll ever be."

They managed it. He could tell she must be in a fair degree of pain because she barely spoke. Doing his best to stop her spine from making the slow, rocking, snake-like undulation that seemed to hurt her so badly, he kept his own hold on her firm to the point of cramping every muscle in his arm. It felt incredibly intimate to him—more so because it was about help and support rather than desire.

"Is it okay if I put my head on your shoulder?" he had to ask, because trying to turn it sideways or tilt it back just didn't work. If he ended up with severe neck strain or a pulled muscle on top of her jarring and pain, they could be in real trouble.

"Go ahead," she told him, and they rode cheek to cheek, looking at the route in front of them, the way they'd drunk champagne cheek to cheek last night.

What was the old Sinatra song about dancing that way? Heaven? In heaven?

This wasn't heaven, it was sheer hell. Feeling Shay's soft skin move against his own face with the rhythm of the horse, smelling her shampoo-scented hair and resting his chin on the slippery silk of her tired blouse, he spent the first kilometer in a state of solid semi-arousal, and if it hadn't been for the distracting effect of the cramping in his arm there would have been no *semi* involved.

If Shay could feel it, she didn't let on.

She *had* to feel it, surely, because he could feel her backside right against him, pert and round and spread against the saddle. Unless she was simply in too much pain…

"How far have we gone?" she finally asked.

"About two kilometers."

"Like yesterday. I guess that's my limit. I'm sorry, Dusty. Having you there helps, but it's not enough. Can we walk again?"

"Sure. You should have said before."

"No. I wanted to go as far as I could, so we'd get home today."

But he already suspected they'd lost their last shot at that.

No point in telling her yet.

He dismounted from Beau then helped Shay down and they began to walk.

## *Chapter Seven*

By late afternoon, their route had brought them close beside the river's main channel, on Roscommon Downs' land. Dusty knew the area well, and could estimate with a good degree of accuracy how far they now were from the homestead. By his calculation, they had around nine or ten kilometers to go—roughly six and a half miles.

Shay had done astonishingly well, but she'd needed a long break over lunch and several more smaller ones since. She'd been blunt and up-front about it each time, saying "Dusty, I need to stop," or, "Get going? Not yet. Sorry. I need a bit longer."

He appreciated the honesty and trusted it now. It was good to know that she would tell him what she needed, that she wouldn't complain too soon or keep going too long.

They didn't have a lot of food or clean water left, however. They'd had a lot of flooded terrain to walk through, including a couple of places where they'd had to battle against the current, and over the past half hour she'd slowed her pace considerably, walking with smaller and slower steps. He thought she wasn't aware of it, while he kept revising their time of likely arrival at the homestead later and later.

When it reached the point where the sun had dipped behind the trees that lined the river, and he'd calculated that they'd have at least four hours of traveling in the dark, he accepted that they weren't going to make it home tonight. Their clothing was wet again, and when the air chilled soon after the sun disappeared, they'd get very cold.

"We need to set up camp," he told her.

She nodded. "I was about to say the same thing. Have we come far enough?"

"About six miles to do tomorrow."

"And today we've done twelve or thirteen? Good." She nodded again. Stiffly. "Good. That's bearable."

"Let me try and massage your back tonight, and rig up some kind of heat pack."

On a mental list he checked everything off. Heat pack, water collection system, fishing line, not to mention the usual tasks of wood gathering and dealing with the horses.

He had a lot to do, and seeing the way she looked, he planned to limit Shay's involvement to unpacking the sleeping bags. There was no overhang in this spot to keep the saddles and saddle blankets free of dew. On the other hand, he could see better possibilities for rigging a kind of lean-to with the plastic sheeting. A carpet of grass and wildflowers would give them a more comfortable night on the ground, provided he removed a few bits of prickly desert vegetation first.

The heat pack was easy, too. Shay helped to gather wood and they soon had a fire. Dusty found a smooth rock that didn't look as if it was native to the area. He suspected it had an aboriginal history, and might once have been used as a seed grinder against a flatter rock embedded in the ground. Its tribal significance wasn't important to him now, however.

He heated the stone beside the blaze then wrapped it in his cotton sweater, which he could do without until the evening grew colder. Next, he rigged up the two saddles as a back support and she leaned against them with the hot rock nudging the small of her back.

The water collection system Shay didn't understand at all.

"Why are you putting Prim's plastic storage bags over the ends of those branches?"

"To get us some more water for tomorrow. The leaves will transpire and the water will collect in the bags."

"Won't it taste…leafy?"

"You'll be surprised. It turns out pretty clean. We can boil the river water, as well, but then there'll be a definite flavor of mud and possibly a bug or two."

"Leafy sounds better."

The peanut butter–coated grasshoppers she found a little bizarre, also, but it was the best fish and yabby bait he could think of right now. The good news was that Channel Country waters should be teeming with bream, golden perch and yabbies, if he could find the right underwater habitat, and some kind of pliable, vine-like branch to act as a line.

"You really think you can catch something?" Shay asked.

"I hope so, or dinner's going to be pretty boring."

"What do we have left?"

"Bread, peanut butter, salt and pepper, sugar, ketchup, tea, coffee and milk."

"You're right. That sounds more like a condiments shelf than a meal."

"And I found some desert lime still fruiting."

"Oh, those green berries you picked at lunch?"

"They're not berries, they're a kind of native citrus. A little past their best since they've been on the tree so long, but they'll give the fish a great flavor."

"If you catch anything." She watched with visible doubt as he transformed some fencing-wire barbs into hooks and prepared his makeshift baits. "I should tell you that the one other time in my life I've had anything to do with fishing, on a vacation in Bermuda, I turned out to be a total fish jinx."

"So you think I should walk downstream a couple of hundred meters, to be out of your aura?"

"Could help."

"And you'll stay here with that hot rock against your back?"

"It feels so good, Dusty, thank you."

He left her and combed the riverbank in search of the right mess of fallen branches under the waterline, which would provide quiet spots for fish and yabbies to shelter. Tramping through a patch of gray-green vegetation that reached to his calves, he smelled a strong odor in the air and realized that this was wild onion. If he did get some fish, he could dig up the corms and they'd be eating Thai style tonight, with a lime, onion and peanut-butter sauce.

He got back to the campfire an hour later, with two nice-sized golden perch. At over thirty centimeters in length—twelve inches, Shay would call it—they were a legal catch. He also had at least a dozen yabbies, and the wild onion corms he'd dug up, and he felt like a cross between an aboriginal tribal hunter and a celebrity chef.

Shay had her eyes closed, but she heard his approach. "I'm not asleep," she said. "And I've kept the fire going."

"It looks good. That's the way we want it, a big bed of coals."

"Do we have something to cook on it?"

"Keep your eyes closed and wait for the smell."

She obeyed him, grinning.

He boiled a billy of the cleanest river water he could get, stripped some smooth, soft pieces of bark from a eucalyptus tree and soaked them in the hot water. Then he scaled and gutted the two dark olive and golden yellow fish and spread them with peanut butter, broken pieces of desert lime and rough slices of wild onion corm. He sprinkled the fish with Prim's little paper packets of salt and pepper, wrapped each fish in layers of sodden bark and buried them in a small pit of burning hot ash.

"It was great sitting here while you were gone," Shay said, still with her eyes closed. "I watched Sally and Beau grazing. You're right, they are like preschoolers holding hands, they're adorable. Then a whole flock of kangaroos... *Flock* doesn't sound right...."

"Pod," he suggested.

"A whole pod of kangaroos came lolloping along, eating the grass and drinking from the river. I never realized they use their tails like a third leg when they're moving slowly. And I just sat here and watched them with the hot rock against my back, and I could easily have fallen asleep, only I heard you." She thought for a moment. "What would you have done, Dusty, if I'd said I couldn't stand another night out in the open and wanted to push through to the homestead tonight?"

"I would have told you no."

"And here I thought Australia was a democracy...."

"Australia is, as it should be. Roscommon Downs is a dictatorship, and I'm the boss."

"Ah."

"You have a problem with that?"

"I'm envisaging some sticky scenarios."

"Knowing I'm the boss is what avoids the sticky scenarios. Sometimes you need one man's vision, not a whole lot of competing claims. We had to stop. The horses were at the end of their strength, even if you weren't. If we'd gone on another two miles we would have moved away from the river."

"Where our dinner came from?"

"Exactly. And I'm the one who knows when the trail moves away from the river, and the one who knows how to catch the dinner. So I'm the boss. Are we okay with it now?"

"I was never not okay with it, Dusty. I am deeply grateful that you are the boss, in a situation like this. I was just curious about how you saw it, that's all."

"Well, that's how I see it. And everyone who works for me knows it."

"You're suggesting that I'd better know it, too."

"While you're here."

With her eyes still closed, she listened to his movements for a little longer. She heard the clank of the billycan, the hiss of water, the sound of his boots on the earth, all of it efficient and sure. "Can I smell something now?" she finally asked.

"It's the chef's special."

"Well, it smells good…."

He had a fresh billy of salted water on the fire and was cooking the yabbies, which turned the six-inch-long freshwater lobsters from green and blue and black to a crab-like pinky red. He flavored them with more of the onion corms, salt and pepper, a sprinkling of sugar and the desert limes.

When the yabbies were done, he broke them open and added the sweet meat to the broth, from which he'd fished out the solid remnants of onion and lime. He added a big dollop of peanut butter and then several slices of crustless bread to thicken the dish into a chunky soup. They'd eat the soup from their enamel mugs and the fish directly from the bark.

Only once it was all laid out did he tell her, "You can open your eyes now."

She did so, and her gaze fell on their feast. "Wow!"

"Tonight your chef is featuring Thai-style yabby and peanut-butter bisque, with ash-baked bark parcels—" By the word *parcels*, she'd started laughing "—of whole golden perch in a peanut, wild onion and desert lime *jus*."

When he got to *jus*, she told him, "Dustin Tanner, you are *such* a show-off! Are you making that up?"

"Nope."

"I guess you're not, because I can smell it, and it smells fabulous. How did you learn to do something like this?"

"It's Prim's fault," he said.

"Yeah?"

"I mean, I learned something about edible bush foods when I was a kid—Mum often used desert lime—but Prim's the kind of person who can teach you things without you even realizing it. You saw her in action with the book discussion."

"I did. She was impressive."

"Letty's begun doing the same thing with her schoolkids. She's pretty bright, too. But Prim has international-cuisine nights, and guess-the-secret-ingredient contests. She's responsible for the word *jus* in my vocabulary, and trust me it's not something I'm proud of."

Shay laughed. "So tell me more about Prim."

They talked without a break all through the meal and, after Shay had washed out the billycan and the mugs, they reheated her rock and made tea and talked all the way through drinking it.

"How's your back?" he asked eventually.

For some time he'd wanted his sweater back because the temperature was plummeting. The fire wasn't enough to keep the chill at bay when he was dressed only in a polo shirt and some thin chambray. They might even get a frost tonight. But Shay still had the sweater-wrapped rock against her back and every now and then she'd shift it a little. He'd reheated it earlier and knew it would be helping her.

She didn't reply to his question, just reached around, unwrapped the rock, balled up the sweater and threw it toward him. "I'm sorry I kept it so long."

"I didn't ask for it back."

"No, you were a perfect gentleman, but as soon as you asked about my back I could see you were freezing. I should have noticed earlier."

"We should be getting to bed, anyhow." He dived into the sweater as soon as he'd said it, remembering what a loaded announcement it had been last night.

He knew the awareness between them was even more powerful tonight, after twenty-four extra hours in each other's company. He also knew that all the reasons he'd already identified for not giving into it still applied.

Last night, however, he'd deliberately positioned himself by the fire and yet she'd still ended up in his arms. Was he kidding himself, thinking he could stay away from her if she gave him the slightest signal that beckoned him closer?

When he emerged through the neck hole of the sweater, he looked at her—at the way she was staring down, avoiding his gaze, her body wrapped snugly in the oilskin stockman's coat that Prim had borrowed from Letty and packed for her—and wondered just what would be so bad about sleeping with her.

He'd seen his share of American television. If it was

even remotely accurate in its depiction of Shay's demographic as a single New York professional woman, she wouldn't exactly be saving herself for marriage. They could pleasure each other now, and say goodbye the day the airstrip came back into service without a skerrick of regret on either side.

All the same, something held him back.

An inkling of danger?

A misguided and way too traditional concept of respect?

He didn't know. He said quickly, "Hey, I noticed you didn't make yourself a pillow last night."

"I didn't think of it. But I saw yours, and I'm going to make one tonight. I don't have much to stuff it with, though. This coat, but it's pretty stiff."

"Take my sweater."

"Then your pillow will be too thin."

"It won't. My shirt's softer than Letty's oilskin, and there's my jeans and T-shirt. They're bulkier than your silk top and those pants. A better pillow might help your shoulders, if not your back."

She nodded. "Thanks. I'm going to take more of Prim's painkillers, too. We have to get to the homestead by tomorrow afternoon, because by then there'll be none left."

"I'm going to check on the horses."

"My luxury bathroom with the Italian marble and gold-plated fittings is fortunately in the opposite direction."

As they'd done last night, they completed their night preparations largely in silence, but this time they lay down side by side in their respective sleeping bags, beneath the plastic lean-to that would keep the frosty dew at bay.

Hearing Shay shift and snuggle like a cat getting comfortable in a basket of laundry, Dusty knew it would be a difficult night.

* * *

Shay waited for the painkillers to work their magic, hoping that their relaxing effect would lull her into sleep. So far, it wasn't happening. She thought that Dusty was still awake, also. Something about his breathing gave it away, as well as the occasional movements she could hear, just a couple of feet from her.

He'd decided not to maintain the fire overnight. With a less demanding journey to face in the morning, he seemed more relaxed about taking longer over breakfast. The benefit of their early start this morning had been outweighed, in any case, by the number of breaks Shay had needed during the day. She only hoped her back was, if not any better, then at least no worse tomorrow.

She shifted again, and massaged her makeshift pillow, trying to plump it up and get it more comfortable. The nylon sleeping-bag cover felt synthetic and unexpectedly rough against her cheek. She didn't like it. Dusty's cotton sweater had felt a lot softer.

She sat up, very aware of the fact that, since she had used most of her clothing for her pillow, all she wore tonight was a cinnamon-and-cream lace and satin bra with matching briefs—the spare underwear that she'd managed to snaffle from her overnight bag before enacting Dusty's decree that she had to leave it behind with the chopper.

How much light did the fire give off? How much of her would Dusty be able to see if he happened to look? Trying to keep the sleeping bag pulled up high around her chest, she took his sweater out of the bag's cover, along with her own silk top and trousers, and remade the pillow completely.

First she rolled up Letty's oilskin and put it inside the trousers. She made the trousers into a compact package that fit inside her top, and then slid the whole mixed bundle of fabric inside Dusty's sweater, folding it in half and using its own sleeves to make a loose tie.

Much better.

Except for the way the sweater smelled.

Like Dusty himself.

With her cheek pressed against it and one arm tucked beneath, it felt as if she were hugging him, especially when she knew that the reality of a hug lay only a few feet away, breathing steadily in the darkness.

Why did he smell so good?

Why did one man smell *right,* while another just... *didn't.*

Personal choices in aftershave and laundry detergent? Surely it couldn't be as simple as that.

Todd had always smelled right. To be honest, in hindsight, this had been the basis for their whole relationship. He'd smelled right, even though in so many other ways he was all wrong.

Adam hadn't even smelled right, but since the Todd episode had convinced Shay that smell was a poor foundation for lifelong love, she'd ignored the nasal dimension to her feelings. Well, he hadn't actively smelled *bad!* She'd put her mourning for the loss of a warm, delicious male neck to bury her face in into the Life's Not Perfect basket.

Jason... She couldn't remember how Jason had smelled. He was years ago.

"Can't get to sleep?" Dusty said out of the darkness.

"Sorry, am I wriggling around?" There was a particular kind of restlessness to her movements, she knew—a heated, tingling, pulsing kind. Her whole body crawled with need, and every particle of that need funneled into the bundle of perfectly scented fabric she held in her arms.

"A bit," Dusty said. "But I think I'd be awake anyway." He let out a particular kind of restless sigh, and Shay heard his body slide against the soft inner fabric of his sleeping bag. She thought he'd shifted a little closer, but she wasn't sure. "How's the pillow now?"

"Perfect. At least," she corrected quickly, "it's much better."

It only smelled perfect.

She wriggled and stretched, protecting her back and shoulders with the movement. Bending her legs to bring her body into a curled position, she felt the puffy edge of Dusty's sleeping bag brush against her down-covered knees.

"Do you think of yourself as a typical New Yorker?" he suddenly asked. "A typical New York woman?"

"Is this how you plan to lull me to sleep?"

"Sorry… It's just… I was just wondering."

"That's fine. I'm teasing. I wasn't sleepy yet." They both considered their shared wakefulness in silence for a moment. "But I'm not big on consigning myself to a stereotype, so even if I am typical, you'd have to back me into a very tight corner before I'd admit it."

There was a thick pause.

"That's what I was thinking about doing, you see," Dusty said slowly. "Backing you into a very tight corner." He went silent again, then added in a lower tone, "Of my sleeping bag."

*"What?"*

"It's okay. Forget it."

She thought.

Of his sleeping bag? Back her into a tight corner of it?

It was quite clear what he meant. Her body crawled and throbbed again. He rolled slightly toward her and their knees pressed harder together.

"Because I'm from New York, and that's what New York women are up for?" She shifted closer without even knowing she was going to do it. If she brought her arm out of the sleeping bag, she'd easily be able to touch him now.

"Yeah, it was clumsy, wasn't it? I was sounding you out, giving you fair warning, or something. But I should have just—" He stopped again, hissed a sigh between his teeth and rolled onto his stomach. The powerful bulk of his upper arm nudged her fingers. As he'd done last night, he'd used his T-shirt as part of his pillow, so his skin was bare.

"Should have just what?"

"Kissed you."

Something slammed into her lower stomach in the thick outback darkness like a kangaroo slamming into a car on a highway at night. How could two words carry that much heat? How could *kissed you* make her so want to be kissed?

"Yeah, that might have been better," she agreed, hearing the way her voice had gone creaky and breathless. She let her fingers press up to his bare, warm flesh, and yet again he shifted closer, making her whole forearm lie against his muscled bicep.

"So is it too late?" he said.

"To—?"

She knew.

But she wanted to hear him say it again.

He did. "To kiss you, of course."

"No," she said softly. "It's not too late."

He eased even closer. Shay could barely breathe. A part of her wanted to meet him halfway, to assert her equality in this most primal form of partnership. A bigger part of her simply waited, in a dizzy and almost painful state of expectation. Her heart beat faster. Her whole body felt hot and ready and aware. She was flooding with desire, melting with it, aching with it, and they hadn't even kissed.

Then she felt his mouth in the darkness—the faintest

whisper of breath and warmth, a rustle of nylon as he moved, followed by taste and pressure and incredible sensation. He smelled perfect, and he kissed... *better.*

He began slowly, exploring her with exquisite patience. His lips felt soft and firm at the same time, angled crookedly against her own mouth. They moved with the same male grace as the rest of his body. There was nothing out of place, nothing clumsy, nothing that jarred. She felt the first hint of moisture and sweetness as his tongue lapped at the sensitive inner skin of her lower lip, and then it disappeared again. The accidental tease made her want so much more.

She had no space in her mind to think it through, but had the hazy understanding that she'd never known a kiss to feel so right, so fast. It was like the meal they'd eaten tonight—unexpected, fabulously fresh, made even better by hunger and by the solitude and the purity of the air.

The whole meaning of her existence narrowed to his exploration of her mouth and her response to him. She heard a little sound escape from her throat—a helpless vocal note that was almost like begging.

*More.*

*Don't stop.*

*Come closer.*

*Never, ever stop.*

Her lips fell farther apart and this time his tongue washed deep into her mouth. She opened her eyes, and in the glow of the firelight she could just see that his eyes were closed, his lashes lying against his cheeks and his lids smooth and relaxed.

It made her feel as if he'd surrendered to this as completely as she had.

There was no need to watch him. She trusted him. She trusted everything that had happened between them since they'd left Jake with the chopper yesterday, and everything that was going to happen once they reached the homestead sometime tomorrow.

Trusted it, and wanted it, and didn't want to mess it all up with the barrage of self-questioning she could so easily launch into.

*What does it* mean? *Where will it* go? *What will he* think? *What's the downside and the risk? Where does it fit in my life? How do I know what I really want, here?*

All of that.

She was so sick of doing that.

Suddenly, kissing him wasn't anywhere near enough. She freed her arms from the sleeping bag and reached for him, needing to know how he felt when she held him, needing to feel every ounce of his weight pressed against her and to map every inch of his contoured body with her hands.

He felt so *strong*.

Why hadn't she ever guessed how good it would feel to hold a man this powerfully physical and honed? Why hadn't she understood about the magical contrast between her own softness and his hard muscle mass, beneath the supple covering of healthy skin.

She couldn't get enough of him. When his tongue pushed deeper, she met it with her own, and when he slid down the side zipper of his sleeping bag and rolled his torso half onto her, she cupped her hands over his tight backside and let out a moan of satisfaction.

Then he began to touch her breasts. He brushed his fingertips across her nipple and, seconds later, the ball of his thumb. Sliding his hand inside the lace, he cupped her, then rolled the hardened peak between his fingers, making an electric connection that arrowed right to her soft, swollen groin. He flicked her bra straps down, one by one, making the lacy cups useless, then he slid around to her back and managed to unsnap the fastening in two economical attempts.

They still weren't close enough together. She fumbled for the zipper on her own bag but suddenly her back spasmed, freezing her with the intensity of the unexpected pain. He felt the tensing in her body at once and dragged his mouth away from another endless kiss.

"I'm hurting you." He stroked the hair back from her forehead and kissed the tip of her nose, then her tingling mouth. "I'm sorry."

"No, it was me. I was looking for the zipper."

"Is it okay again now?" His question was tender and totally focused. She appreciated it, knowing that in some men the subtext would have been purely *when can we keep going?*

"My back's okay," she said. "For the moment. It's weird. Sometimes just the slightest bend and twist sets it off. But I can't get the zipper, and I want to. I want to be closer, touching you, Dusty."

He slid a little, so that he was sharing her makeshift pillow. He kissed her shoulder with sweet heat, and kept his hand lightly cupped on her sensitized breast. "Maybe it's best to leave the zipper," he said.

She could hear the reluctance slowing his words and didn't understand. "Leave it? You mean leave it closed?"

"If we get any nearer to each other, you know what will happen."

"Yes. Isn't that the whole point?" She brushed his lips with her fingertips—she loved the shape of his mouth, loved how much better she knew it, now—and he grabbed her wrist and breathed hot kisses into her palm and against the sensitive skin at the base of her fingers.

"Well…yes, it could be the whole point, if you want it to be, I guess."

"I do want it to be. Don't you?" She hadn't expected this hesitation and holding back from him.

"Very much. But what kind of contraception are you using?" he asked softly. "I'm not doing this unless it's safe. Shouldn't you consider that, too?"

The question hit her so suddenly that it jarred her mood almost as much as yesterday's chopper crash had jarred her body. She thought about it for a moment, thought about all the implications, and all the past history she didn't want to have to share with him, then blurted out, "Can't you take it on trust?"

"No, I can't."

"Shoot, Dusty, you can't take it this far and then refuse to go all the way!"

"That's supposed to be my line, isn't it?" She heard the smile in his voice, felt the push of his breathing against her body.

"We're not going to argue over who's saying the wrong thing!"

"Is that what you usually expect, though? For a man to take it on trust?"

"Usually…" she echoed vaguely, then spoke with an edge. "There's no *usually*. That makes it sound as if— I'm not that promiscuous, Dusty. I don't— You know, I've had steady boyfriends. Just a handful of them. I'm not in and out of bed with every man I meet. This is what your typical New York woman question was about. Again. If you want me to analyze why this feels so right… No. Please don't make me do that!"

"My question isn't about your morals, or your past." He swore, as if her misunderstanding was a huge frustration, an affront to his sense of honor. "It's not about analyzing, either. It's about whether this is safe. For both of us. I have no protection. I have nothing unpleasant to pass onto you, either, I'm certain of that."

"Same from me to you!"

His voice dropped low, more tender than anything she'd yet heard from him. "Don't get angry, Shay." He brushed her mouth and she wanted to hunt down the too-brief kiss and get it back. "Isn't it something that needs to be talked about? Isn't it something that protects you even more than it protects me?"

She didn't know how to answer. Her ob-gyn specialist had already told her that unwanted pregnancy was likely to be the least of her problems. The woman was only a few years older than Shay herself and was one of those super-human creatures who juggled motherhood with a Manhattan medical practice.

Dr. Chin had been pretty blunt during a checkup just a few months ago. "If you want kids, Shay, don't put it on the back burner, okay? It's only going to get harder for you with every month that goes by. You're probably already looking at some kind of intervention if you want to conceive. Three or four years from now, you'll be looking for a miracle."

"I'm not even sure if I do want kids," she'd answered, numb with surprise.

"You don't have the luxury of a lot of time to anguish over it, Shay."

"I see. Thanks."

Dr. Chin had gone on to apologize for her honesty. "But I'm not going to have you saying to me, 'Why didn't anyone tell me before it was too late?'"

The whole conversation had stayed with her, word for word, especially what she'd said herself.

*I'm not even sure if I do want kids.*

Now, halfway around the world from Dr. Chin's exclusive and highly regarded practice, Shay could allay Dusty's concerns about contraception by passing on the message from her doctor in a couple of stark sentences.

She began. "If you're talking about pregnancy, Dusty, you don't have to worry. It's safe."

"Famous last words."

*Okay, say it Shay.*

*My doctor says I'm going to have to work to conceive.*

The words didn't come. Other words came instead.

"I don't even know if I want to have children," she blurted out. She curled her fingers against his back and had to consciously relax them to keep from digging her nails into his skin. "I mean, it's such a huge commitment. There's so much to consider. I look at my friend Sarah, who's seriously asthmatic, and has twins and a third one due in the fall, and she never has a second to herself. She never goes out. She never sleeps, as far as I can see. She wears sweatpants and running shoes ninety-five percent of the time. People say that the rewards cancel out all that, but I just don't know that I'd make a good mother. My own parents… Well, we talked about that, didn't we? I look at various things about myself and I think, would I pass that on? Would I royally stuff up my child by some huge fault in my parenting? I can see that it would be satisfying once they got older, and you could be proud of their achievements, and have adult conversations with them."

In the darkness, she smiled a little at an imaginary daughter—competent, interesting, intelligent and gorgeous. It was a precious image.

"But then I think about the kinds of conversations I have with my own parents and, let me tell you, they're not by choice and they're definitely not satisfying. It's such a powerful, scary relationship. So if I kill my career and my body and my entire lifestyle by sacrificing everything to this person, or people, who are then going to choose not to want to be with me the moment they're old enough to be any use as equals or friends…" She took a breath, hearing the way her words had sped up. "…Then what's the point? And yet, the idea of little arms reaching up to me, and of me actually *wanting* to make some of those sacrifices, which is a desire that does seem to kick in for most people once they actually have the baby—"

"Shay?" he whispered, pressing his fingers over her lips.

"Yes?" She grabbed his hand and took it away—it was a distraction, with all the stuff she was groping to say.

"Are you writing a book on this?"

"Well, no, I hadn't considered that, but—"

"Because I think you're already up to about chapter five."

"Sorry." She tensed. "I didn't realize you wanted the condensed version."

"But don't you think it's a hell of a lot simpler than what you're suggesting?"

"No. I don't." She'd been fretting about it for months. "I think it is."

"How in the heck can it be simple? It's the most complicated decision I've ever faced! My friends and I—"

"Talk about it for hours. Somehow I guessed."

"Okay." She gritted her teeth. "I overanalyze. I know that."

"But as for how it can be simple… Don't you think some of those big life things just are?"

He lay back and began stroking her body again, as a background to his words. She wanted to grab his hand and say *stop,* and yet there was something good about this. They seemed to be arguing, but it didn't feel angry or unequal or part of an unbridgeable distance.

"Like when you fall in love with someone," he went on, "you don't think, but what if they get hairy in strange places twenty years from now and I can't stand it? What if we run out of things to talk about? What if I lose sleep over them some day because they have to go in for surgery and I'm worried?"

"What are you saying?"

"Don't you think sometimes your heart pulls you so hard, there's no choice and you just have to go where it takes you? You just have to…follow it home?"

Yeah, maybe.

It was a very appealing idea, somehow. Follow her heart home. Could she do that? How did she find out where her heart lived?

"So you want kids?" she asked.

"Yes."

"In one word? Really, Dusty? Just like that. No questions or doubts."

"I can go a little deeper if you want," he drawled. "I can give you the book-length account."

"Please." She ignored his sarcasm. "Tell me why it's easy for you. Tell me why you're so sure, and what you think the benefits are, when to me this is one of the major decisions of my life, and I don't have forever to make it. At all!" Again, there was a tiny moment when she could have told him what Dr. Chin had said. Again, she didn't. Instead, she finished, "And I'm totally unsure about what the decision-making process should even be."

"Well, okay, you want detail? For a start, I'm absolutely bound and determined to have somebody around to do my laundry for me when I'm ninety-five."

"Seriously."

"I am serious. I like the idea that there's hopefully going to be someone who still cares about me that much if I get that old."

"All right, but laundry?"

"Those practical things are a symbol of the way people

# An Important Message from the Editors

Dear Reader,

Because you've chosen to read one of our fine romance novels, we'd like to say "thank you!" And, as a **special** way to thank you, we've selected <u>two more</u> of the books you love so well **plus** two exciting Mystery Gifts to send you—absolutely <u>FREE</u>!

Please enjoy them with our compliments...

*Pam Powers*

Lift here

# How to validate your Editor's
## "Thank You"
# FREE GIFTS

1. Peel off gift seal from front cover. Place it in space provided at right. This automatically entitles you to receive 2 FREE BOOKS and 2 FREE mystery gifts.

2. Send back this card and you'll get 2 new Silhouette *Special Edition*® novels. These books have a cover price of $4.99 or more each in the U.S. and $5.99 or more each in Canada, but they are yours to keep absolutely free.

3. There's no catch. You're under no obligation to buy anything. We charge nothing—ZERO—for your first shipment. And you don't have to make any minimum number of purchases— not even one!

4. The fact is, thousands of readers enjoy receiving their books by mail from The Silhouette Reader Service™. They enjoy the convenience of home delivery...they like getting the best new novels at discount prices BEFORE they're available in stores... and they love their Reader to Reader subscriber newsletter featuring author news, special book offers, book reviews and much more!

5. We hope that after receiving your free books you'll want to remain a subscriber. But the choice is yours— to continue or cancel, any time at all! So why not take us up on our invitation, with no risk of any kind. You'll be glad you did!

GET TWO *Free* MYSTERY GIFTS...

*SURPRISE MYSTERY GIFTS COULD BE YOURS **FREE** AS A SPECIAL "THANK YOU" FROM THE EDITORS*

DETACH AND MAIL CARD TODAY!

# Yes!

I have placed my Editor's "Thank You" seal in the space provided at right. Please send me 2 free books and 2 free mystery gifts. I understand I am under no obligation to purchase any books, as explained on the back and on the opposite page.

PLACE
FREE GIFTS
SEAL
HERE

335 SDL EFYR          235 SDL EFXG

| | |
|---|---|
| FIRST NAME | LAST NAME |

ADDRESS

| | |
|---|---|
| APT.# | CITY |

| | |
|---|---|
| STATE/PROV. | ZIP/POSTAL CODE |

(S-SE-08/06)

## Thank You!

should care about each other. Although I do recognize that this is one of the bad reasons for wanting kids—loneliness insurance."

She laughed. "Loneliness insurance. I'll have to add that to the plus column on my pro-and-con list."

"Do me a favor, Shay. Do not ever show me that list."

"So what are the other reasons?"

"*All* the reasons, okay? I want kids for all the reasons. Name a reason for having kids, whether it's good or bad, and it's on my list."

"All the bad reasons are on your list?"

"Well, not the evil bad ones, obviously. Just the normal human bad ones, like hoping I might one day get to be proud of something they did so I could boast about them, and show their photos to total strangers, thus embarrassing the kids and boring the total strangers to tears."

"You are funny. And strange."

"Because I know I want kids?"

"Because it doesn't seem to be *conflicting* you to any extent, when it's such a huge thing."

"Seriously, I think the huge things are sometimes the most obvious. Plus I now understand why contraception is not an issue for you."

The hair on the back of her neck stood up. "Oh?" What had she given away, in that rambling five-chapter piece of self-contemplation? He was absolutely right, she'd gone on way too long, and way too little of it had made any sense.

"Your conflict regarding the childbearing issue is the most effective bloody mood dampener I've ever met. We're never going to get as far as needing contraception in a million years."

"Oh, Dusty…" She buried her head in the pillow.

"Sorry," he said after a moment. "That was too blunt."

"No. I liked it."

"Yeah?"

She thought, then said, "I did. It might be good for me to get slapped in the face by a wet fish more often."

What had she decided just recently about herself and her friends? That they had crisis meetings more often than relaxed, pressure-free get-togethers?

It was true.

She'd dumped that whole rambling piece about whether or not to have kids on Leah and Alicia the last time they'd seen each other, and all three of them had ended up nodding and listening empathetically to each other for hours, tying themselves in emotional knots, no closer to any real insight than they'd been when they'd started.

It had felt good at the time, but now she wondered.

Maybe the whole point about men—the whole reason you might love one and need him in your life on a permanent basis—was that they tackled things differently. They refreshed your outlook. They wouldn't let you get away with certain female weirdness, the way you wouldn't let them get away with being too typically male. You balanced each other out.

Meanwhile, Dusty just wanted to have kids for "all the reasons" and if he occasionally bored total strangers with family photographs, so be it. There was something refreshing about this. Something endearing and healthy and safe.

But then, it was definitely easier for a man.

Which brought her back to where she'd begun.

"Um, if you're still interested, Dusty…"

He shifted and stretched like a lazy lion. "I could be. If you promise to shut up soon."

She laughed. "I promise. And look…you don't have to worry about me getting pregnant, okay? It's—it's—" she stopped and cleared her throat "—just not going to happen. Trust me on it? Can you, please?"

Her voice had gone a little too high. He said nothing, so she borrowed some of his own honesty, got stubborn about not messing this up with too much head stuff, and added very deliberately, "So now you can kiss me again, if you want."

## Chapter Eight

"You are making this really hard for me, do you know that?" Dusty growled.

He'd already refused to kiss her about three times, but she wasn't taking no for an answer. He'd drawn his line in the sand and she'd simply reached out with one dainty big toe and rubbed it out, to leave a big mess there instead.

"Here I am," he said, "doing the right thing, and you're punishing me for it."

"I'm not." He could hear the need and impatience and heat in her breathy voice. "*Punishing* is the wrong word."

She shifted her hips and settled more intimately on top of him. Her legs straddled his thighs, and even though there were still two sleeping bags between them from the waist down, there was no such barrier between her silky-skinned stomach and his tensed-up rib cage, or between her breasts and his chest.

He could feel two fabulous, round soft-skinned shapes

pushing against him, and the brush of her peaked nipples, and he knew that every time she made the slightest movement, she did it with total, merciless intent. What had happened to her?

And what had happened to him?

He was on fire.

"In fact, who's punishing who?" she demanded. She cupped his jaw with a feather-light touch and gave him a kiss like a ripe, juicy peach. "Are you still saying no? Really? Seriously?"

"Yes. I have to." He clenched his teeth.

"I really, really don't want you to." Another peach of a kiss, the kind that left your lips glistening and your tongue sweet and dripping.

"Yeah, well, you're making that delightfully obvious," he managed to say.

"I might have to make it even more delightfully obvious if you keep refusing to cooperate."

"Please…do that," he heard himself rasp out.

"So you're mine? I can have my wicked way?"

"You're making it impossible to say no."

He didn't care anymore. He was only human. And he felt so close to her, as if the two of them were the only people who mattered in the entire world. He tried to tell himself that this was just because of their isolation, because of what they'd shared over the past two days, but this didn't make sense or feel like the truth. There was more to it than that.

She was such a maddening woman, and her own worst enemy, asking herself all those complicated, angst-ridden, unnecessary questions about her life because for some reason the simple, necessary questions just scared her too much. He found it a compelling quality. It made him want to laugh at her and rescue her from herself at the same time.

*Shay, sweetheart, you don't have to live your life this way.*

And it reminded him of someone.

It reminded him of…himself.

Shoot!

But yes, it really did. Not his normal attitude to life, but the way he'd been with Mandy, when he'd tied himself in all those knots of rationalization because the whole relationship had just fallen into his lap thanks to *Today's Woman* magazine. With Mandy herself making all the moves and seeming so sure, he hadn't wanted to let go of something that effortless and easy.

He hadn't asked any of the right questions—hadn't asked the *simple* questions, the ones he'd urged on Shay. He'd dug himself into a trap of his own making.

Next time, he wouldn't make the same mistake. Meanwhile—

Meanwhile…

Ah hell, how was he supposed to do the right thing when Shay so plainly didn't want him to, and when she seemed to know exactly how to get right inside his skin?

"I'm going to forget the jammed zipper on my bag," she whispered. "I'm just going to get inside yours. It might be a challenge. There won't be a lot of room. But that'll make it…interesting…don't you think?"

With a rustle and a slither, she freed herself from her bag.

"It's not going to work," he told her, balanced on the knife edge of surrender. He'd forgotten every reason for saying no.

"Ooh, do you really think you have that much will-power left?"

"That's not what I meant. I meant there really won't be room."

"Mmm, tell me what you're envisaging, in that case. It sounds athletic."

"Oh hell, Shay," he groaned, "what suddenly turned you into such a tease?"

"I'm not teasing. Teasing means promising and taking away. I'm not going to go back on anything I say. My promises are genuine."

"Such a vixen, then."

She gave a throaty laugh. "Vixen? I just know when I have to bring out all my weaponry, that's all."

"Because you're not letting me say no?"

"That's right."

He felt her slide down the zipper on his sleeping bag about two feet, making the top gape. He thought, *I'll just close my eyes and whatever happens will be her doing, not mine.*

"I'm taking this slow," she explained seriously, "because of my back."

Her back? Who was she kidding? Her back was merely a transparent excuse. She slid herself into the bag, her legs slipping silkily past his. One inner thigh brushed right down his body, soft and scented from the soothing cream she'd been using, and he felt the rougher texture of the lace triangle that barely covered the most intimate part of her. He was so ready for this.

"Can you support me a little, please? My shoulders are still pretty sore. When I prop myself on your chest like this, on my elbows, there's a strain."

"A vixen and a tease," he whispered.

Then her back spasmed again and as he held her and waited for the pain to settle, it reminded him of something else he'd learned about her—her vulnerability. What had she said earlier?

*You don't have to worry about me getting pregnant, okay? Trust me on it? Can you, please?*

Her tone had contained something, an emotion he

hadn't identified at the time and couldn't identify now. It rang alarm bells, though. *Trust me* wasn't another way of saying *I'm on the Pill*. He'd already learned that she was straightforward about certain things. If she were on the Pill, that's surely what she would have said. No, there was something more complicated going on. He'd trusted the women in his life before, and they'd betrayed him and let him down. He didn't intend to let it scar him…but he wasn't a fool, either.

Although every cell in his body clamored its masculinity and told him to forget the issue, he heard himself say, "So while you're lying on me, Shay, before we really get going, here, tell me why I should trust you about the pregnancy thing. What protection have you got in place that makes you so sure?"

As soon as he felt the tension that pulled at her body, he knew they weren't going to make love to each other tonight.

Shay had never slept so tightly cocooned with a man before. The ground felt so much softer beneath her, with her discarded sleeping bag providing a piece of narrow mattress for them both. She braced her back against Dusty and he held her with his whole body curved against hers.

Every nerve ending and every inch of her skin felt as if it were on fire from frustration and wanting, and she couldn't believe that he'd managed to say no to such a primal need. The other kinds of pleasure they'd given each other after they'd finally finished talking might have temporarily eased the aching—enough to allow Dusty himself to sleep—but their effect hadn't lasted in her own body.

Dusty was right.

Everything was so much simpler than she'd ever thought.

It was *incredibly* simple, when it came to the point.

She wanted him inside her.

Nothing else would do.

She couldn't understand quite how she'd ended up telling him so much.

How had he been so persistent and skillful in extracting the story of her medical history and Dr. Chin's warning?

And she absolutely couldn't understand why it wasn't enough for him.

"Probably need medical intervention if you want to conceive?" he'd said. "That's not good enough, Shay. She was scaring you into thinking about your priorities, that's all."

"You think she was *lying?*"

"Lying, no. Presenting a worst-case scenario, yes."

"I mean, that's occurred to me, too, but—"

"I'd probably do it, too, if I were in her position. You said she runs an infertility program."

"Which means she knows what she's talking about."

"She does, and she said *probably.*"

"*Probably,* to give me some hope, Dusty, to soften the reality!"

He ignored her. "And I'd imagine you *probably* don't want to get pregnant tonight, and even if you're *probably* not at the right point in your cycle, I'll *probably* be able to face myself in the mirror sometime tomorrow with a better conscience if I do the right thing."

"Shoot, you have willpower!"

"No, not much, right now, but I definitely have principles!"

Which had brought her to this current state of unbearable physical frustration and nourishing emotional safety at the same time.

She could feel Dusty's arm brushing the undersides of her breasts, reminding her of the way he'd touched them and kissed them so lavishly. When he slid it lower to curve against her hip in his sleep, she wanted to move his touch to a more intimate place, wanted to roll toward him and feel him harden and fill her the way she craved.

There would be other chances.

There had to be.

She might die if there weren't.

And meanwhile she felt strangely happy…. Really… just happy… Ready to sleep, too. Yes…

She only awoke hours later when he eased himself away from her. The whole sky had lightened, even though the sun wasn't yet up. "Stay," she mumbled.

"You stay," he whispered back. "I'm going to get the fire started."

"I'll help."

"You'll have stiffened up again. Let me do it, and I'll heat that rock for you."

"I don't feel stiff."

"Well, I'll take that as a compliment, after all the things we did and didn't do." He gave her his heart-stopping grin. "But stay in the sleeping bag all the same. We still have six miles to go."


Six uneventful miles, as it turned out.

They ate peanut butter on slightly smoky toast for breakfast, and drank the last of the instant coffee. Then Shay doused the fire and rolled the sleeping bags while Dusty saddled the horses. Was this really only their second morning in the wilderness together? She thought about the couple from the 1930s whom Dusty had told her about— the ones who couldn't sleep indoors. She understood them a little better now, she thought.

And then, at around noon, they saw the homestead and outbuildings of Roscommon Downs appear slowly around a bend in the river channel, and Shay cried with relief at the thought of reaching home…even if the home wasn't hers.

"Thank you," she said to Dusty, during their last few moments alone.

"Yeah? Why?"

"Because I can't think of anyone I'd rather be lost in the desert with—even though I really can't believe this is ever a desert, and I know we weren't lost."

He laughed. "You were a pretty satisfactory traveling companion, yourself."

The screen door on the veranda of the single men's quarters flapped and they saw Prim. "You took your time," she called out to them. "We were giving you three more hours then calling for an aerial search."

She thumped down the steps and came toward them, her round and not-very-pretty face lit up in the most brilliant smile. Shay remembered what Dusty had said to her beside the campfire on their first night—that a pretty smile was more important than a pretty face. She wondered if he'd learned this from his station cook.

"Shay hurt her back and couldn't ride," Dusty said to Prim. "So we walked most of the way."

"I could kiss you for putting in the first-aid kit, Prim," Shay came in. "Its stock of painkillers needs replenishing at this point, as well as that fabulous cream."

"You must have run out of food, too."

"Dusty turns out to be a pretty resourceful bush chef. We ate Thai-style seafood."

Prim threw back her head and laughed her deep, throaty laugh. "I am going to have to hear a lot more about this adventure of yours over dinner tonight." The words contained an echo of significance that Prim herself wouldn't understand.

*I want to look at Dusty,* Shay thought, *but I'm not going to.*

*I want to smile at Dusty, like two people with the best secret in the world.*

*And already everything feels different, now that we're back. We're not alone anymore.*

"Boss!" said a man's voice. Someone Shay hadn't met. One of the married men, she guessed, who would have his own cottage in the widespread grouping of homestead buildings.

"Yeah, Dave," Dusty said.

Dave strode up and punched him in the arm, then shook his hand heartily. "Took the long way home, did you?"

"Yes. Had a very scenic detour, thanks to the water over Wilandra Crossing getting visibly deeper while I watched, on the way out. Shay's riding skills aren't quite up to swimming a horse across a flood current, yet."

"Shay's riding skills weren't even up to sitting on straight," she said.

"That was your back," he consoled her easily. "When it's better, I'll teach you to ride. Let's get you inside. I'm sure you want a shower."

He put a hand on Shay's shoulder and nudged her toward the house. She went willingly, feeling a sudden selfish and pretty terrifying need to have the man to herself, the way she had for the past forty-eight hours. The adrenaline and determination that had been coursing through her on and off for days suddenly plummeted and she felt miserable and lost.

"Dave, can you get one of the useless mugs around here to take care of Sally and Beau?" Dusty said, behind Shay. "I'm going to wash and change, these clothes are getting pretty bad." Like Shay's, the legs of his pants were stained to thigh level like a high-tide mark on a waterfront pier.

He was going to come into the house with her, which made her spirits flutter briefly back into life. It was that selfishness, again. She didn't want to lose him to all the demands of the huge cattle station.

But then he added, "I won't be long."

She felt foolish for having thought he might stay with her. What, sipping tea on the veranda? He was a busy man.

"Prim, if there's anything involving peanut butter on the menu for tonight," he called back to his cook, "change it, okay? I like the stuff, but five meals in a row is too much of a good thing."

By the time Shay came out of the shower, wrapped in a towel, Dusty had gone. He'd left a pile of clothing on the bed, and a note.

*There's stuff I need to do, so I'll see you later. Make yourself at home. Clothes courtesy of Letty.*

She picked up the pile of casual tops, pants, shorts and very practical pairs of clean cotton socks and let them fall untidily back on the bed, wondering when *later* meant.

At dinner? That was hours away.

And so, presumably, was her laptop, still with Jake, wherever he now was.

Seriously, you had to laugh. How much progress had she made since she'd first surveyed this tranquil, pretty spare room almost three days ago? She was no closer to getting to New York or even Sydney. She'd been separated from her laptop and might never see it again.

And in its place she had the much weightier baggage of a new and incredibly inconvenient connection to a man who didn't remotely fit into her life.

She chose a pink tank top, cropped denim jeans and pink socks, and dressed with movements that felt both automatic and still stiff. The shower had soothed her back, but it remained fragile and sore and liable to spasm at any moment.

The thought that she didn't have to push herself to tramp through the wilderness, sleep on the ground, and eat any more peanut butter brought a catlike lift to her bedraggled spirits. There was a lot to be said for creature comforts—for being clean and comfortable, well-fed and permitted to sleep—and she celebrated in style with a ham, mustard and lettuce sandwich, a glass of iced coffee with a large blob of chocolate ice cream on top, and a two-hour nap on top of the clean and fragrant puffy pastel cotton quilt.

When she woke up again, it was almost three-thirty and the house was still quiet. She phoned Sonya in Sydney and told her, "I'm still stuck in the flooding, but at least I'm back at Roscommon Downs."

Sonya wanted more detail. "Because Tom was pretty skeptical about the whole story, I have to tell you."

"You mean he thought I'd *faked* involvement in a helicopter crash as an excuse for not getting to New York? Who is he? Donald Trump?"

"Well, I think you should call him. He says you have to take your vacation days to cover the entire period that you're…wherever you are."

"Southwest Queensland."

"Right. But I think he's pretty much expecting you to keep working, even so. By the way, I have nine feature-article proposals for upcoming issues that need to be okayed, is there an e-mail address I can send them to?"

Shay gave her Dusty's.

"When are you flying out?" Sonya asked.

Good question.

"Two weeks," she said firmly. She had at least that much vacation time owing to her.

"Two *weeks?*"

"If Tom wants to have another editor-in-chief in place at the magazine by then, fine."

*Am I bluffing?*

Shay honestly didn't know. She wasn't sure that she knew anything about her life, right now.

"Tell her to pack the contents of my desk into boxes," she went on, "and I'll pick them up if I get out of here alive. I've already nearly died trying. Now I'm going to accept that it's not meant to be."

The call to Sonya left her oddly exhilarated and free, but with this feeling came a restlessness she didn't like. What was wrong with her? She drank a glass of cold water and ate an apple, then went out onto the veranda and circled it. It ran all the way around the house, keeping out the harsh sun and adding a tranquil buffer of space that would be a gorgeous place to spend lazy afternoon hours or hot summer evenings.

There was little sign of life. In the distance, she heard the grinding rumble of a heavy engine and the buzz of something lighter—a motorcycle, maybe, or one of the four-wheeler farm bikes she knew they used on properties like this one.

The four-wheeler came into view, and its rider might have been Dusty. She watched, hoping the vehicle and rider would head in this direction, but they didn't. Soon they had disappeared, cut off from her line of sight by the outline of a broad shed. On a low rise farther off, she saw a huge mob of cattle like a red-brown shadow across the land, and guessed that they were being mustered to fresh pasture, or away from the still-rising waters.

She envied Dusty, having work to do.

Back in the house, she discovered his office, which she hadn't seen on her first day here. It contained the usual computer and filing cabinets, as well as bookshelves stacked with farming journals. On the walls, however, there were framed photos of race-winning horses, and these were what grabbed her attention most. The horses were so sleek and perfect.

She didn't know much about horse racing, nor why the photos took pride of place. Her journalist's instincts kicked in and she started reading the printed captions listing the details. Horse's name, race name, distance and type, date, winning jockey, trainer, owners.

Ah, owners.

D. Tanner, B. Smith, C. Woods, R. Middleton.

Or sometimes D. Tanner, B. Smith, C. Woods, P. Morris.

Whatever the combination, Dusty's name always came first.

"Hi," said his voice from the office doorway, and she couldn't help the way her face lit up at the sight of him.

He wore clean jeans and a navy-blue polo shirt, with his sunglasses folded and tucked into the open neck, and he must already have been working hard because jeans, shirt and tanned skin were all streaked with mud. The evidence of his physical lifestyle only made him sexier—which was a new reaction, in her life's experience.

"Hi, yourself." She'd even gone breathless. "You're back."

"To see how you're doing," Dusty explained, even though he knew it had to be obvious.

Her smile almost knocked him over. She hadn't tried to hide her pleasure at seeing him. It was scary how much he just wanted to wrap her in his arms and kiss every bit of skin and silky hair that he could reach.

Yeah, very scary.

He held himself back, feeling that everything was different now, even if their attraction to each other hadn't changed.

"You own racehorses," she said. The tone was a little awkward and almost accusatory, a kind of why-don't-I-already-know-this, as if they should have covered their entire life stories out there in the flooded desert.

He nodded vaguely. He'd looked for her in her room, in the kitchen and living room, on the veranda, a little concerned when the house had seemed so quiet. He'd abandoned her for nearly four hours, and felt bad about it, but too many people had needed his input around the station.

"Part own them," he told her. "With my mates Brant and Callan. Our trainers usually kick in for a ten percent share, too."

Why was he going into this detail? He hadn't thought about the photos in months, hadn't framed any new ones recently. The pleasure he took in the racing syndicate with Callan and Brant was only partly about pride, much more about friendship.

"Brant?" Shay said.

"You interested in racing?"

Was it possible that they'd actually found something they had in common, at last, beyond a shared taste for Thai-style seafood beside an open fire?

"I know nothing about it," she answered.

Okay, no, it wasn't possible. He should have known. And he shouldn't feel this disappointed.

"Well…" she went on. "Last year I flew down to Melbourne, dressed up in a ridiculous hat, four-inch heels and a floaty dress and went to the Melbourne Cup, but that's the sum total of my experience."

"The four-inch heels count for something, I guess," he drawled at her, hoping to get a laugh.

But her thoughts had apparently tracked elsewhere. "Dusty, you just mentioned someone called Brant."

"Yeah, Branton Smith, one of my best mates." He struggled to get this onto a more personal level, to find the right way to talk to her, the way they had when they'd been on their own. "I think it's what the three of us like best about owning the horses—keeps the friendship going. If either of them ever tell me they want to pull out of the whole deal, I'll be gutted. It was my—" He stopped.

So much for spilling his feelings. She wasn't listening.

She'd pressed her fingertips against her temples. "The same Brant Smith I interviewed for the magazine last month? He's a sheep farmer at a place called—"

"Inverlochie," he supplied. Good grief, she'd interviewed Brant for the magazine? Why?

"That's right," she said.

"Brant didn't tell me you interviewed him."

They hadn't spoken to each other for a couple of weeks. Dusty knew that Brant had been stretched lately. Wool prices were down, and his move into the fat lamb market had risks attached. They'd kept the conversation mainly to the subject of racing, with a sidebar on their fellow racing syndicate member Callan's recent engagement to a women he'd met through *Today's Woman* magazine's "Wanted: Outback Wives" campaign.

"…met through the magazine's 'Wanted: Outback Wives' campaign," he heard Shay say. "The story appeared in our June issue. It came out about four weeks ago, and I was really pleased with it."

"I'm sorry?" he said blankly.

"Brant," she clarified with heavy patience, jutting her chin.

He could imagine her speaking to her magazine staff like this—heavy frown, strong jaw, flashing jade eyes, abrupt tone—when they were being slow to grasp an idea. The career woman had been on vacation for the past couple of days, but now she was back. He understood her a little better now. He could see more of the complex woman beneath her facade. He even liked her.

"Yes, but…" he said vaguely, then got a grip. "No, it's my other mate Callan who's engaged to a woman he met through the magazine. And of course I was, too, to Mandy. Seemed like a pretty good strike rate."

"Strike rate?" She frowned again, and the muscles at his temples tightened in frustration.

They weren't communicating very well.

She had a faint red indentation on her cheek and her hair was slightly mussed, although silky clean and a lot less frizzy. He guessed she'd taken a long nap after her shower and was still a little groggy. And maybe he was already too deeply caught up in the responsibility of running Roscommon Downs because the closeness they'd discovered on their trek through the floodwaters had almost gone.

Not that there was any hostility.

They just weren't quite connecting.

"Strike rate," he repeated. "It's a racing term. Percentage of winners to races run. Callan, Brant and I all took part in your Outback Wives thing."

"Callan." Shay frowned. "I remember him. Blue eyes. From South Australia. His wife had died. He was at the cocktail party we held in February. I knew you'd had a couple of friends involved with 'Wanted: Outback Wives,' also, but I couldn't remember who."

"Yes, we all sent in our photos and our details, Callan, Brant and me. It was Brant's sister's idea. Callan lost his wife nearly five years ago to cancer, and…we don't quite know what happened…we think he might have tried to jump into another relationship too soon and he got burned.

Anyhow, he seemed so lost, he didn't know where to start, to get his life back. Nuala thought if we all sent our photos and details in to the magazine, he might at least get some encouraging letters."

"We had a fantastic response," Shay said. "Way better than I'd dared to hope. Sales jumped that month."

She frowned. Maybe the high sales hadn't lasted.

"And Callan did meet someone," Dusty told her. "Jacinda. American, like you. She's a screenwriter, and she was running away from a very bad divorce, needed a place to hide. Callan had her staying with him, with her little daughter, and it went from there. So there was a point where both of us were engaged. Two out of the three of us, a strike rate of sixty-six point six percent."

"But I interviewed Brant, not Callan," Shay insisted, stubborn on the subject.

"Callan and Jacinda didn't want to go public with their story."

"And Brant is engaged to a woman called Michelle. Mish, she called herself. If I had a copy of the magazine, or even my laptop—" She broke off and sighed. "Am I ever going to see my laptop again, Dusty?"

"You can use my computer, if you want." He gestured toward it, feeling stuck—stranded in an awkward impasse more effectively than they'd been stranded by the floodwaters.

She looked just as ill at ease. A little of the stressed-out executive had returned, and he was torn between admiring her single-minded drive and wanting to protect her from herself—her workaholic tendencies—the way he'd have protected a child from snakes and sunburn.

Tonight hovered like a great big question mark in the sky. They'd had a kind of shipwreck romance over the past couple of nights. Such things did happen. Two people thrown together in extraordinary circumstances found an illusory connection that evaporated within hours once their normal lives resumed.

Was this what Shay wanted? A kind of thanks-for-the-memories end to something that had never fully begun? Almost certainly, she did. Her renewed tension suggested it, and it was the only outcome that made any sense.

Or should he check in with Prim this afternoon and find out what supplies she kept in her Aladdin's Cave of a storeroom to equip a love-hungry single stockman planning a night on the town?

"I will e-mail the office, Dusty, I will get them to send an electronic copy of our June issue and I will show you the story!" she said, heated and impatient, as if it mattered. "Your friend is engaged. She speaks with a slight Dutch accent, but—"

"Dutch? That was years ago. Beatrix. That's long gone."

"A Dutch accent, but she's American."

"So Callan, Brant and I have a strike rate of one hundred percent now? That's what you're saying? Two American fiancées and one Aussie ex, all of whom saw our photos in your magazine?"

"She's very pretty. Gorgeous, actually. Brunette with blue eyes. Her hair could use a better stylist, I did think."

"Beatrix was a redhead."

"I'm telling you, it's not Beatrix! It's Michelle. Mish. She seemed really happy on his farm. Even the dogs adored her. I promise you, Dusty."

"He would have told me," Dusty insisted, while wondering why they were arguing about such a weird and unlikely thing. "It's how many weeks ago? That you interviewed him and this Michelle? Six? He would not have kept something like that a secret! This is the craziest conversation I've had in—"

"I'm sorry," she suddenly cut in, and he looked at her to find her eyes narrowed with concern. She stepped closer and her hand hovered at her side as if it wanted to be somewhere else.

"What for?"

"For arguing, and being a pain in the butt." The hand came up, landed on his shoulder. He let it stay.

"I like it when you're a pain in the butt," he said. "I like how you stand your ground. You know, some things change, when your life gets back to normal. But some things don't. Some things are constant, and real." He only thought it through as he said it. "The things I like about you. They're real."

She slowed down at last, enough to say quietly, "The things I like about you, too, Dusty. I'd rather have a healthy argument any day, than have nothing to talk about at all."

And suddenly everything they'd both felt over the past couple of days was back in the air again, superheating it, charging it with electricity, filling it with meaning. He could have kissed her in a heartbeat, but if he did that, he knew he wouldn't want to stop, and he had Dave and Wayne and Steve waiting for him in the machinery shed.

This would have to wait, but at least he could make it a wait that held the right promise.

"Do you want to eat in the house tonight?" he asked. "I can have Prim send something over for us, and we could open a bottle of wine."

She nodded, her eyes wide. "Let's do that. We need to, don't we?"

"Yeah, I think we do," he answered gruffly, knowing he definitely had to find time to see Prim about the inventory in a certain section of her storeroom this afternoon.

## Chapter Nine

Shay knocked at the front door of the head stockman's house. Before her knuckles even touched the dark green painted wood, she knew that the reason for her visit was a crazy one, but it was too late to bail out now.

"Hi, Jane," she rehearsed cynically, under her breath. "It's nice to meet you. I'm Shay. And I was wondering if you happened to have any spare contraception hanging around your bathroom that you could pass on to a girl in need."

No.

Even the more delicate way she intended to approach the subject in reality seemed fraught with pitfalls. And judging by the number of kids' voices she could hear inside the house, what were the chances that Jane and her husband had heard of contraception, anyhow?

"Mu-u-u-um? Someone's at the door!" Shay heard.

"Well, answer it then!" said someone else—a boy, she thought.

"I'm making a snack," said the first voice.

"Harry, answer the door!" This was presumably Mum.

"Just a minute."

"Don't let Gemma open it!"

Finally, after a lot of handle rattling, it opened and there stood a little blond angel, of surely no more than two or three years old, with a face covered in some kind of chocolate substance.

"Tum in," said the angel.

"Should I wait for your mom?"

But the chocolate angel had toddled off.

Shay "tame in" as instructed, shut the door behind her and discovered that missy must have had the chocolate substance on her hands as well as her face, because it was all over the inside door handle and now smeared on Shay's own palm.

Hmm.

It wasn't chocolate, she discovered when she cautiously sniffed it. It was Vegemite.

As editor-in-chief of an Australian magazine, Shay had been given a crash course on Australian cultural icons and, bizarrely enough, Vegemite was one of them. Australians loved the stuff. They took jars of it with them when they traveled out of the country, or hunted down international suppliers on the Internet. Providing healthy quantities of B vitamins, it *looked* like chocolate, but it was in fact made of yeast, and was very salty and strongly flavored.

Sonya had shown Shay her own personal version of how best to enjoy Vegemite. She spread it very thinly on slices of crusty French bread along with a generous smear of butter and crunched the whole lot down in big, happy mouthfuls. Shay had conceded that it was edible this way. Tasty, even. But she hadn't gone out and purchased her own jar.

Now she had it all over her hand. What should she do? Lick it off?

"Oh, bliddy hell!" said a cheerful—and pregnant—woman of about thirty-five, appearing in the cool, dim front hall. "Did Gemma let you in?"

"The blond angel with the Vegemite face?"

"I'm sorry. Those are her two current crazes—helping herself to Vegemite straight from the jar and answering the front door. Each one is bad enough on its own, but together they're a disaster!"

"It's fine." Shay instantly liked this woman's open approach.

"You must be Shay. We've heard all about your adventures. I'm so glad you stopped in. I'm Jane. Do you mind washing it off in the kitchen sink?"

Half an hour later, Shay had decided that if there was anyone in the world from whom she *could* ask to borrow contraception without feeling very self-conscious and lamentably disorganized, it would be Jane Portman, but even Jane's casual, cheerful attitude didn't quite get her that far at their first meeting.

Maybe she could work up to it over the next few days… if she and Dusty could wait that long.

No, she decided a moment later, it would be so indiscreet. The news would soon spread. She just wasn't that… brash, or something.

Meanwhile, Gemma turned out to be Shay's favorite kind of angel—into everything and convinced, probably correctly, that "Wanna tiss, Mummy?" would earn her instant forgiveness for any minor mishap such as accidentally dropping a kilogram tub of strawberry yogurt on the kitchen floor and then tracking it everywhere as she "helped" to clean it up. The other four kids, as well as two more who belonged to other families at Roscommon Downs, created similar if slightly less toddler-ish distractions.

Jane attempted to make Shay a cup of tea during all this, and announced eventually, "There! That only took twenty-five minutes!" as she put the two steaming mugs on the kitchen table. "Dinner is scheduled for midnight tonight, I think."

"Why don't you let me help with something?" Shay asked. "I mean it."

Because she'd already offered twice and Jane had said no.

This time the other woman threw out a skeptical glance. "If you keep saying that, I'll take you up on it."

"Do!"

"You said you don't have kids."

"No, but it's obvious I should get in some practice in case one day I do," she said recklessly. *I don't even know if I want kids, Dr. Chin.* "This is full on!"

"Well, not everyone's crazy enough to have five in seven years."

Ooh, window of opportunity on the contraception topic! Shay couldn't do it.

The magazine that the Australian edition of *Today's Woman* was descended from, a thick periodical called *The Ladies' Weekly Round* had offered some very progressive, cryptically worded pieces of advice on "limiting family size" in the 1930s, in its From Your Family Doctor column. They would have been aimed at just such extravagant examples of motherhood as Jane Portman, even though it was clear that Jane was perfectly happy with her large brood.

But wouldn't it make an interesting article, Shay suddenly thought, to look up some of those old bits of medical and family advice and examine whether any of it still had something to offer women today?

"I've just had an idea," she blurted out to Jane, who had just returned from breaking up an argument between two of the boys. She told her all about it.

"Sounds like great fun," Jane said. "I'd read it. I'd even contribute to it! I have an old Country Women's Association recipe book with some hand-written additions in the back of it, including something called, 'Special Wash for Women.' We think it was my great grandmother who wrote it, but we're not sure."

"You'll have to show me."

But maybe not today. The voices of the two boys were rising in anger again.

Over the top of them, Jane said, "Hey, if you're serious about helping, Gemma would love to have you supervise her bath."

"I'd love it, too."

"You'll get wet. I laugh when they talk about kids' electronic toys being 'interactive.' Gemma's bath will give you the true meaning of the word."

When Shay finally left, with patches of strawberry-scented bathwater decorating Letty's borrowed shirt and jeans, it was after six o'clock. The other kids had gone home and Jane was able to promise Dave, who'd then immediately disappeared to have a shower, "Dinner's in twenty minutes."

Shay hadn't gotten close to the initial incentive for her visit, but she'd come away with something important, anyhow.

If only she could work out what it was.

"Pasta sauce," Prim said to Dusty. "How's that? Too basic?"

"It's fine."

"Because I could think for a minute and come up with something better."

"Really, Prim, Bolognese sauce is fine."

"Some of our fresh fruit and veg is getting a bit low since I can't get into Longreach to stock up, but I could whip you up some mini-quiches with—"

"It's fine, okay?"

"But not very…" She trailed off, making vague loops in the air with her hands. "…Seductive."

"Oh, hell, Prim!" he burst out. "How did you know?"

"I didn't." She grinned, totally unrepentant. "But I do now."

He took a steadying breath. "Actually, on the same subject, I've got a small problem I need help with."

"Yeah?"

"Hoping you might have certain supplies in your storeroom."

She did.

He walked across to the homestead several minutes later, as darkness gathered over Roscommon Downs, still somewhat embarrassed and having sworn Prim to secrecy, but equipped for a very nice evening.

Or, more accurately, twelve nice evenings.

Shay wasn't back. She'd told him she might go and introduce herself to some of the other people on the station this afternoon, so she was probably with Jane Portman or Bronwyn Hemming. Dusty used the opportunity to track down the inexplicable mystery of Brant's supposed engagement to a slightly-but-not-quite-Dutch brunette named Michelle, and called him at Inverlochie.

The engagement story wasn't true.

He knew it couldn't have been.

He and Callan and Brant didn't chat on the phone for hours at a stretch, or call each other to report every little detail of their lives, but they always covered the important stuff. If Brant had got himself engaged, if something that significant had developed in his life, he would have said something about it before this.

And yet…

"I'm flying to Langemark on Sunday," he announced abruptly to Dusty, just when Dusty thought that their conversation was almost over.

"Langemark, the country? In Europe?"

"You mean, as opposed to Langemark, the capital of Mars? Yes, of course Langemark, the country." Brant sounded tense and not particularly happy, suddenly.

Or maybe not suddenly.

In hindsight, he'd been a bit tense throughout the conversation. His initial *Of course I'm not engaged,* Dusty had read as meaning, *Of course I would have told you if I was,* but now he wondered. What else was going on?

"Why?" he asked. "Do they breed good sheep there?" Those places in the north of Europe were really better known for their cattle and horse breeds than for sheep. Friesians, Warmbloods, Hanoverians—

"There's more to my life than sheep, Dusty."

"I know. So tell me why you're going to Langemark."

Because he was in love with Langemark's princess— Artemisia Helena, known to her family and friends as Misha—or, when traveling incognito, as Michelle. Brant's sister, Nuala, was apparently one of those friends, and Misha was Shay's not-quite-Dutch blue-eyed brunette from the magazine interview—only the brunette part was a wig put on as a disguise, the engagement had been a pretense, also—and she was really a blonde.

"You tricked Shay Russell?"

"To get the magazine off my back, and the women who kept making contact. You have no idea, Dusty."

"She's a professional. You know, people give journalists a bad rap, and some of them deserve it, but not all of them. Some of them sincerely try to bring their readers the right stories, and if you're happy to *fake* something for a national magazine—" He stopped, knowing Brant wouldn't understand why he was angry on Shay's behalf, and not having the remotest desire to explain.

Brant was too caught up in his own problems, anyhow, which was probably fair enough. There were two sides to a heck of a lot of life's important stories. He should let this one go.

"She was only here for three and a half weeks," Brant said. "I don't think it was real. It can't have been real. She wanted to stay but I wouldn't let her. I wasn't going to get us both into this stupid, ill-thought situation that both of us would soon regret."

*Like my engagement to Mandy,* Dusty thought.

He didn't say it out loud.

"I sent her back to deal with her life," Brant went on, sounding anguished about it. "She had to make a formal announcement to the people of Langemark that her wedding was off—she was supposed to marry Gian-Marco Ponti."

"The Formula One driver?"

"As opposed to Gian-Marco Ponti the vacuum-cleaner salesman?"

"Okay, Brant, I get it. Langemark the country, Misha the princess, Ponti the race-car driver. You have to admit—"

Brant wasn't interested in what he had to admit.

"But I can't just let it go," he said. "I've given her three and a half weeks, the same amount of time she was here. If there was any reality to it at all, we should know it when we see each other again. If there wasn't, I'm going to get a twenty-foot-tall medieval castle door studded with bolts and carved royal crests slammed in my face—"

"Or else maybe this long braid of hair rolled up like a rope ladder from a window, while a witch with a wart on her nose chases you, brandishing a broomstick like a lethal weapon."

"Something like that." Even over the phone, Dusty could hear the gritted teeth.

"You have your plane ticket?" he asked.

"Yes, and I'm bloody scared it's not going to work out. She's…pretty incredible."

What did you say to a strangled announcement like that?

Dusty had no idea. Brant sounded as if he'd prefer to have all his teeth pulled at once with no anesthesia than to make such statements.

And at that moment, Dusty heard Shay coming into the house. "Listen, mate," he said, "it'll be all right, okay? Whatever happens. It'll work out."

"I don't know if it will."

"I have to go, okay? Talk to you soon? How long are you going for?"

Dumb question, given the uncertain outcome of the trip. Brant didn't answer it.

"Anyhow," Dusty went on quickly, "talk to you when you get back."

"Yeah. And if I go to Melbourne for the spring racing carnival…"

"I might fly down myself. Definitely. That'd be great. Talk to you before then, anyhow."

After a couple more stilted, repetitive phrases, they managed to get off the phone.

"Hi," said Shay, in the same breathless, wide-eyed way she'd said it in his office four hours earlier, when they'd first trespassed into the whole ridiculous question of whether Brant Smith was engaged.

As Dusty had just established, he wasn't. He considered giving her the information…

Considered it for about one quarter of a second and then decided that instead of another tense, pointless argument, he'd prefer to have a great evening. "We're eating spaghetti Bolognese," he said, "and Prim's chocolate mousse for dessert."

"Ooh, not a vitamin in sight!"

"She's getting a bit strapped for fresh food, since the roads are closed. She did offer a side dish of frozen peas and corn. Want me to go over and—?"

"No." She shook her head emphatically, laughing. "I want you to stay right here, close all the curtains and take the phone off the hook."

"Sounds good to me."

Darkness had fallen outside and, with his mother's thick yet summery curtains pulled, the house felt almost as private and peaceful as an outback campfire beneath the stars. Dusty opened a bottle of ruby-red Shiraz and left it to breathe while he and Shay put the sauce into a cooking pot to reheat and water into a bigger pot to boil. They'd be able to eat very soon.

He could almost feel the expectancy in the air between them. Shay kept looking at him when she thought his attention was focused elsewhere. She had color in her cheeks that toned with Letty's pink tank top—and with the socks—and it made her look…not younger, exactly, because thirty-one years old was quite youthful enough for him, thank you very much…but softer, somehow. Happier, too, he thought.

They hadn't touched each other all day.

He wanted to, quite desperately, but even more desperate was the sense that he wanted to get it right, wanted no clumsiness, no rush, no misunderstandings. While he stirred the pasta sauce, she set the dining table, and when he went in there he found music playing and the overhead lighting dimmed.

Shay held two long and elegant red candles in her hands. "Is this too hokey? Candlelight? I just loved the fire so much, while we were camping. I loved talking while we watched the flames."

"There are some crystal candleholders in the drawer right there, I think," was all he said. "I'll bring matches from the kitchen."

She nodded and smiled.

The water was boiling. He added the long strands of spaghetti with unsteady fingers, then went to light the candles. The table looked like a play on the colors of the American flag—white cloth, dark red candles and napkins, wide blue-and-white ceramic bowls. With her back to him, Shay stood surveying her work and this time he didn't second-guess his reaction, he simply stepped close behind her and wrapped his arms around her, lowering his chin to her shoulder and pressing his cheek against hers.

She turned to him and he kissed her long and sweet and deep, and neither of them spoke a word.

They talked later, as they ate.

She told him about her visit to Jane's, and the hectic atmosphere created by so many kids—Gemma and the Vegemite, Gemma in the bath, dinner preparations and even brewing a pot of tea had turned into marathon accomplishments.

"But I like it. And Jane is great."

"She is. You have to be pretty relaxed to have that many kids so close, and another one due in three months. Or if you weren't relaxed before, the kids change you that way."

Her attention sharpened. "You think kids change their parents? Isn't it the other way around?"

"I've heard Jane say that's the way it goes. Babies come into the world with their natures fully formed. Parents are the ones who get shaped by the whole experience, like a piece of wet clay."

"Speaking of wet clay, I did some laundry."

"You're billing Williamson International Pastoral Holdings for the blouse, I hope."

"It's looking that way. Prim gave me some stain soaker, but it may be too strong for silk."

"Oh, you saw Prim?"

Before his own visit to her storeroom?

"Um, yes, just now, on my way back from Jane's," she said, and her cheeks went a darker pink. "As well as the stain soaker, there was a particular item I was hoping she had in stock. A drugstore item."

"And did she?"

He knew what she'd say.

"Someone else had beaten me to it, taken the last twelve-pack, and she had none left…."

They looked at each other, giddy and happy and silly and self-conscious, like a pair of teenage kids. No further words on the subject were needed. Shay hid her smile behind a forkful of pasta and sauce.

"This is good, isn't it?" Dusty said.

"So is the wine."

Even so, neither of them managed to finish a full glass. They had far better things to do.

*I'm falling in love with him.*

It couldn't be true, Shay decided, because it made too little sense. This strange, fabulous feeling had to have some other name. Or if it really was falling in love, then she should remember having done it…felt it…before, with Adam or Todd, because hadn't she been in love with them?

She tried to remember.

This big pool of warmth inside her.

This giddy happiness.

This sense of trust.

This fascination with every moment they spent together and every word they said, every detail they discovered in common, every intriguing difference between them.

She *must* have felt this way before.

"Hey," Dusty growled at her. "What's happening?"

"Nothing. I'm just…thinking."

"Well, stop!"

He tightened his arms around her and kissed her with such an aura of command that she could barely breathe. She felt the nip and scrape of his teeth teasing out the fullness of her lower lip, and the thrusting caress of his tongue. He tasted of red wine and smelled the way he always did—like himself, and perfect.

She surrendered to the heat of his mouth and the press of his thigh between her legs, and the line of thought she'd been trying to follow drifted away like a jet trail in a blue sky. Nothing else existed but this.

They were still in the dining room. At some point she vaguely thought that they would have to move, get to a bed, some place flat and horizontal, at least, but that would mean stopping, or talking, and both of those things seemed too hard when all she wanted was to follow her body's command.

But then Dusty said with a harsh caress of breath and mouth against her ear, "Oh hell, Shay, I just want to have you right here, right now," and she said, "Yes," and that was the end of it.

He tore off his own shirt, pulled the little pink tank over her head and cupped his hands over her lace-covered breasts, his touch verging on rough in his impatience, but never crossing the line. He tore at her bra, slipping the straps down, wrenching at the fastening, letting the garment slip between them and not caring whether it fell to the floor or what. He just wanted her breasts.

His thumbs found the push of her peaked nipples and traced the line where her soft fullness met her ribs. He bent toward her and used his mouth, sucking her until her nipples were like ice-hot pebbles, grazed and throbbing and wet.

His impatience and hunger pulled at her and made her melt. She gasped and arched her body, and he pressed her against the wall and kissed every inch of skin he could reach while she kneaded her fingers in the muscles of his bare back and pulled him higher or pushed him lower, exactly where she wanted him and where he wanted to be.

It was like opening a floodgate.

They'd wanted this so much last night and had held back. Now they didn't have to. He pulled open his jeans and slid them and his briefs down his tight butt and tighter thighs while she watched shamelessly, loving the sight of his arousal springing free, totally ready for her.

She kicked off Letty's white leather trainers, pink socks and cropped jeans, but when she reached for her own lacy panties, Dusty stopped her. "Let me."

He slid them down, using it as an open excuse to touch her, to run his hands over her bared backside and press his mouth hot against her lower stomach before coming higher to bury his face between her breasts once more.

She ran her hands through his hair and held on to him because she wasn't sure that she'd be able to stand straight without the contact. Her strength was plugged right into his, and she needed him the way she'd never needed anything in her life.

They kissed, their bodies locked together and their hands everywhere.

The phone rang. Dusty had forgotten to take it off the hook. They both ignored it and eventually it stopped. Somewhere, a screen door flapped and a dog barked, and they ignored those things, too. Almost nothing could have stopped this.

She was throbbing and damp and achingly ready for him by the time he whispered, "Now?"

"Yes. Now." Her breathing came in ragged pants and she had to squeeze her own thighs together to slow herself down.

He was as close to the edge as she was, she knew it as clearly as she knew her own name.

In his jeans he had the packets he'd gotten from Prim. It didn't take him long to retrieve one, while Shay held on to him from behind, totally unable to let him go, or to think beyond the moment.

"Wrap your legs around me," he said, turning her in his arms.

They weren't even going to get as far as the floor.

She lifted her body against his, tightened her arms around his neck, let him ease her back against the wall once more. He was so strong. How many men could have done this?

He entered her deep and hard and she shuddered at the sensation of throbbing fullness, the feeling of connection and completion and bliss. They moved together, stretching and rocking, straining to get even closer.

She kissed his neck, tasting his skin and feeling the muscles tighten beneath, with the strain of holding her. "It's too much," she whispered. Too much for his strength.

But it wasn't.

"Oh yes, way too much…" he said. "Way too—" He couldn't even finish.

His breathing began to race and hers raced with it and they clung to each other like shipwreck survivors clinging to a floating log, while need and heat tossed them around like corks in wave upon wave of release that seemed to last for minutes, climbing higher than she'd imagined possible before they slowly settled back to earth.

"Did it hurt your back?" he said, as soon as they were both still.

He hadn't yet lowered her feet to the floor. She was still wrapped around him, holding him tight, closer to him than she'd ever been to anyone. She could feel his chest wall pushing in and out, nudging at her still acutely sensitized breasts.

Her head was spinning.

Or maybe it was the whole earth.

"No, it was fine," she answered. "I don't know why. You'd think it should have hurt. But it was fine."

"It was very fine," he said, drawing out the last two words, his voice as deep and dark as a well. "Shay, it was amazing."

They eased away from each other and he cupped his palms at the tops of her thighs and lowered her slowly and gently from his body. As soon as she was standing he pulled her close again and she felt the way he was shaking. "It was too much for you, Dusty."

"It was perfect. Shh. Stop." He pressed his fingertips against her lips.

She took them away, holding his wrist, then kissed his palm and cradled it against her own cheek. She wanted to speak, wanted to say something big and momentous—something that just might begin to encompass the huge pool of feeling stirring inside her, but nothing would come, so she just kept his hand pressed against her face and stroked it and smiled at him.

He smiled back, and it was so, so goofy. It had to be. She could imagine. If someone had seen them, looking at each other like this, as soppy as Sally and Beau, they would have laughed.

She didn't care.

She wanted more of it.

As much as she could get, for as long as it could last.

## *Chapter Ten*

The grader plowed back and forth across the red-brown dirt of the airstrip, transforming the messy sheet of dry-baked mud into a smooth, hard expanse under the bright morning light.

Shay sat on the hood of Dusty's four-wheel drive, parked at the side of the strip, and watched, while the rumbling sound of the engine spread into the air and drifted away on a breeze. She had her forearms resting on her knees, a broad-brimmed felt farmer's hat pulled low over her forehead and sunglasses shading her eyes, and the camouflage was a good thing because she suspected that at any moment she might start to cry.

The sun had been so bright and strong for the past two weeks, without a drop of rain, either here or farther up-stream in the catchment headwaters. At first it had shim-mered and sparkled on acres of floodwater, stretching almost to the horizon, then on narrower channels and shrinking ponds as the waters ebbed, and finally on mud.

Now, even much of the mud had dried.

The river crossings on the roads out of here were expected to be open again within the next couple of days; Prim was itching to get into Longreach to replenish her supplies; and Dusty and his grader driver Steve had walked the length of the airstrip before breakfast this morning and decreed that it could be smoothed out and tested with a couple of heavy vehicles. If all went well, then the mail plane would be summoned this afternoon to take Shay away.

Her stomach churned at the thought, and she couldn't reconcile the way she felt now with the desperation she'd felt about getting out of here just nineteen days earlier. The helicopter crash had changed something at a deep, vital level.

If she'd never gotten into that chopper and tried with such spectacular lack of success to leave this place, she could imagine she might still have considered herself a prisoner. She might never have built the powerful connection with Dusty that had grown during the two days they'd walked through the floodwaters back to Roscommon Downs with only Sally and Beau as companions.

But you couldn't think about those maybes and if onlys.

The chopper crash *had* happened.

And now, two weeks later, the airstrip was dry.

She had to leave this place—the place where Dusty had taught her to ride and shown her his cattle and all the beauty of his vast acreage; the place where she'd talked about books and kids and horses with Prim and Letty and Jane, and about weather and farm machines with Dave and Wayne and Steve; the place where everyone worked hard, but somehow meetings and time management and schedules and deadlines didn't seem so important; the place where she and Dusty had come together with so much perfect, unexpected heat, time after time.

He came up to her. "Looking good."

"Looking great," she agreed.

They smiled uncertainly at each other, with too much to say and no way to say it.

She'd learned a lot about him over the past two weeks. She'd seen the truth in what he'd told her by the campfire on their second night—that he'd never ask his men to do anything he wouldn't do himself, that he was the boss here and this meant doing things his way.

It worked because of the kind of man he was, because he was fair and clear-sighted and capable and honest. So different to Tom in his ivory tower high-rise in Manhattan—Tom who played power games because he could, who made people jump through hoops just to prove his own control, who made decisions then blamed someone else if they turned out wrong.

Caring about a man like Dusty was like knowing your house was founded on solid rock. There was a whole, crucial area of uncertainty and doubt that you never needed to have. Nonetheless, they'd only known each other for two and a half weeks. It would end today, and there was nothing she could do about it because there was no precedent in her life for asking for something different.

*Dusty, I don't want this to be goodbye.*

How could it possibly work? How could she bare her heart like that with no plan to back it up?

She couldn't.

"Let me run you back to the house so you can pack," he said. "And you probably want to call your office. Are you still going to New York?"

"I—I don't know. I'll fly to Sydney first, and make sure things are running smoothly, find out what Tom really wants. If I still have a job, for example," she joked, then added quickly, "So you definitely think the strip will be firm enough? You were afraid there might be some wash-aways…"

"Only a couple, and they're minor. Steve is filling them in fine with the grader and anyway they're right at one edge of the strip. You'll get out of here today."

She nodded. "Good."

She flicked a glance at him and saw him look quickly away.

"Let me run you back to the house," he repeated, as if he didn't remember saying it before.

He did that thing with his sunglasses that she'd noticed at their very first meeting, pushing them up on the top of his head, then rubbing a frown away with his fingers. She'd never gotten used to the amazing color of his eyes— the warm brandy that she could so easily drown in.

The house was cool and quiet, as usual, after the power-ful force of the sun in this part of the world, even in July, the middle of winter. Dusty called the air charter company that ran the mail flights and Roscommon Downs was added back onto their regular route, with a one-off stop this after-noon to pick up Shay. It was all arranged in a few minutes.

"Longreach?" she heard Dusty say at one point. "That'll be fine." When he got off the phone, he told her, "Your overnight bag is in Longreach. You'll be able to pick it up there, at the airport. And your laptop."

"My laptop? My laptop is there?" Why didn't this feel more like good news?

"Yes, it's being held for you at the main office."

"That's great! Um…going to stay in the house for a bit?" she asked him lightly, trying to hide how much she hoped that he would.

So that they could make love for the last time…the last

perfect time… Or eat together. Or even just sit on the veranda and talk, the way they'd now done so often, sometimes alone, sometimes with people like Letty or Prim or
Jane and Dave.

"Too much to do," he said, his tone clipped. "I'm sorry,
Shay. There's no point in—" He stopped.

"No point in what?"

"We had last night. We've had all those nights…and
days." He dropped his voice lower. "Would it really be any
better, saying to ourselves, *This is for the last time?*"

"No. I guess it wouldn't. Maybe."

"It wouldn't. It would be way worse," he said, sounding
almost angry, and he left the house again a minute later,
after stopping only long enough to grab a glass of cold
water from the fridge in the kitchen.

Shay had a lot to do, also.

She made flight reservations that would get her to Sydney late tonight, provided the mail flight got her to Longreach by five, as well as making a tentative one for New
York for the day after tomorrow, if Tom still wanted her
to go. She wasn't going to get into that issue with him until
she was back in the office with more of a handle on how
things had gone in her absence.

Not that she'd been totally out of touch. From Sonya and
others, she'd received e-mails with lengthy attachments to
them almost every day, and had spent hours working on
Dusty's computer. There was a lot you could achieve via the
Internet from a home office, in the twenty-first century. Still,
it wasn't the same. After a certain point, you needed to be
in the thick of things, or you lost your edge and your over-
view.

She knew that. She wasn't kidding herself that she
could justify staying here so much as one more day.

When she'd made her reservations, she gathered up all

of Letty's borrowed clothes and threw them in the washing machine, wearing a T-shirt of Dusty's over her black trousers, instead of the ruined silk blouse. It hung on her…and it smelled like him. She didn't plan on giving it back.

There was a spiderweb-shaped clothesline behind the house. In the strong sunshine, Letty's things would be dry in time to be ironed and folded ready to return to her well before the mail plane was due.

She was going to miss Letty. And Prim. And Jane.

Everyone.

They were friends now.

And she'd really progressed with learning to ride. After several days of treating her back with respect and doing only some careful stretching exercises, she'd felt confident enough to get back on Sally, under Dusty's instruction, and take some big loops around the homestead buildings. He had even convinced her to try a canter and a trot, and she hadn't wanted him to know how nervous she'd been so she'd tried both and loved both, and could imagine that one day she might actually be good at this.

Riding. This was something she could take with her, something concrete about her that had changed. She mentally added it as an item to a small, sad little list in her mind.

Riding.

Rejecting helicopters as a viable form of transportation.

Appreciating the flavor of golden perch cooked in peanut butter and desert lime.

Understanding just how fabulous an outback cattleman could be.

She packed her few belongings into a canvas sports bag that Dusty had found for her. He'd given her a pocket diary that he didn't need, for when she'd wanted to check dates as she worked, and she flipped through it. She should take it. It had some notes in it that she should follow up on.

Speaking of checking dates…

She looked at today's, and did some woolly-witted cal-
culations. Her cycle was normally as regular as clockwork. Relentlessly so. Every fourth Monday signaled the
start of heaviness and pain, usually before she even got out
of bed in the morning, and always by lunchtime. It seemed
to get worse every month, and Dr. Chin had told her this
was the effect of the endometriosis.

Today was one of those Mondays, but so far nothing
had happened. No doubt it soon would.

She didn't know if Dusty planned to come back to the
house for lunch. Probably not, judging by the way he'd
acted when he'd told her that there was "no point" in
spending any of her last hours here together. She made
herself a toasted sandwich and a pot of hot leaf tea, feeling
bloated and irritable the way she always did on a fourth
Monday. After she'd eaten, she checked the clothes on the
line and found them dry. She had just begun to unpeg
them, folding them as she went, when Dusty appeared.

Was it time to go already?

Surely not.

Please, not!

Before she could ask, he lunged toward her, took her in
his arms and said in a shaky voice, "I've changed my
mind."

"About—about the airstrip being ready?"

"About our last time." He swore. "I'm sorry. I can't let
you go without…" He lowered his voice and whispered
something so hot and graphic into her ear that she flushed
and laughed, even while her body began to throb with
need.

How could she possibly say no?

He took her hand and she forgot about Letty's clothes.
They managed to make it as far as the bedroom, which

had been by no means a guaranteed thing on several occasions. Oh Lord, his body felt so familiar now! She knew the way he responded, the sounds he made, and the tiny imperfections of a cattleman's healthy skin—the callouses, the sun damage, a couple of minor scars. She loved all of it.

She loved how hungry and impatient and desperate he seemed today—loved it to the point of tears because it matched the way she felt herself. How could he ever have claimed that they could say goodbye without this?

"My T-shirt's way too big for you," he whispered, as he pulled it over her head.

"It smells like you. Don't try to get me to mail it to you. It's mine, now."

He took her face in his hands and looked into her eyes. "You want to keep it because it smells like me?"

"Can I?"

"Oh hell, Shay, do you have to ask?" He brushed his thumb across her lower lip, then touched his mouth there in its place.

They kissed sweetly and feverishly, while he pulled her hips against his so she knew how much he wanted her. She rocked a little, the slow bump of her body driving him wild, while she exalted in the power they had over each other. She'd given so much of herself to him, and yet she felt safe because she knew he'd given just as much in return.

They were both naked in showing what they wanted from each other today. When it was over, they'd both suffer the same loss.

Did it have to happen?

She knew it did—knew it even while she shimmied out of her clothing, watched him doing the same and waited till she could have his hot body back.

This wasn't one of the romantic stories she'd been chasing to cap her magazine's "Wanted: Outback Wives" campaign. She believed in those stories very much. They happened. They were real. Dusty's friend Callan was happily engaged—although apparently his other friend, Brant, was not. Another once-lonely farmer from one of the wine-growing regions in southern New South Wales had written to the magazine, announcing that thanks to the appearance of his photo in the February issue, he'd married his new city-girl soulmate in June, after a whirlwind romance.

But her own reality with Dusty was harsher.

They'd had less than three weeks together. Surrounded by floodwaters, it really felt like a shipwreck romance—intense but incompatible with their regular lives. Dusty's future lay here at Roscommon Downs. Her own was ultimately not even in this country, but in New York.

Today…now…would be their last time.

"Hold me," she said to him suddenly. "Don't kiss me. Just hold me."

She didn't want this to end too soon. He'd tear himself away as soon as they'd made love, she knew he would, because looking each other in the eye afterward with nothing left that they could safely say would be way too hard.

"Hold you?" he whispered, even though he already had.

"Yes. Just quietly, so I can hear your heart." She pressed her ear against his chest and they both stood there in motionless silence for a long time.

"Shay, if you don't want to do this…" he said at last, his voice creaky as if he hadn't used it in months.

"I do."

"But we've stopped."

"No, we haven't. We haven't!" She cupped his jaw in her palms and kissed him, proving the point. "See?" she whispered, brushing her body with a sinuous, seductive motion against his. "We haven't."

"Good."

"Very good."

"Always." His hands seared against her skin, and neither of them needed to speak another word for minutes more.

At two-fifteen, Dusty drove her out to the airstrip again, to meet the incoming plane. Even when she saw it approaching the ground she hoped it might loop up into the air again at the last minute, hoped the pilot might spot some impediment to the landing. But it came down smoothly and safely, and she knew this was really happening. It was time to say goodbye.

Bizarrely, the clockwork every-fourth-Monday mechanism of her body hadn't gotten going yet. She'd waited for it after that final heartfelt session of lovemaking, expecting it to unleash even more suddenly than usual, but it hadn't. It was now officially six hours late.

Well, two hours, if you wanted to be cautious.

Not significant.

It would be insane to conclude that it was significant. They'd been using contraception, which all along she'd thought unnecessary anyhow.

Nevertheless, thinking back on how long it was since this kind of a delay had happened, she could count over a year of fourth Monday mornings since her arrival in Australia, and not one of them had left her in suspense as long as this.

The tiniest, faintest nuance of a thought that she might be pregnant whispered at the edge of her mind, and she wanted to laugh at herself. Two hours late, and she was pregnant? Two hours late, some heartfelt new questions about whether she wanted children, and suddenly she'd already conceived? Women all over the world, from their teens to their fifties, would live in a perpetual cycle of terror or happy expectancy if two hours late meant pregnancy.

She wanted to laugh at herself, but she couldn't. She felt as if she were hiding something important from Dusty, and wondered how appalled he'd be if she gave him the details.

Two hours late. He'd think she was crazy.

*It's all in your head, Shay.*

*These past two and a half weeks haven't messed with your emotions enough, so now you're inventing extra reasons to feel like your life has been turned upside down?*

"I have your e-mail address at the magazine," Dusty said.

"And I have yours, here."

"Let me know how your laptop survived."

"I will."

It was the kind of meaningless small talk that everyone fell into as they waited for the final moment of parting. It was stupid. Why didn't people either say the important stuff, or say nothing at all? It was unbearable.

"Don't wait," she told him.

"I'd better. In case…You know, there could be a mechanical problem, or something. We always wait until the plane goes."

She nodded.

"And he'll have mail for us, anyhow."

"Of course." She'd treasured so much about this period of isolation, she'd almost forgotten that the station people were hanging out for fresh supplies, mail deliveries and the opportunity to go into Longreach or Windorah in a day or two, to see friends or have some entertainment.

The plane had almost reached them now. It was slowing. It had stopped. The propellers were at first invisible, then they became a circular blur, then separate blades. The pilot who'd brought Shay here a million heartbeats ago stepped onto the ground, went around to the cargo hatch and pulled out two big mail sacks. He held them up to Dusty as a kind of greeting, and Dusty thumbed toward the open rear door of the four-wheel drive, as a greeting in return.

"I remember you," the pilot said, when he got closer and saw Shay. Grant was his name, she hazily recalled.

"You should," she drawled. "You flew off before I discovered I didn't need to be here, and the floodwaters came up and I've been stuck. Not that it was a problem, in the end," she added quickly, since she hadn't intended to sound rude.

From the corner of her eye, she saw Dusty glance at her, but didn't know what he was thinking.

"Had a bit of a heli-mustering drama, too, didn't you, trying to get out of here?" the pilot said.

"Word gets around."

"Out here, yes! There've been a few stories to tell, with these floods. Biggest in a while."

"But we'll have no problem getting to Longreach today?"

"It's my next stop."

Dusty took the mailbags from him and loaded them into the four-wheel drive.

"This your stuff?" the pilot asked Shay, taking the borrowed sports bag from her before she replied.

This was the moment. This was when she had to turn to Dusty and say something. The right goodbye. The right thanks for…for…things she couldn't remotely put into words. Oh hell, it was just hopeless. Painful. There was no way in the world to make this moment right.

She gulped down some air and it got stuck in her throat. "Bye," she rasped out.

"Bye."

"And thanks."

"Shay—"

"I know. I know." She flapped her hands, keeping him away. She was wound so tightly that she thought she'd throw up if he touched her. "There's no need to thank you."

Okay, this was it.

She couldn't say anything else.

She just had to go.

Turning from him, she walked to the plane, stopping one final time just before she climbed in, to wave at him. He waved back. When she was seated and strapped, she saw him still standing there almost motionless beside the four-wheel drive, but he was too far away for her to read his face.

Dusty's stomach felt like a rock as he drove back to the homestead, after he'd watched the plane climbing in the sky until it had disappeared.

Shay had gone.

He'd watched it all happen like watching a train crash, powerless to stop it, not fully believing it until all the evidence was spread out in a tangled wreck in front of him. He'd wanted to hold her against his body and say something insane and extravagant like, "Marry me!" but he'd said that to Mandy just a few months ago—she'd made it pretty clear that she wanted him to, had practically put the words into his mouth—and he wasn't going to repeat that mistake.

Mandy had at least made him believe that she wanted to be here, that she would be proud to call herself the boss's wife at Roscommon Downs. He knew Shay couldn't possibly feel the same.

They'd known each other for two and a half weeks.

This would fade.

He wasn't going to act on blind faith and blind need; he was going to act on certainties.

Getting out of the vehicle after he'd parked it in front

of the house, his legs moved mechanically and he'd totally lost track of what he was supposed to do next.

*Oh yeah, that's right.* Drive out to Four Mile Crossing to see if the track was passable yet, heading into Number Three Paddock, or if Steve would need to regrade it. He'd told Steve that he'd look at a couple of other tracks today, too, and Number Three Paddock itself might be fit for restocking as long as the fence line beside the creek had held. He should check it.

But first he needed to talk to Prim. He'd forgotten why, but he was sure he did. When he saw her, it would surely come back to him.

On those same mechanical legs, he stepped up to the veranda of the single men's quarters and met her coming out of the back kitchen door. "Boss," she said.

"Yeah…" he answered vaguely.

"Shay's gone?"

"Yep."

"She was nice. I liked her."

"So did I."

Prim looked at him, waiting for more.

"What else do you want me to say?" he snapped at her.

Prim could never take a hint. "Are you going to keep in contact?"

"She lives in New York."

"Sydney."

"When she's got the Australian edition of the magazine running smoothly, they'll put in a local editor-in-chief and she'll be pulled back to New York for another project."

"You might like New York," Prim said lightly. "For a change of scene."

"Yeah, right!"

"By the way, I thought I should tell you…" She looked uncomfortable, which was pretty rare for Prim.

Rare or not, he wasn't in the mood. "What?"

"Those storeroom supplies you…uh…had me find for you a couple of weeks ago…"

She hesitated again, but this time he just stood there waiting until she spilled the story, whatever it was. He knew what "supplies" she was talking about. Couldn't imagine why she needed to bring the subject up.

"I took a look at the box, just now, when I was tidying up in there, throwing out empty containers and getting ready to reorder. You know, we haven't had anyone calling on their use in a while, so I haven't needed to restock."

"Get to the point, Prim," he growled.

"I checked the date. The pack expired two years ago."

Was that all?

Remembering what Shay had told him about her doctor's warning, he told his station cook, "It won't be a problem," and walked away. Whatever he'd needed to talk to her about could wait because he needed some time on his own.

## *Chapter Eleven*

New York City in the middle of July was its usual hot, steamy self. Locked in meetings for the past two days, Shay had nonetheless managed to squeeze in a hair appointment first thing this morning to deal with her frizz, but she doubted the effect would last.

Through the thickly glazed windows of *Today's Woman* magazine's headquarters, on the thirty-eighth level of a sleek Madison Avenue office building, she could faintly hear the sounds of the traffic below—pumpkin-colored rivers of taxis protesting the slightest delay, the sirens of emergency vehicles on their way to a hospital or police building.

There would be crowds of people streaming along the sidewalks like turbulent rivers, every one of them in a hurry to get somewhere important, there would be power lunches taking place in expensive restaurants, money shifting from one bank account to another in massive amounts.

New York contained the beating heart of fashion and music and art and advertising and so much more.

It was all so familiar, and for so long she'd thrived on it. She'd always felt as if plugging into the city's irrepressible energy was an automatic sign of success, and that negotiating the difficulties of daily life in such a fast-moving, crowded, fascinating place was just what you did to survive.

It strengthened you.

It was necessary.

Today, she'd lost her certainty about all this.

Tom, as expected, had made her jump through all sorts of hoops, and then just as she'd begun to wait for the ax to fall, he'd shown her the Australian edition's latest circulation figures.

Up.

Significantly up.

"You're getting it right," he'd told her. "I wasn't sure that you could pull it off, but you have. Whatever it is you're doing, do more."

Which should have been the point at which she pumped her fist in the air and went, "Yesss!" but instead she'd felt a fresh wave of jet-lagged fatigue and had only nodded at him. "More? Sure. I can do that."

Her period hadn't started yet.

She could point to all sorts of reasons for this. A lot of women had disrupted cycles when they traveled, when they were unusually stressed or when they lost weight. Of those particular boxes, she could check all three. She'd lost several pounds at Roscommon Downs, first during the arduous trek from the stricken helicopter and then because she'd been so absorbed in her shipwreck romance with Dusty that she just hadn't felt like eating three big meals a day.

Even now that the huge cattle station was only a memory, her appetite hadn't returned. She couldn't get Dusty out of her head, and her body remembered his so vividly that if she closed her eyes she could almost feel his mouth on her skin. Two nights ago in Sydney, she'd buried her face in his T-shirt and inhaled his scent.

She honestly didn't believe she could be pregnant, and yet she toyed with the idea in every spare moment—toyed with it and tortured herself with it.

She was seeing Sarah tonight for dinner, and she knew what Sarah would tell her. "Stop letting it mess with your head and just take a test."

But even taking a test…actually going into a drugstore, choosing one, paying good money for it and putting it discreetly into a paper bag…gave the whole thing a reality that she stubbornly didn't want.

The test would be negative and she would have wasted her money.

She would feel like a sad, deluded fool.

She'd have lost her last excuse to think about Dusty, and to rehearse some magical, emotional moment when they might see each other again.

Dear Lord, did she *want* to be having his baby, then? Did she want to be having a baby at all?

They were stark questions, and she was way too confused and emotional to have an easy answer to them.

Her final meeting ended at five-thirty and she took the subway downtown to Tribeca, where Sarah lived with her husband and three-year-old twins in a converted loft. Not for much longer, it turned out. They'd just purchased a craft gallery in Vermont with an old farmhouse attached, and they hoped to be fully settled there before the middle of fall, when Sarah's baby was due.

"Tell me…tell me…how you could make a decision as huge as that," Shay asked as they lingered over Swiss chocolate almond ice cream for dessert, curled up on a squishy couch in front of a blast of air-conditioning. Sarah's husband was out with friends, and the twins were asleep. Her blond hair looked rather limp and damp, but her cheeks and eyes were glowing.

"You mean *explain your craziness?*" she said.

"No! I don't mean that at all. I mean, what was your process? Was it sudden? A lightbulb moment? Did it feel like an act of desperation to save your lives, or—I'm not making sense, I know. Did it come on gradually? Did you argue much about your options? Were you rejecting this lifestyle, or embracing a new one, or—?"

"Hey, slow down. Pregnant people can't follow when you throw up that many questions that fast. They have overheated brains and toxic hormones raging inside them." Sarah's brown eyes widened. "You mean... Are you thinking of not coming back to New York, yourself?"

"No," Shay said quickly. "Not at all. I love New York. I'm just wondering about you."

"Do you know what?" Sarah stretched and rubbed her lower spine. "It was actually pretty simple. We listened to our hearts, and this was what they said, loud and clear, so we made a commitment to working it out."

"That easy?"

"The heart and the commitment was easy. The working it out took longer. We've been talking about it since the twins had their first birthday. It took us a year to find the right place and do a proper business plan, work out the right safety nets."

"You never said a word about leaving the city."

"We don't tell people our baby-name ideas in advance, either."

"There, I'm not seeing the connection."

"Before the baby's born, people will shoot your names

down in flames. Once it's a done deal, no matter what they really think, they'll tell you it's a lovely name, and since it's nobody's business but ours, *lovely* is all I want to hear. Same with Vermont. It's locked in now, so people are thrilled for us. Are you thrilled, Shay?"

She laughed. "On the basis of the argument you've just given me, you'll never truly know, will you? Yes, I'm thrilled. Now tell me your baby names."

"Absolutely not!"

They talked until Sarah began to yawn. Pregnant people got tired early in the evenings, and with her asthma always an impediment, Sarah had to take extra care. Shay tore herself away, feeling that she might have spilled a lot more if they'd just had a little longer to get to the subject. She wished they did have longer, and she was deeply relieved that they didn't.

Which was about as logical as not buying a pregnancy test because she didn't know what she wanted the result to be.

The following day, she flew back to Sydney, skipping Sunday completely when she crossed the international date line. She touched down early on Monday morning.

The fifth Monday morning, not the fourth, and her period still hadn't come.

At the office, to which she took a taxi direct from the airport, everyone congratulated her on the rising circulation figures, including the three women who had a chance of winning her own editor-in-chief position once she relinquished it to return permanently to New York. They saw job security and a possible promotion in the news, and she understood their hunger.

Understood it, but didn't share it.

Maybe she was just too tired.

At three in the afternoon, Sonya told her, "You have a double dose of jet lag. Go home!"

Shay went.

Via the pharmacy two doors down from her high-rise apartment building, with its Darling Harbor views.

She took ages to choose between a surely unnecessary number of test-kit options, felt just as foolish and secretive about the purchase as she'd known she would, and hid the test in her purse.

In the lobby of her building, someone was waiting for her. He stood up like a jack-in-the-box as soon as he saw her, and her legs turned to perished elastic. Her mind flashed to the moment when he'd reached her through the floodwaters, more than three weeks ago, beside the stricken helicopter. She remembered the physical rush of emotion and relief she'd experienced then, as well as her bone-deep appreciation of his strength and competence and heroism.

Remembering the power of those feelings, she wished desperately that she could feel them again now, but she just didn't. She was back in her real life; she was too much of a mess and, considering what she had in her purse, his timing could hardly have been worse.

"Dusty…What are you doing here?"

"Good to see you, too, Shay," he drawled.

"I didn't mean—"

"It's okay," he cut in. "It's a reasonable question. Maybe I should have phoned first. I did call your office to make sure you were in town, and then again from a cab on the way here to discover you'd left for the day. But I didn't want to give you a chance to say no."

"No? Dusty—"

"Because I would have come anyway," he finished simply. "I wanted to see you again."

They looked at each other, while Shay's purse began to emit this deafening radioactive howling sound because of the pregnancy test kit hidden inside it.

Well, no, of course it didn't, but that was how she felt. She wanted to shield the black leather from Dusty's view, as if it had suddenly become transparent. She wanted him here *so much*, for so many reasons, only not right at this moment.

Not until she *knew.*

"Come up," she said.

"Can I kiss you first?"

"No." Romantically, she felt as if she might throw up if he did that. Not a good look for a senior publishing executive in a granite-floored lobby. "Let's—" She didn't know what to suggest. "How long are you here?"

"There's a couple of horses I have to look at. How long do you want me?"

She closed her eyes. "I—I don't know."

Silence.

She opened her eyes again and looked at him, every muscle in her body aching with tension. "Was that the wrong answer?"

"I guess *forever*'s not realistic at this point, is it, for either of us?" His brandy-brown eyes narrowed, as if she were a page of bad handwriting and he was trying to read her.

"No." She pressed the elevator button, then blurted out, "Did you think this through?"

An older woman joined them in their wait for the elevator, and Dusty dropped his voice very low. He bent his head toward Shay and she felt an overwhelming rush of awareness and familiarity that orientated something in her universe once again.

Whatever else was or wasn't happening, this man's body belonged to hers, in this moment, in a way she could never explain and never deny. Standing this close, she could have touched him anywhere she wanted, and even the fabric of his clothing would have felt sensual beneath her touch because of the shape of his body beneath.

"Of course I didn't think it through," he said. "Have either of us been any good at that so far, with each other? I just came. The horses were an excuse. And I thought you might not think it through, either, you might just—" He stopped, and his gaze arrowed to her mouth.

"Kiss you," she said, understanding.

"Don't you want to?" His mouth barely moved.

"Yes, I do."

So much!

He was still leaning close, his hands poised uncertainly in the air as if he wanted to touch and hold her but didn't know how. She could smell the familiar *rightness* of him— another thing that made no sense but was possibly even more powerful because of the very fact that she couldn't understand it. She could see in detail the beautiful, familiar shape of his lips, the tawny fire deep in his eyes, and somehow they brought her home.

"Well, that's something!" he muttered.

The elevator arrived and they stepped into it. The woman stepped in after them, then squeezed herself into the corner by the control panel, as if whatever fatal disease they had contracted was highly contagious. Seeing herself in the mirrored elevator wall, Shay understood the stranger's reaction. She looked horribly pale, with blue half circles beneath her eyes, while the eyes themselves stood out like chips of glittering jade on white velvet.

"Could you press twenty-seven, please?" she asked, and the woman complied with the flicker of a polite smile.

"When do you head to New York?" Dusty asked. He leaned his powerful forearm against the mirrored wall.

"When? I've already been!"

"You mean since you left Roscommon Downs?"

"Yes, I flew out Wednesday, and I got back this morning."

"That's crazy. No wonder you look so tired." He brushed his thumb against the puffy skin beneath her eye, then tucked a strand of hair behind her ear. Her whole body tingled.

"I'm fine."

Dusty raised his eyebrows but didn't reply.

The elevator whooshed up to the twenty-seventh level, leaving Shay's stomach behind. She would be okay once she was safely inside her apartment, she told herself, but then realized this wasn't true. She wouldn't be remotely okay until she'd taken the pregnancy test, and how could she do that with Dusty here?

She'd just have to.

She knew it. No matter how much the task got in the way of everything else thrown up by his unexpected appearance, now that she'd bought the kit, she had to get it over with and know the truth for sure.

Having been forcibly separated from her whole Stressed Out Executive persona for most of the time she'd been at Roscommon Downs, she understood it a little better now that it was back again. There was a certain piece of critical information that she needed before she could move on to formulate her next set of plans, and she needed that information *now*.

The entire universe…in the form of Dustin Tanner…had entered a conspiracy to prevent her from acquiring the information, apparently, but she refused to let the universe win.

"Do you want some tea, Dusty?" she asked him as soon as they were shut inside her apartment.

"Sure," he answered vaguely, looking around as if he weren't convinced this place would even have a kitchen.

It did, but admittedly Shay hadn't often cooked anything in it.

Having gone directly from the airport to her office this morning, she hadn't yet been back here since last week, when she'd sandwiched two unsettled nights in her own bed before heading for New York. The air smelled stale and chemical. She had a cleaner who came in for an hour and a half on Friday mornings, and the faint odor of the products she used still hung around. This didn't help Shay's stomach to behave.

And would the milk she'd bought last Tuesday for her breakfast coffee still be any good?

She filled the electric kettle and switched it on, sniffed at the milk and decided it would just do if Dusty wanted it, checked her supply of horrible chamomile tea bags and discovered she only had two left. Probably a good thing, since she didn't intend to drink chamomile tea-bag tea ever again. As soon as possible, she was going to invest in a china pot, and the kind of black leaf tea they drank at Roscommon Downs.

One concrete plan for her future, at least.

Dusty was waiting in the other room. She peeked out at him. He'd picked up last week's newspaper. He folded it back, read a couple of lines, folded it the other way, dropped it back on the coffee table.

He might be the father of her child.

The kettle began to sing, but she couldn't wait for it, couldn't just calmly make tea beneath the massive question mark that hung over her life. Coming out of the kitchen, she said to Dusty, "Could you excuse me for a moment? I'll finish the tea in a minute."

She grabbed her purse from where she'd flung it on the couch, dived for the sanctuary of the bathroom, and opened the pharmacy bag and the box inside it with shaking hands.

* * *

Left on his own, Dusty considered the fact that so far his visit hadn't gone according to plan.

Well, the plan had been pretty basic.

Check that Shay was actually in Sydney, fly down, tell her he wanted to keep seeing her, have her fall rapturously into his arms…then into her bed…and work out the details later.

He paced through the apartment. It seemed sleek and clean and unlived in, and the granite-and-glass bathroom gave the impression of taking up half the space. He found a framed photo of three people who had to be her parents and her sister, but he suspected it only occupied this space on the teak shelf because that was what people did—they had photos of their family on display. The absence of such a photo would invite more questions Shay didn't want to answer than would the photo itself.

There were two more photos. One showed Shay receiving a journalism award that she'd never mentioned to him, and there was another in which she was almost unrecognizable, grinning into the camera with a pair of identical little girls, aged around two, squishing their plump rosy cheeks against hers on either side.

His heart did something uncomfortable in his chest.

The three faces of Shay.

Ill-adjusted daughter, proud and steely-determined executive, loving human being.

He knew which of the three had traveled up to the apartment with him just now.

The executive.

But why did the executive need to hide in the bathroom?

When she finally came out several minutes later, he remembered that there was a fourth face to Shay—the one he'd seen when he reached her at the helicopter, the one that had first arrowed its way into his heart, the face of a lost child needing rescue.

"What's wrong?" he demanded as soon as he saw her.

She put on a smile. "Nothing. Bit of a stomach upset, that's all. Forty-eight hours of airplane food in one week, what were the odds? Did the kettle boil?"

"Forget the kettle."

"I'd really like a hot cup of tea." She dredged up a laugh that was even less sincere than the smile. "I'm turning into an Australian."

"Let me make it, then," he offered. "Sit down. You look like you wouldn't even get as far as the kitchen."

He put his arm around her shoulder and she tilted her head and, with her eyes closed, pressed her cheek against his hand like a cat. His protective instincts surged, and he decided he wasn't leaving her alone yet, no matter what they ended up saying to each other, even if this meant that all he did was watch over her while she slept.

"Sit," he repeated, and she nodded and dropped to the smoky blue leather couch. "Would you like a pillow and a quilt? Get yourself comfortable, in case you fall asleep."

"I won't," she predicted at once, but he couldn't see what would keep her awake. Himself?

So far, she hadn't given any indication that he held that much power.

Stubbornly, he refused to consider that his showing up here might have been a mistake. He would push through this. He'd left Dave in charge at the station, and had warned him that he might be gone for a week or longer. Dave could reach him by phone if he needed to.

He found the pillow from her bed, and on a chest at the foot of the bed there was a folded white quilt patterned with flowers, so he gathered that up as well. Both items gave off Shay's scent. He had no name for it, and no descriptive words. He just knew it was sweeter and warmer than he would once…a long time ago…have expected for a high-powered publishing executive.

When he reentered the living room, she'd kicked off her shoes, left them lying under the coffee table and gone back to the kitchen to finish pouring the tea.

"Hey, I said I'd do it," he told her, taking the two steaming mugs from her grip. Their fingers touched, and the heel of his hand brushed her wrist.

She smiled thinly. "I couldn't wait that long."

"Not sure how long I can wait, either," he said, dropping his voice low. He could feel the way her body pulled toward his. This wasn't one-sided. Even though she was holding back, a part of her reacted exactly the way he did, wanting him, finding a home in his arms.

She sat back on the couch, silent as she took her first few sips of tea.

"Good?" He wanted more from her. He was accustomed to her honesty, not to this polite, tired shield, and he liked the honesty a lot better.

"Revolting," she said.

"Wha-at?" He let out a relieved laugh. Well, this was honest!

"You've spoiled me. I told you that. I've discovered just how much I really do hate chamomile."

"I could have gone out and got you some other kind, while you were in the bathroom."

He thought he felt her flinch at the word *bathroom*, which didn't make sense. Something was so wrong about this. He'd never seen her with this brittle facade before. It made the ruthless self-absorption of her first few hours at Roscommon Downs seem healthy by comparison.

He'd been able to deal with that.

Easily.

He'd simply attacked back.

Dealing with this was like trying to grab onto handfuls of smoke.

She must be exhausted, he reminded himself, and forced back his instinct to confront her and demand to know what was wrong. It could wait.

In the warm semicircle of Dusty's arm, Shay longed to tell him about the pregnancy test in the bathroom wastebasket, the way she imagined an interrogation subject longed to spill everything under the influence of truth drugs.

Yes, she was exhausted.

And she was pregnant.

The knowledge clanged like a ceaseless bell in her head, drowning out the possibility of hearing what her heart told her, or even thinking about what decisions she would need to make.

She was pregnant.

And she'd had enough discussions with Dusty on the subject of having children to know that he would never be content to act as an accidental sperm donor and then conveniently disappear, to leave her as a single executive mom.

He was a strong, simple, successful, honorable man. He had traditional values. He was accustomed to being his own boss, and to directing others. He would have his own ideas about being involved with this child, and he would expect those ideas to hold sway—ideas about inheritance and influence and day-to-day contact, fitting somewhere in between feudal kingdoms and white picket fences.

Feudal cattle kingdoms.

White picket fences stained red with outback dust.

He'd want his child to grow up at Roscommon Downs.

*Welcome back to your life, Shay.*

*You knew from the first moment that he wasn't your type. Now the knowledge has come back to haunt you in a way you never imagined.*

*Don't tell him,* said a little red cartoon Shay-devil sitting on her left shoulder.

On her other shoulder, there should be a little white Shay-angel with a halo and wings, providing a different answer, but if there was a Shay-angel, she was hiding under Shay's hair and speaking too indistinctly for her to hear.

*Don't tell him.*

It began to seem like a good idea.

The pregnancy wasn't planned, after all. In fact, they'd tied themselves in knots trying to keep away from each other until they had contraception taken care of—as it turned out, unreliably—and that had been at Dusty's insistence. He'd talked about wanting children, but he'd been quite determined not to father a child with her!

It would be the easiest thing in the world, surely, to ride out his time in Sydney, tell him she didn't want to see him again—skip over a few inconvenient details such as the tender state of her heart, at this point—and send him back to Roscommon Downs in ignorance.

Hurrah.

Problem solved.

The bell in her brain began to clang more softly, and her whirl of thoughts about the pregnancy settled to a deeper level, somehow.

At which point a feathery little Shay-angel tapped her on the shoulder and said, "Excuse me? I got tangled in your hair—you really need an appointment with your stylist— and I'm not sure if you heard me clearly enough just now…"

"Go away," she muttered to the Shay-angel. "Tell me again when I've had some sleep."

*Shay, he needs to know…*

No.

She couldn't tell him.

Not yet.

Not until she had some idea about what *she* wanted, instead of the dust-stained white picket fence, and some idea about how she was going to get it.

At this deeper level in her thoughts, dark, frightening scenarios began to unfold. She saw personal arguments escalating until they became court battles. She saw lawyers pushing her to demand things from Dusty that she didn't even want, purely as a strategy for achieving what she really needed. It could go on for years. This child of theirs, bred in an uneasy limbo between the city and the outback, the U.S. and Australia, could tangle them in legal wrangling until they had a teenager ready for dating instead of a toddler in diapers.

With all the uncertainties she had about parenthood, one thing Shay knew down to the marrow of her bones was that she didn't ever want to treat a child like a possession or a weapon, exchanged or fired back and forth across the biggest ocean in the world, and yet the seeds of exactly this might already be in place.

It wasn't a far-fetched nightmare. It was a possibility as real as floodwaters in the desert, and the Milky Way overhead.

And she couldn't risk a child's well-being that way.

Which meant, didn't it, that she couldn't tell Dusty about the baby until she was sure the legal wrangling wouldn't happen.

And that might mean she couldn't tell him…ever.

The light began to fade. She put her unfinished tea

down on the coffee table and sank back into Dusty's arms, not sure if he should even still be in her apartment. She should have just asked him to go; she should have told him she didn't want to see him again *before* she'd taken the test....

Which didn't make the remotest sense because if she hadn't been pregnant, if she hadn't had a trans-Pacific, outback-versus-city, possession-slash-weapon of a tiny, precious, defenseless baby growing inside her—oh, wow, it was hard to grasp!—she would want what he seemed to want, a joyful, easy, open-ended continuation.

*I wanted to see you again,* he'd told her, and she felt the same.

Out of the gathering darkness, and after several tortured minutes of silence, she finally heard his voice. "Listen, I know you're not okay. Maybe it's the jet lag, maybe it's something else."

"I—"

"I'm not asking for an explanation, Shay," he cut in, with his usual authority. "I'm telling you it's okay not to give me one. Just to sit. To fall asleep if you want."

"I'm not going to fall asleep." Even with fatigue over-taking her like paralysis, she couldn't imagine it. The impossible baby, the baby who didn't belong in the outback and couldn't belong in Shay's life, would keep her awake all night long.

"I hope you do," Dusty said.

"Yeah?"

"Yes, because I'd like to sit here holding you while you do. And then tomorrow I'll bring you flowers and take you out to dinner and we can talk."

Talk.

The word scared her.

Talking would be the start of it—of the trans-Pacific,

city and outback, legal battle impossibility of her baby's future.

She knew she'd flinched at the word, the way she'd flinched about the bathroom when he'd mentioned it earlier, and she knew he would have felt the movement. In fact, their bodies were so attuned that she could *feel* him feeling it and then letting it go, putting it into a too-hard basket called *tomorrow,* along with the dinner and the flowers, when she'd had time to rest.

But when she'd had time to rest, she knew, nothing would change.

"Sleep, Shay," he said, pulling her closer.

"Tell me a bedtime story."

He laughed, then took a slow breath and said softly, with his cheek pressed lightly against her hair, "Once upon a time there was a magazine executive from New York who didn't know what was good for her...."

She listened, and his words spooled out like ribbon. He made her laugh, and he made her catch her breath, and very soon she came to a point where she knew she could either keep listening to this and therefore inevitably end up telling him what she'd learned in the bathroom—the thing that might have them hating each other one day— or she could kiss him and get him to stop.

No contest.

No contest at all.

Needing only a tiny movement, she turned her face toward his, brushed her mouth against his lips to drown out the words *firelight* and *under the stars,* and made a powerful bid for his response.

## Chapter Twelve

It was the softest, sweetest, laziest kiss Shay had ever had, and it went on forever. Only once they'd wrapped their arms around each other and tasted each other and let their mouths melt together did she realize just how hungry she had been for his touch this past week when she'd flown halfway around the world and back, and hadn't seen him.

"You're too tired for this," he whispered, pulling away a little, but he meant it halfheartedly, and she knew it.

"No," she whispered in reply, and ran the tips of her fingers down his neck and then up into his hair at the back. "It's what I want."

Deliberately, she let her gaze fall to his mouth, with her own lips softened with kissing and just an inch or two away. She saw his tongue lap his lower lip and let her mouth drift closer. She knew it would drive him wild—this close, but not touching. She saw the fan of his lashes against his cheeks as he looked down at her mouth, and then he looked up again and their eyes met and he groaned between gritted teeth.

He gave in, kissing her more hungrily and more deeply until she felt dizzy and breathless and more precious to him than ever. He slid off her clothes, garment by garment. The tailored jacket, the tailored pants, the silk shell blouse, the thread of gold around her neck, and she did the same to him. They laughed a little bit when a button wouldn't push through, and when he couldn't find the hook of her bra. They gasped when they touched each other in places they hadn't touched for a whole long difficult week.

He touched her breasts, covered their tender peaks with his hot mouth, cupped her as if her breasts were made of spun sugar. She realized that she'd already grown fuller there, one of the pregnancy symptoms Sarah had talked about. If he knew her body well enough to notice, he didn't say anything, but he went on touching her and suckling her until her breathing went out of control and she had to grip his shoulders to keep from flying apart.

They came together like two puzzle pieces—warm, soft, living puzzle pieces that had been made to fit. Her brain buzzed and burned with fatigue, but her body didn't care. His hands and mouth brought her back to life, shut out the whole world, made sense of everything. When he filled her, pushing deep as if he could never get deep enough, she had to hold on to him even tighter, for fear she'd lose contact with the earth itself, this felt so powerful and right.

And when their perfect rhythm had settled into stillness, she fell asleep with tears on her cheeks.

She hadn't slept so soundly in a long time. She never felt him stir, never felt the quilt tucking around her, or the pillow puffing closer against her cheek. It was three-fifteen in the morning when she woke up again, according to the clock beside the TV.

No Dusty.

Wide awake, she wrapped herself in the quilt and looked for him, expecting he might have gone to sleep in her bed, since she'd taken the couch. But he wasn't in the apartment at all. She found his note in the kitchen.

*I've booked into a hotel.* He gave its name and telephone number—a place not far from here, on the opposite side of Darling Harbor. *I'm seeing those horses tomorrow. Pick you up at six for dinner? If I don't hear from you, that's what I'll do. D.*

And if he did hear from her?

She thought about it, working distractedly on her laptop, with first coffee then hot oatmeal at her elbow, until the sun had risen without her noticing and it was time to get out of her robe, shower, dress and head into the office.

If he was "seeing horses," that meant he'd be out for a good part of the day. Sale yards? Racetrack? She had no idea, but could still pick the most likely time. Eleven. She couldn't imagine a man like Dusty hanging around in his hotel room at eleven on a sunny morning, in Sydney's mild winter weather. She could easily leave him a voice-mail message.

She rehearsed it half under her breath, standing beside the phone, wondering if this could really be the Shay Russell she'd known for thirty-one years, running out on her responsibility just because it was scary and tough.

"Last night was a mistake, Dusty, and I don't think dinner's a good idea, either. I've had some time, now, and some sleep, and I don't think we should see each other again. There's no future to this, and I don't see how… *why*," she revised, "…two people would want to maintain a long-distance relationship without a future. I mean, do you? See why? It just doesn't make sense."

She stopped, knowing that if she'd been with her friends

in New York having a crisis meeting over coffee, they could have run with this subject for an hour, talking the whole thing out like squeezing the juice from an orange until there was nothing left but a battered, sticky mess, even without the subject of her pregnancy coming into the picture.

Her whole body suddenly went hot, and she felt as if she'd been wrapped in someone else's skin. It felt wrong on her body. It didn't fit right, and the feeling scared her.

*I'm having a baby.*

*I'm having Dusty's baby.*

*And that's the way he's going to think about it. He has rights, and he's going to want them to count—in the most honorable and decent and responsible way possible. He'll be the best father in the world, but on his own terms, in his own world, the way he's a great boss at Roscommon Downs but on his own terms and in his own world there, also.*

Could those terms ever be hers?

Could she ever belong in that world?

"It's simple. If you're not going to tell him about it, then you shouldn't see him tonight," said the shoulder-dwelling Shay-angel and Shay-devil in unison, although they didn't speak in quite the same voice. One sounded sneaky, the other noble and self-sacrificing.

Frankly, Shay couldn't stand either of them.

She circled away from the phone and slumped onto the couch, knowing she wasn't going to call his hotel to cancel.

She had to tell him about the baby.

She *would* tell him about the baby.

The decision felt right, if not comfortable.

Right, not comfortable, and terrifying.

Still wrapped in a stranger's skin, she took the commuter train to North Sydney for work.

* * *

Shay looked beautiful.

Dusty had never seen her dressed up for an evening out. Her hair was silky and shimmery and soft, curving to frame her cheekbones and jawline in a natural way that left several strands brushing her skin and tempted his fingers into a caress that he was determined to give her tonight. She wore a simple sleeveless dress in a pinky kind of beige, with a wide V neckline tucking between her breasts, and a skirt that floated around her calves.

Her skin-toned high heels lengthened her legs, she had touches of gold jewelry at her ears and throat and she'd done something to her eyes…makeup, which he wasn't an expert on…because they looker softer and grayer today.

Did they?

He got closer, and saw yesterday's glittery green chips beyond the illusion given by shadow and liner. She looked beautiful…and tense…and terrified. For a moment, it disturbed him, the way an animal got disturbed by an approaching storm, but then he remembered that, to be honest, he was terrified, too.

You didn't bother to get terrified in a situation like this unless it was important.

Important was good.

His heart lifted.

He'd come so close to leaving a message with her assistant at *Today's Woman* to say he'd flown back to Queensland. He'd been ninety percent convinced that she would have greeted the news with relief, even though she could easily have called to cancel herself and hadn't, so that had to be a plus, didn't it?

In the end, he hadn't canceled either, he'd instead gone all out to ensure that this would be a night to remember, whatever they ended up saying to each other.

And now here she was, standing in the doorway of her apartment, leaning slightly on the handle as if she wasn't fully confident of her strength and he had to consider that, beyond their shared nerves, her stunning appearance was a kind of gift to him—a gift or an apology.

"You look great," he said, packing enough heartfelt sincerity into the three words to make up for their lack of fluency.

"Thank you." She smiled, took his hand and drew him inside, and he wanted her at once, in the most primal male way possible. "So do you."

Because he'd tried!

Gone were the cattleman's jeans, shirts and boots in which he felt at home. He'd put on his only suit, a dark charcoal one with a pale blue shirt underneath. He'd left the shirt open at the neck because a tie would quite possibly choke him when his throat already felt so tight, but maybe she liked this casual touch, because she reached up and brushed his bare skin there with the backs of her fingers—they shook slightly—and he had to fight to keep his breathing steady.

She smiled in a tentative way. "Let me just pick up my purse. Are we taking a cab?"

"Yes, and you should bring a jacket, too."

She nodded and came back with a beaded purse that matched her shoes and a pale gray spring coat that didn't match anything, but still looked great on her, as far as he was any judge. "Will this do?"

He thought about saying, "Yes, but how about you take it all off for half an hour or so, because what's underneath is even better." In the end, something stopped the words in his throat and he accepted that he'd spend the whole evening in a state of dizzying, hypnotic frustration.

"We have to walk down to the waterfront at Darling Harbor," he managed to say instead. "We're taking a water taxi and eating overlooking the yachts in Rose Bay. And I can't drop that casually into the conversation as if I take water taxis and eat in swish restaurants every day, Shay, because I don't, but…hell…" His fluency deserted him again, suddenly.

*I've tried*, he wanted to say. *Credit me with that, no matter how this evening ends up.*

She slid her arm through his and squeezed him, but said nothing and he felt the weight of something unspoken hanging between them like summer humidity hanging in the air.

"We're going to have a good evening," she finally said, having held the words back until they left the lobby of her building and reached the street.

"Well, yes, I hope so."

It was already dark, and the night air would be colder on the water. They walked down to Darling Harbor together, with Shay's heels cracking on the pavement and the traffic still noisy and unrelenting on the city streets.

Dusty liked cities. Brisbane, with its wide, winding river, lush gardens and houses set in odd locations in the often steep terrain. Melbourne, which he only ever saw in spring racing season, when the weather could range from windy and wet to scorching hot and still. And this city, Sydney, a frivolous, dramatic, cosmopolitan place where the inhabitants would allegedly sell their souls for a water view.

Could he live in one, though?

He'd never considered before that he might have to. Cities had always meant time out for him—a break and a chance to experience something new. Real life was one and a quarter million of his own acres of richly grassed flood plain and red desert, where the gratification was a lot less instant, the work was harder, but the rewards lasted longer, too.

Would he abandon all that—*could* he, even if it was only

for a few years—to be with Shay? He wasn't at all sure that he could.

"You're quiet," she said.

"So are you."

"How were the horses?"

"Promising. They're up for sale in a couple of weeks. I'm going to report back to Callan and Brant, see what our trainers think. One of them I'd like to bid on."

"How does that work?"

"Well, there's a couple of major avenues for buying thoroughbreds in this country…."

*We're remembering how to talk to each other,* he thought, after he'd given her more detail and she'd asked her usual alert, interested kind of questions. He liked talking to her, didn't matter what the subject was. He liked the places where their thinking met, and the places where it was different. She seemed interested in exploring the differences, as he was, and that was good.

They reached the waterfront and the taxi was waiting for them. He helped her aboard, then kept her hand in his and they smiled at each other, and he jumped the gun totally and leaned close to whisper in her ear, "I want to see you tomorrow, too, if we can find some time."

She closed her eyes and nodded, and both the pleasure and the terror were clear on her face again, and since pleasure and terror about summed up the contradictory nature of his own feelings, he let it go.

The water taxi zoomed away from the wharf and around under the Harbor Bridge, past the Opera House with its backdrop of city neon and glass and blue-black night sky, past the stretch of lush darkened greenery that was the Botanical Gardens, past the naval dockyards at Garden Island and the distant forest of masts on the yachts moored in Rushcutters Bay.

And with the fresh salt air in his lungs and Shay's warm hand in his, Dusty was so sure that they could do this, that they could make it work for as long as they wanted it to, *somehow,* that he left the taxi man a fifty-dollar tip.

Then, later in the evening, she told him her news….

Over dessert.

She'd say it then.

No, over coffee, Shay revised, because during dessert they happened to be talking about legendary Australian racehorses, and the life story of Makybe Diva, who'd won the Melbourne Cup an unprecedented three years in a row, and it was too interesting and too off-topic…and too much of a good excuse to hold off a little longer.

The coffee made Shay jittery, and she had a buzz of fatigue behind the jitteriness, like the buzz of white noise.

How did you do something like this?

How did you say it?

*I know we've only known each other for three and a half weeks. I know this is going to put our relationship under a kind of pressure you never envisaged when you flew down here yesterday. I know I was just as happy to see you as you were to see me, even though I couldn't show it then.*

*There's a reason I couldn't show it, Dusty.*

He watched her fiddling with her coffee spoon, just as he'd watched her struggling with her shrimp and salad and steak.

"Spit it out, Shay," he suddenly said. "What didn't you tell me yesterday?" He thought for a moment, and there was a harder edge in his voice when he added, "Or should it be, what didn't you tell me at Roscommon Downs?"

"Nothing. Not at—"

"Come on…" He pushed his chair back, as if about to get up to leave, and she remembered that he knew how to get angry when he needed to—when there was a result he wanted, when he needed to be the boss, the one with clarity and control. "Is this something I've been through before? With Mandy or Rebecca? Is it suddenly going to turn out that there's baggage or a hidden agenda you never mentioned or even hinted at?"

She grabbed his wrists across the table and said quickly, "I didn't tell you because I didn't know about it at Roscommon Downs. It only happened at Roscommon Downs, and I didn't know about it until yesterday, after you got here." He swore and she thought he must have guessed, so she just blurted it out. "I'm pregnant, and I don't know what I'm going to do about it, yet."

But he hadn't guessed, it turned out.

"*Do* about it?" he echoed, then backtracked, his voice suddenly even tighter and harsher. *"Pregnant?"* She still enclosed his wrists with her grip and now he gripped back, enough to hurt her, although she doubted he knew it.

She could see his reaction, that same feeling she'd had—was still having—of being wrapped in a stranger's skin that didn't fit.

*I didn't handle it right,* she knew at once.

*For either of us.*

And yet she didn't know how she could have handled it better for him. Slower? More cryptic? More upbeat?

How to handle it better for herself… Suddenly she couldn't hold back the words. She'd always found it best to be honest with him.

"I'm scared of what you're going to want, Dusty. I—I thought about not telling you at all, so that what you might want wouldn't matter."

She couldn't look at him anymore, his eyes were blazing so much. Instead, she dropped her gaze and watched the monkey grip they were both locked in across the table, his big hands effortlessly cuffed around her forearms.

"I don't want it signed and sealed on the spot that this is going to be an outback baby," she went on, faster. "Your baby, raised on Roscommon Downs, miles from my world. That's…that's more than a lifestyle adjustment, and it's about more than whether we care for each other enough to keep seeing each other. It's a huge thing, and I'm scared," she repeated, looking up again. "This baby is mine more than it's yours—"

"More?" His eyes narrowed, glaring icily from behind his half-closed lids in a way that eyes of such a warm color had no right to glare.

"I know there has to be a compromise. I know you're going to want…" The word that fell out of her mouth was "…Control," which was a mistake, but she couldn't take it back and maybe it was best to have her fears right on the table in their starkest terms.

"Control?"

"Don't just echo my words."

"Your words are making my jaw drop. You think the baby is more yours than mine, but you think I'm the one who is going to want control?"

"Am I wrong, though?"

"I've had two minutes to think about it, for heck's sake!" His voice rose, and someone at a nearby table turned to look.

"I knew in two minutes what you'd want," Shay said, leaning toward him, trying to keep this private. "Tell me I'm wrong. If I say to you, this baby is mine—"

"You just did say that, Shay. You said exactly that."

"—and that I want it raised in my world, not yours, tell me you'd say that's okay, that's fine. I know you wouldn't!"

He didn't answer, just pulled his wrists out of her grip. She could see his hands shaking. With anger?

She waited.

"Tell me how this can have happened," he finally demanded, as if he'd been tricked in some way. He might seriously think he had, she realized. The thought that he didn't yet trust her honesty hurt her. "Your doctor told you you'd have to work to conceive—you said."

"And you told me she was probably presenting a worst-case scenario. You were right. She must have been. The contraceptive failure I'm not so clear on. Is this really what we want to be talking about? Aren't there more—?"

"I have to take it step by step. And I can explain the contraception. Prim looked at the empty carton last week, before she threw it away. The whole batch expired two years ago." He laughed, although nothing was funny. "I told her it wouldn't matter."

"Did you tell her why?"

"No."

"I believed my doctor, Dusty."

Silence. Shay contemplated the people at Roscommon Downs and wondered what they'd think, what Dusty would tell them.

"I don't like your assumptions," he said.

"No, I can see that. And I hadn't intended to…" she spread out her hand "…lay them on the table, just like that. But now that I have, I'm not sorry, because I need to know if it's how you feel. What do you want, Dusty?"

"Shoot, how can I answer that, when you've just preempted what I might want by telling me it's unacceptable! How can I tell you, yes, I do want this baby raised on Roscommon Downs, I do want my child to understand its heritage, I do want the chance to be the kind of father I've always imagined I'd be, when you've made all of that sound like a crime on my part. You've sprung this on me…."

"The lapsed expiry date sprang it on me. The pregnancy test sprang it on me *yesterday* in my bathroom, three minutes after we both walked through my front door. I can't soft soap everything I'm scared of, Dusty! It's too important. You have to know I'm terrified of how much we could fight about this."

"Because you think all I want is control."

"Because I'm *scared* all you want is control."

"Which means I can't say, yes, I want a large degree of involvement—Is that control? I don't know—without sounding like a monster. Listen, the whole restaurant is listening to this."

"Then the restaurant owners should give us a cut of their profits for providing their patrons with entertainment."

"Don't you care?"

"You want us to go?"

"I'm going." He rubbed his fingers over his eyes, a gesture she knew. "We both need breathing space. I don't want to think about how much we could fight over this, either. Lawyers on two continents."

He shook his head, sounding scared about it, and his fear gave her a glimmer of hope because at least it was something they shared.

"That's what I'm afraid of, too," she whispered. "Lawyers on two continents."

He didn't answer directly. "I'll get you home, and then I'll head to my hotel."

"I can get myself home."

"Just like you can raise our baby on your own. I'm sure you can. Both things. But I'd like to take you home." He looked around and caught their waiter's attention at once.

He brought the check and Dusty snapped a card into the black folder.

Shay stayed silent, afraid that if she argued about something as trivial as him seeing her home, then they wouldn't have a chance in hell of communicating or coming to an agreement on the vastly more important subject of the baby.

When the waiter returned, he murmured to Dusty, "Shall I bring…?"

"Yes, please."

The man nodded and skimmed off again, returning with flowers. Gorgeous flowers in a riot of color and scent, beautifully wrapped. Shay stood and took them, touching her face to the cool petals as she inhaled their fragrance.

They were fabulous.

And they were so wrong.

Dusty had obviously arranged to have them delivered to the restaurant as a final flourish to the evening, but now… Several people at adjacent tables were still covertly staring, wondering how the flowers fit with the raised voices and hostile looks.

"You're right," Shay murmured to Dusty. "It would be impossible to keep talking about it here."

"Do you want the baby at all?" he asked abruptly.

Tears stung in her eyes. "Yes!" She hadn't said it before, not even to herself, not in such a simple way. "Yes, I want the baby, with all my heart."

He gave a short nod, and she couldn't tell if he'd wanted this answer or something starkly different.

## Chapter Thirteen

"We have scores back from three of the five judges on the short-story competition," Sonya told Shay, coming in to her office, "And they've all put 'Misty Blue' in first place."

"Oh, that story was my favorite, too!" Shay said.

She felt a momentary spurt of satisfaction. Her judgment was in line with *some* people's, then. It wasn't in line with Dusty's. They'd shared a taxi as far as her apartment the night before last, and he'd asked the driver to wait while he made the unnecessary gesture of showing her right to her twenty-seventh-level front door.

"But I won't come in tonight," he'd said.

"Not with that meter running."

"Even without a meter running."

"O-kay."

"Because this is all we're going to do tonight, Shay. We're going to snap and fight."

"But if we—"

"And I'm seriously not going to argue about the possibility of us not snapping and fighting if we try hard enough, because it's already getting circular and I think we're trying as hard as we can."

"It bodes well for the future, doesn't it?"

"It bodes bloody nothing! I'll see you, okay? When we've both had a chance to think, and to cool down."

He hadn't been any more specific about when that might be, so here she was in her office a day and a half later, desperately pretending she knew what she was doing, and that she cared about it. And since she was a professional, she was probably managing to fool everyone but herself.

There, she had no place to hide.

She was a mess.

Except during certain odd, unpredictable moments that came several times a day, when the one thing she really understood about her feelings came wafting over her like a rain-scented breeze and made her feel happy, simply happy, in a way she'd never felt before.

She wanted the baby.

She was absolutely over the moon about the baby.

She was over the moon to feel the way her body was already changing, all by itself. Her body knew what to do. It was amazing. She could have hidden her head in the sand over the pregnancy-test issue for weeks longer, ambivalent about it in every waking moment, and still her body would have taken no notice of the foolish head games. It would simply have gone on with its task, the way it was doing now.

Her breasts felt sore. Her taste buds had begun to react strangely. Coffee didn't taste right anymore and toothpaste smelled terrible. Her emotions balanced on a knife edge, and she knew that inside her body, she was making more blood, her ligaments were softening, her hormones were changing.

It was a miracle, and her heart wanted it.

"It's simple," Dusty had said to her out in the flooded desert, when they'd talked about children. "You just follow your heart home."

She hadn't believed him then. How could it be simple? But she believed him now because it had happened.

Had they both somehow intuitively known it would?

Ridiculous.

"We'll wait for the other two judges, and then we'll tee up a story on the winner as soon as we can," she told her assistant. "I so hope she's interesting!"

"Everyone's interesting," Sonya said. "You've taught me that, Shay. Everyone has a story if you ask the right questions. You've really helped me to see that, and I've been wanting to tell you for a while how much I appreciate it."

Shay blinked in surprise. "Oh." She added awkwardly, "Thank you. I forget it myself, sometimes."

Sonya paused in the doorway and tilted her dark head. "Are you okay?"

"Just tired." Shay pasted on a smile.

"A guy phoned for you earlier. He didn't leave a message, or his name. In fact, as soon as I told him you were in a meeting, he seemed to think that was all he needed to know. His voice sounded familiar. I know he's called here before."

"His voice sounded…?"

Like Dusty?

"…Like he knows what he's doing," Sonya said. "If that makes sense."

"It does."

"Should I have pushed him for his contact details?"

"No, it's fine."

Sonya left the office and Shay felt her pulse start to flutter. She knew what would happen. She'd emerge for lunch half an hour from now and he would be waiting. If she didn't emerge, he would talk his way past reception, unglue her from her desk and march her away because it was time for them to deal with each other and they both knew it.

Sure enough, when she'd faked her way through a little more work, she found him seated in the waiting area, flipping through back copies of *Today's Woman* the way he'd have done in a doctor's office. He had the June issue folded back at the spine and she recognized the photo of his friend Branton Smith and the woman Dusty had insisted wasn't Brant's fiancée posed with a sheepdog on a mud-spattered four-wheeler.

What was the dog's name? Suzy? Shep? Sox?

Sox.

Got it.

Like it mattered.

"Hi," he said, patting the magazine a couple of times with the flat of his hand and then putting it down.

"That's your friend."

"Yeah." He looked as if he wanted to say something more.

Well, they both had so much to say, and what they didn't say now, lawyers might one day say for them. Their shared awkwardness—and their fear?—vibrated in the air like a buzz saw, making Shay try to recall irrelevant facts such as the name of a dog she would never see again and causing Dusty to slap a magazine with an orator's hand as if he wanted to make a speech about it.

"Shall we go?" she said.

"How long do you have?" He sounded skeptical, as if

expecting the news that she had five minutes because of another meeting.

"I have as long as we need. Dusty, I do recognize when things are important, other than the magazine."

He gave a short nod. "I could do with some air and some space."

"We could get on a ferry, or something," she suggested.

"Following through on the surrounded-by-water motif from earlier in our relationship?"

She laughed. She forgot, sometimes, that he wasn't always the strong, silent type. He had a way with words, when he wanted to, and she enjoyed it. "It could be appropriate, couldn't it?" she agreed.

Sydney was famous for its harbor, and the commuter ferries were the best way to get out on it, short of hiring a private yacht. They took the train from her North Sydney office to Circular Quay, bought tickets and hopped on the green-and-yellow boat that went to Manly, a half-hour ride.

Shay had begun to feel, sometimes, as if this were *her city*. She loved New York, but didn't have this same sense, there. New York belonged to too many other people, perhaps.

Well, Sydney did, too, so it wasn't logical.

Maybe because, in her snatched hours of weekend spare time, she'd explored Sydney in a different way to how she'd explored New York? She'd ridden a lot of these ferries. She'd walked a lot of waterfront trails and pathways, through the lush, semitropical greenery of the North Shore, or over the windswept sandstone cliffs between Eastern Suburbs beaches such as Coogee and Bronte and Bondi.

"If you want air, we should sit outside," she told Dusty as they boarded, so they sat on an open-air bench midway down the port side of the ferry and the blue-green harbor water slapped past, along with an oil tanker, a couple of smaller ferries and some pleasure boats out for a mid-week sail.

Window dressing, all of it.

They were here to talk.

"Tell me what you want," Dusty said.

His shoulder pressed against her body. It felt like a statement of companionship, but it wasn't enough. She reached down and entwined her fingers through his, and he squeezed her hand. Keeping the contact, they rested their hands where their thighs touched.

Now it was a statement of companionship, and one of hope, which was better.

"The baby," she answered. "I want the baby. I'm happy. I think I…forgot to say it, the other night. Maybe I didn't know it then. I don't think I did. But I'm very happy, Dusty."

"What else do you want?"

"Tell me what you want, first." Because she wasn't sure how to frame her own needs and desires. She didn't want to lose her sense of herself. She did want to slow her life down, make the right space in it for this child. Where was her middle ground?

"No," Dusty said.

She tried to laugh. "So how come you get to go second? Second is the power position."

"That's why," he growled.

"Because you think it's your right."

"Because I've really thought about this. Because I've come up with something…a plan…and I can't see that there's any other fair option." His voice dropped lower as he spoke, until it came from deep in his chest, sounding half like a whisper of passion, half like a tree creaking in the wind. It melted her, totally beyond her control. "So I'm hoping that what you say fits in with that." He looked at her steadily, and she couldn't look away. "And I want to hear it first."

"First," she echoed, indignant. And this time, she really did laugh, untangling her fingers from his grip to brush them against his cheek. "Look at us! This is impossible!"

"Yeah?"

"I'm getting ready to fight with you, and I still want to kiss you."

"Yeah…?" he said again, more softly.

"I always want to kiss you," she admitted.

"You're right, then. It's impossible." His mouth met hers a fraction of a second later.

The kiss was sweeter, Shay thought, because it was so uncertain—because it was the last kiss they might ever have before reaching an impasse that would make any more kisses impossible and unwanted.

She closed her eyes and gave herself to it completely, knowing she'd never forget it. The slow rumble and rock of the ferry, the freshness of the air, the sun on the side of her face, the taste of his mouth, the feel of his skin when she curved her palm softly against his neck, the sensation of giving, of entrusting her senses to his care.

Breaking the contact almost hurt.

"Tell me what you want," he said.

"Oh, are we back to that?" She brushed the frown from his forehead with the ball of her thumb.

"The ferry's halfway to Manly."

"And you get to say what you want on the return journey, is that the system?"

"I thought we'd walk across to the beach and get ice cream, first."

"Ice cream can be good."

"You see? In a whole lot of areas we're in complete agreement."

Suddenly, however, the lightness had gone. "We're putting it off, aren't we?" she said softly. "Kissing each other and— Because it's too hard and we're scared of what's going to happen when we put our cards down on the table."

"Is that what we should do? Put it off longer? Just spend some more time the way we'd be doing if you weren't…"

"Pregnant. It's such a big word."

She touched his cheek again, looked at those eyes and that mouth, imagined what he'd suggested. Imagined just going to Manly on the ferry and eating ice cream as they wandered along the beach-side walkway, enjoying the new sensation of being together in her world instead of his.

"If we don't talk about it now, we'll just be pretending. It won't count for anything, Dusty."

"No, it won't. You're shaking, Shay."

She didn't try to hide her fear. "How much are we going to fight, Dusty?"

"We don't fight when our goals are the same. Have you noticed that? Did we fight, when we were trekking back to the homestead with Sally and Beau? We didn't. Because we wanted the same thing. To get home safe."

"Sounds good. I'm not buying it. Go first." She closed her eyes.

"Listen, if I go first, you don't get to go at all. If there's something you want, then say it now."

Her eyes flashed open again. "I want to stay the person I am, Dusty. That's as far as I've got. And I know we talked about Jane's theory that kids change parents more than parents change kids, but if you somehow enact this feudal dictate that our baby has to be raised at Roscommon Downs…"

She shook her head.

Dusty said nothing, so she went on, "Where am I in that? Where is my part of our baby's heritage in that? Where is my career? Where is my well-being? There's no room for compromise when the distances are so great. Weekend access or shared custody is not going to work between your land and…well, anywhere else in the entire world."

Still without answering, he stood up and went to the ferry boat rail, leaned his forearm on it and watched the harbor. Then he turned back to her.

"You know me, and I know you. I'm thirty-four years old, and you're thirty-one, and neither one of us is stupid. You don't get to our age, you don't make the mistakes we've both made in relationships in the past without learning something. You're right that I want this on my own terms. Isn't it better if we're both clear on that from the beginning? All you have to decide now is whether they're terms you like."

"A take it or leave it proposition?"

"I've thought about this!"

"A take it or leave it proposition," she repeated.

It wasn't a question this time, and he nodded.

"Go ahead. I'm listening," she said.

"My brother will come home and manage the property. He would have done that in a year or two, anyhow, sharing it with me, but now he'll do it sooner, and on his own. I know he'll be okay about it. We'll stay in Sydney for the whole pregnancy, you and I, and for the birth. Until the baby's around two or even three years old. I know you'd have concerns about a baby so far from medical care, and it'll give you a transition period to work out what you want and what's possible with your career." He spoke in clipped sentences. "What you choose to do about working or maternity leave is up to you, and whatever it is, I'll support it. After that, we'll move to Roscommon Downs until our child is old enough to give us some signals about what he or she wants."

"When will that be?"

"At a guess, around eleven or twelve? Maybe later. Toward the end of high school."

"You're talking about fifteen years of my life!"

"Of your life, mine and the baby's, Shay. Your career will have to scale down. That's clear. But there must be ways to work it so that you can freelance. Read manuscripts, like you did with those short stories. Or by then you may have decided you'd like to try something else. Something creative of your own. A new skill you'd like to focus on. There's a lot to do at the station, and you might find it—"

"Stop!"

"What?"

"This is your plan?"

"Yes."

"The thing I'm not allowed to argue against, because you can't see any other option. Take it or leave it."

"That's right." His face muscles barely moved, apart from what was needed to narrow his eyes down to tight slits.

"No! *I* was right!" she burst out. "It's feudal! You've offered a little window dressing, but it's feudal all the same."

"It's reasonable. It keeps you in the city for three or four more years."

"And in purgatory for at least ten." He flinched at her suggestion that Roscommon Downs counted as hell on earth, and she didn't care. All of this was too new.

"It stops us and our lawyers from tearing each other apart, along with our child." His voice had gone quiet. "That's more important, isn't it? I've thought about it," he repeated.

"And now I have to take it or leave it."

"What have you thought of, that achieves those same goals?"

To this, she had no answer. She only knew that something was wrong with everything he'd said, something drastically important was missing from it, and he wasn't going to listen to her when she tried to tell him so.

The ferry shuddered and slowed, the pitch of its engine sounds changed and she realized they'd almost reached the terminal at Manly.

The end of the line…

"Leave it," Shay whispered as the engines slowed. "That's my choice."

"Shay?"

For a long moment, she couldn't speak, but finally she gasped out the words. "You said take it or leave it. I'm leaving it."

Dusty felt as if he'd been punched in the gut. He could see that she was as hurt and angry and at sea as he was, but he didn't know what he could do about it. He had a painful, nagging feeling that he'd missed something, there was something he hadn't said, but he had no idea what it was. Surely the feeling was wrong. He'd been so careful to keep his proposition clear.

Shay blinked back tears and he wanted to take her in his arms, but knew it would be a mistake. He wasn't so very far from the same state, himself. Not tears. More like blocked plumbing—a thick, painful constriction in his throat that made even his breathing hurt.

Hell, he'd tried so hard, just now! He'd tried to be as precise and honest and straightforward as he could. No false promises, no aimless generalizations, no manipulation. They couldn't afford any of that, with a baby in the picture—a baby and so much geographical distance—so he'd been incredibly careful not to fall into it.

Shay had reacted as if he'd suddenly sprouted horns.

"You really mean that?" he said.

"Take it. Leave it. Two choices. Doesn't take long."

"No, I suppose it doesn't," he muttered.

He felt promises and assurances and compromises and flowery words rising inside him and dammed them back, feeling as if the tables had turned on their whole—short—relationship. He was the one who'd told her that the decision to have a child was simple. You just followed your heart home.

Now he was resisting his heart with all his strength because his heart told him, *Promise her whatever she wants. Tell her we can work it out because we want to work it out, and wanting is enough.*

How stupid had he been to tell her it would be simple?

"I'm going back," she said.

"Back?"

"On the next ferry. This one, I guess. It'll make the round-trip."

A crewman slid the gangway into place as she spoke and passengers began to disembark. The two of them didn't have long to keep talking.

Dusty couldn't go back with her. Prolonging their contact would only make the gulf between them even deeper. The gulf deeper, and the connection more painful.

Without the baby, none of this would be happening.

For a moment, he felt a spurt of anger against his unborn child that was so powerful it made him nauseous. *Why are you here? Why are you so damned important, when you didn't exist a month ago? Why do I care about you, and feel responsible for you, and want the best for you, when I don't even know who you are?*

Slowly, slowly, he let the anger go, and was left only with the knowledge that his ultimatum and Shay's choice had already effectively taken his child out of his life. It would be a city baby not an outback baby, now. It couldn't be both.

It would ride the New York subway, not the shaggy little Shetland pony that Roscommon Downs kids sat on almost before they could walk. It would take classes in a heated gym, instead of swimming in a shaded billabong. It would rub shoulders with a thousand strangers every day.

And that wasn't bad. Millions of kids grew up that way. Talents and skills and strengths developed differently in the city, but they developed just as much.

But not for my child…my daughter…my son.

Not for a child who was heir to the heritage of more than a million acres of Channel Country land.

"I'm going to walk along the beach for a while," he told Shay.

"Then you'd better get off the boat." She threaded a wobbly smile across her mouth.

"This isn't the end," he blurted out.

"I guess we'll work something out. Contact. If you want it. Photos of the baby by e-mail." She stopped.

"I don't know if I can do it that way." Because he really thought it might be too hard to acknowledge that he had a child at all, when it was a child he never saw, who had a mother he'd been involved with for only a few weeks.

"Get off the boat, Dusty, please, if you're going."

*Or I'll start screaming,* said her body language.

He went without saying goodbye, and she watched him—he didn't look directly, but could see her in his peripheral vision, still standing there as he crossed the gangway—and he knew that neither of them intended the no-goodbye thing as a statement of any kind; it had just somehow got lost in the middle of too much emotion.

At his hotel he called Rae Middleton, their horse trainer near Brant, and told her that he and Brant and Callan wouldn't be bidding on either of the fillies at the thorough-bred sale this week, and flew back to Roscommon Downs the next morning.

## *Chapter Fourteen*

Shay hadn't known it was possible to feel this ill without respite.

It felt more like chemotherapy than pregnancy. Nausea ambushed her when she sat at her desk, when she rolled over in bed in her sleep, and the moment she woke up in the mornings, and she was lucky if she made it to the shower before the heaving began.

She learned to have bottled water beside her bed, in the bathroom, on her desk, in her purse, everywhere she went, all the time. Bottled water, tissues, a towel and an empty plastic bowl.

Oh, and chips.

She ate salted potato chips as if they were illegal and she was a long-term user. She lay down on the carpeted floor of her office for a ten-minute nap every two hours because staving off fatigue seemed to relieve a fraction of the nausea. She vainly attempted to take public transportation without breathing, to drink decaf coffee without tasting it, and to watch any TV commercial featuring a kitten, a baby or, for some weird reason, a house-cleaning product, without crying.

At eight weeks from her last period, she had a first prenatal checkup with an obstetrician whose name she'd been given by the family practice doctor—a general practitioner, he was called in Australia—whom she'd seen a couple of times over the past year, and her first question to the man was "Why am I feeling this bad?"

His answer reminded her of what Dusty had once said about why he wanted kids. "For all the reasons."

In the case of her nausea, these reasons ranged from "Some women just do," through to, "And you're on your own, you said. That makes it harder. If you have any unresolved issues about what's happening, and about your plans for the future—well, any source of stress doesn't help, especially when you're also dealing with a demanding career."

"Our magazine did an article a couple of months ago about the superwoman myth," she murmured. One of their staff writers had put it together and Shay had only read it as part of her work. She hadn't let it speak to her. In fact, had she subconsciously closed her ears to everything it had said?

"Exactly," the obstetrician said. "The modern woman can have it all…but sometimes that means she gets the pregnancy symptoms to match."

"Mmm, it's a theory."

"But we'll take a closer look at a few things, anyhow, to make sure there's nothing else going on."

Nothing was.

Various tests showed healthy levels of every pregnancy hormone and bit of body chemistry known to womankind, and a beautiful Thumbelina-sized baby actually—wow!—bouncing around...almost swimming...in its grainy pool of fluid on the ultrasound.

Which left Shay at nine weeks with the same unrelenting nausea and a new and even starker knowledge that her real problem wasn't physical or career-superwoman related or any of that.

It was about Dusty.

His impossible choices.

All the things he hadn't said.

The way his disappearance from her life had left a huge, horrible hole in a part of herself she hadn't even known about before.

She was so angry with him.

And she loved him.

The word tasted strange in her mouth. Overdramatic, wasn't it? But it was the only word that fit with the huge, horrible hole, so...so...

So, oh, against all logic and plans and good sense, she loved him, and no wonder she felt nauseous at least twenty-three hours a day!

At nine and a half weeks of official pregnancy—why did doctors count it that way? Technically, it meant she'd been pregnant before she and Dusty had even met!—and eight weeks since she'd first flown to Roscommon Downs, she made plans to fly there again. Whether this was to tell him she loved him or that she was so angry with him that her stomach had turned permanently inside out, she had no idea.

She didn't tell him in advance that she was coming. The mail plane dropped her off like a big, queasy, potato-chip-and-bottled-water-toting parcel on Thursday afternoon, and there he stood beside a four-wheel drive at the edge of the airstrip, meeting the flight but not knowing that he'd be meeting her.

His strong body was silhouetted against the yawning blue of an outback sky, and even though the airstrip was no longer surrounded by a pretty lake, she could hear and see the pelicans and pink cockatoos in the distance, where one of the river's main channels ran. It was so familiar, and so scary, too.

Dusty would normally have moved toward the plane at this point, to take the two boxes of deliveries. Shay actually saw and recognized the way his body was about to uncoil from its lazy shoulder lean against the vehicle, but as soon as he realized who she was, he froze.

She reached him and just one word broke from his lips.

"Shay…" He flipped his sunglasses up and wiped his fingers across his eyes before dropping the dark lenses back into place.

"I am so angry with you!" she said and burst into tears.

He reached out his arms and she stumbled into them. "Yeah, and I'm pretty angry with both of us." His voice vibrated in his chest, right against her ear.

She heard the thud of Grant's boots on the hard dirt. "Uh, Dusty? You want me to put these beside the vehicle?"

"Thanks," Dusty said, over her head.

"Looks like you're busy, so…" Grant didn't finish.

As the pilot returned to the plane, Dusty added in a low tone, "And I've never been happier to see anyone in my life. Oh hell, Shay…"

She balled her hands into fists and tried to push him away. "Hell is right. I am so ill. I throw up five times a day. It would be ten times a day if I didn't suck constantly on salt and fat and carbs."

"As a very wise woman once said to me, a broken heart is *the* best flavor enhancer."

"No, it's not!" she sobbed. "Nothing enhances any flavor, right now, and my broken heart is killing me."

"You and me, both, sweetheart," he whispered. "What can we do about it? There must be something we can do."

"Tell me you love me! That's all. It's pathetic, isn't it? To come all this way just to beg you to say that?"

"No, dear God, not when it's true, not if it's how you feel, too…"

She hardly heard him. She was crying too hard. "But that's what I want. And you never said it in Sydney, when you told me what you wanted for our child. You never even said, 'I know we can't talk about love so soon, but let's make a commitment to each other for the sake of the baby.' You said nothing!"

"I didn't mean it that way."

"You left me with two impossible choices and no ground for either of them to take root in, and I'm ill about it and I'm angry and I love you anyway. I must, because nothing else makes sense. You gave me your ultimatum, Dusty, so here's mine." She raised her head, not caring what kind of a swollen, red-eyed mess she was in, nor that the tears still streamed down her cheeks while the sobs shook her shoulders. "If you don't love me…if you can't use that word to fill the huge, horrible hole inside you…if you don't have a huge, horrible hole the way I do…then tell me so. If you love me, then say it, because you were right, before. It's simple. It's so simple. And I can't stop crying."

"I love you, Shay." He tightened his arms around her and her fists relaxed back into hands—hands that wanted to hold him hard and never let him go. He kissed her neck in a long, sweet trail, and he smelled, as always, perfect.

"I love you, too, Dusty. I love you. See? Do you see?" She dragged in a shaky breath through her swollen nose.

He found a clean cotton handkerchief in his pocket and whispered, "Here…" and she wiped her eyes. Fifty yards away, the mail plane's engines began to rev up and its propellers began to whirl.

"It's crazy," she said, "but it fills the hole."

"But is it really simple?" He stroked her hair back from her forehead, touched her cheek and her neck and her mouth as if he couldn't yet believe she was real. "That's where I get stuck, Shay. I always thought it would be. I've looked for it. With Rebecca. With Mandy. I thought it would be simple right up until the moment when you told me about the baby and then—" He stopped.

The plane began to taxi along the strip of red dirt, but her words defied the noise of the engine. "I'm coming to live at Roscommon Downs."

"What?" he yelled. "You said—"

"Because if we love each other, it makes sense. That's where it's simple. That's where you were right, Dusty. If I follow my heart, it takes me home."

"And home could be here? Not in Sydney or New York?" He shook his head, as if he didn't believe her. "You made it sound like a life sentence. You seemed to hate me for it. You turned around on that ferry. We didn't even say goodbye. We haven't e-mailed or spoken or—"

She stopped him with her fingers pressed to his lips. "Yes. Home could be here. Home is here. If we're a family, not two separate, uncommitted people making a plan to protect the baby's heritage. If we love each other and stay true to that. If that's what leads us forward."

"It's what led me, in Sydney."

"But you never said it, you didn't say anything like it."

"Because I didn't know. Not how strong it was. Not until I got back here and there was the huge, horrible void. And because I was so determined to be clear about the plan. I didn't want to make vague promises, the kind I've sometimes heard Jane make to her kids when she's frazzled and tired. 'We'll see…' when really it means, 'The answer's no, but I don't want to fight about it right now.' I thought if were going to fight about Roscommon Downs versus the city it had to be now, and it had to be honest. I had to be honest about how important it was to me that our child should know this life, this place. You had to know that three or four years in the city, and a promise to move back there later on if our child…our children…aren't interested in cattle farming, was the best I could do. It's still the best I can do, Shay."

He looked into her eyes and she understood the value of what he was telling her, and the sacrifice, understood the sacrifices she was prepared to make, too, and suddenly they didn't seem like sacrifices at all.

"It's more than enough," she whispered.

"Are you sure? So fast?"

She told him about her talk with Sarah in New York, and about the doubts she'd begun to acknowledge in her heart even before she'd first come here, and finished, "Besides, throwing up five times a day since you left doesn't tell you I'm sure?"

"Sweetheart, it tells me you're pregnant…." He kissed her, and held her, and then they drove across the red dirt, following their hearts home.

## *Epilogue*

"So that's why I told Rae not to go ahead and bid on the filly," Dusty said. He turned his head to smile at Shay. "Even though the horse looked to have energy and heart and legs, with the breeding to match."

"Sometimes, you have to go with your gut," Callan agreed.

Brant nodded, also. "And sometimes your gut makes up its mind pretty fast."

"I don't know, *gut?*" His fiancée, Misha, also known as Princess Artemisia Helena of Langemark, wrinkled her nose and grinned at him. "Ladies, we can't argue the *pretty fast* part, since we each fell in love with one of these guys within a few weeks of meeting him, you, Shay, and you, Jacinda, thanks to the 'Wanted: Outback Wives' campaign and me in spite of its pernicious influence, but are we in agreement that it's the gut that's involved, here? I don't think so!"

"It's definitely the heart," Shay said. She felt Dusty's hand slip into hers, with a feeling of belonging that felt so familiar and so right. "I don't suppose we'd ever get our men to use the word in mixed company, but they know it's the heart not the gut."

"Hey," Dusty protested. "Who was it who detailed to me exactly how many times a day she was throwing up, largely because things looked like they hadn't worked out for us? That's the gut talking, not the heart."

"That's—" Shay stopped.

That was the baby.

She'd almost reached the end of her first trimester, now. She'd begun to feel a lot better, and hadn't yet started to show. The pregnancy was still a secret between herself and Dusty, however, and they hadn't yet talked about how or when they would share it. If they weren't careful, their friends would soon guess.

The next race was due to run in a few minutes. Was now the moment to spill the news to Callan and Jacinda, and Misha and Brant? She and Dusty looked at each other, smiled at each other, couldn't look away.

"You two…" said Jacinda. "What haven't you told us?"

She was a willowy brunette, who'd been engaged to Callan Woods for almost four months now. They'd left their kids—Callan's two boys and Jacinda's four-year-old daughter—with Callan's mother to make the short hop by air to Birdsville for the annual spring racing carnival. Shay had only met Jac for the first time last night, but already felt as if the two of them would soon be friends.

"Yes, you two, spill!" Misha commanded—because *commanded* was really the only word you could use.

She did that sometimes.

She was a princess and she issued commands.

Shay had trouble getting rid of the mental image of a

glittering tiara on her Scandinavian blond head, and even more trouble equating this woman with the down-to-earth farm girl in the curly brown wig whom she'd interviewed for the magazine back in May.

*…Although that's my fault more than hers*, Shay knew.

She'd spent too long working in magazine journalism to find it easy to treat celebrities of Misha's status as normal human beings. Spoiled prima donnas, yes. Normal human beings, no. Misha didn't seem to be a prima donna, and she was clearly seriously in love with Brant, who'd pursued her all the way to Langemark to make sure of what they each felt, but Shay suspected that the imaginary tiara might stick around for a while, all the same.

"So should we spill?" Dusty said, leaning to say the words softly in her ear, then brushing her mouth with a quick, crooked kiss.

"Let's," she whispered back.

"We're having a baby!" he announced, then added with pride, as if this were a credit to his own personal testosterone levels, "Shay's been sick as a dog."

Since he'd never failed to bring her bottled water, potato chips, tissues, a towel or a bowl when she'd needed them, and had twice during the past two weeks cooked her Prim's bean-and-pasta soup recipe at ten o'clock at night, once in the homestead kitchen at Roscommon Downs and once in her apartment in Sydney, because it was the only thing that seemed as if it might taste right and settle her stomach enough for her to get to sleep without a long and unpleasant side trip to the bathroom…she didn't hit him.

Misha clapped her hands. "A baby? Really? By accident? You know what? I think there's a lot to be said for that! Well…when it's with the right person, which it obviously is for you two, and—" She stopped, and took Shay totally by surprise with a big, warm hug. "It's wonderful! I am so happy for you!"

"Thank you!" Shay hugged her back. "Thank you! We're happy, too!"

Misha pulled back enough to hold her at arm's length. "And you look great, not as if you've been sick as a dog at all."

She was smiling.

Shay smiled back.

Misha looked different, somehow. What had suddenly changed?

Oh.

The imaginary tiara had gone.

"The horses are going into the barrier," Callan reported.

"We have Saltbush Bachelor running in this one, right?" Jacinda said, leaning close against him and stealing his binoculars. He used the opportunity to squeeze her tush.

"It's his fifty-second start," he said. "I'm not sure how much he's got left. But one of the bookies said number three, in the red-and-green silks, is going for auction soon. He's had three wins and a second out of seven starts, good-tempered stallion, lively but easy to handle, and the bookie thought the owner might consider an offer today. We should look at him in the race as much as we look at Salty."

"Salty's not sure about getting into the gate, it looks like," Brant said.

"Pete wasn't sure about entering him," Dusty told the others. "But he decided he was fit. It's really a question of whether the horse wants it."

"Whether he's got the—" Brant stopped.

"The heart, darling?" Misha teased him.

"Well, yeah. You can talk about a horse's heart, as an outback man, it's when you start talking about your own

that it gets just that little bit unmasculine." He looked
down at her, with a softness in his eyes that said he was
pretty capable of unmasculine language where his own
personal princess was concerned. It was exactly the same
way that Dusty looked at Shay.

The horse finally agreed to go where he was meant to,
the barrier light came on, and a moment later the an-
nouncer over the loudspeaker system said, "They're racing!" which brought an electric tension to the entire crowd.

Callan stole the binoculars back from Jacinda and glued
them to his face. "Come on, Salty," Shay heard him mutter.
"Don't get yourself hemmed in at the rail."

Dusty and Brant exchanged a significant, satisfied look,
and from what Dusty had told her about Callan, Shay understood what it meant. Callan cared about their horses
again, cared about his whole future again, thanks to
Jacinda's appearance in his life, and Shay knew it would
never have happened without her magazine—the magazine she would be resigning from, she and Dusty had decided, two weeks before the baby was due.

It was still a little scary, and she wondered sometimes if one day she might be ambushed with regret.
How did you reach that final state of certainty, she wondered. Not just certainty about love, because this certainty she already had. Certainty about shared lives, for
better or for worse, all the decisions and choices and
compromises two people had to make together during
the course of a marriage.

"Salty, get out a bit wider and make your run," Callan
said. To the jockey, he added, "Come on, Garrett, doesn't
he have anything left?"

"I don't think he does, Callan," Dusty said. "I think he's
looking forward to a cushy future in stud. But look at
number three in the red and green."

Even as he spoke, the trouble came. Number three began to make his run just as another horse veered out slightly wider from the rail and there was a misstep and a clash of hooves. For a moment, the jockey in the red-and-green silks looked as if he'd lost control and might also lose his ride. If he fell, there were at least three horses coming right behind him who could trample him into the red outback dust. Shay saw the ambulance start around the outside of the track and her spine began to crawl.

But then the horse got its footing back and you'd have sworn he almost flipped his jockey right back into the saddle. The collective breath of the crowd let out and, even though the ambulance kept moving, it wasn't needed now. The horse had lost ground, but he didn't seem to care. He simply stretched out a little farther, almost flew across the ground and came home by half a length, ahead of a tangle of horsey names that Shay couldn't make out over the indistinct public address system.

"…and Saltbush Bachelor is last of all," the race caller said.

Well, that had been clear enough!

Callan, Dusty and Brant shook their heads ruefully, and stayed silent with disappointment for a while.

"But I tell you what, let's make the owner of number three an offer," Callan finally said. "What's his name? I couldn't hear."

"Rock-a-bye Baby," Brant said. "Which could be an appropriate omen, right?"

"We'll make the offer," Dusty said. "Shay? Do you think? Sweetheart?" He tightened his hold on her and looked into her face, seeking confirmation.

"Yes," she said, and the word tasted good in her mouth. "Yes! I've never been a part of buying a racehorse before. Yes, let's do it!"

"Just like that?" Misha grinned. "Now, what is that? Gut or heart? Or more of a rash, illogical impulse?"

"Definitely a rash, illogical impulse," Dusty said.

The three men looked at each other, reading faces, making decisions, looking at the women they loved. It was a nice moment. Shay felt something settle and cement itself deep inside her—a calm and total certainty about the future, and the decisions she'd made and would go on making with Dusty down the years.

She was having a baby. She and Dusty would get married in some quiet, simple way, and she would become friends with these two women, Jacinda and the princess, and the friendship and her marriage would last the rest of her life.

The little niggle of fear evaporated like water in the desert.

This was right.

All of it.

"So?" she said, grinning, as the certainty spread like heat inside her. "We're making an offer on a horse we've seen in just one race?"

The men knew each other pretty well, and Dusty spoke for all of them…and not just about horses…when he laced Shay's fingers through his, leaned his long, hard body against her and said with a slow, steady smile, "What can I say? Sometimes you just know."

\* \* \* \* \*

*Experience the anticipation, the thrill of the chase
and the sheer rush of falling in love!
Turn the page for a sneak preview of a new book
from Harlequin Romance
THE REBEL PRINCE by Raye Morgan
On sale August 29th wherever books are sold*

"Oh, no!"

The reaction slipped out before Emma Valentine could stop it, for there stood the very man she most wanted to avoid seeing again.

He didn't look any happier to see her.

"Well, come on, get on board," he said gruffly. "I won't bite." One eyebrow rose. "Though I might nibble a little," he added, mostly to amuse himself.

But she wasn't paying any attention to what he was saying. She was staring at him, taking in the royal blue uniform he was wearing, with gold braid and glistening badges decorating the sleeves, epaulettes and an upright collar. Ribbons and medals covered the breast of the short, fitted jacket. A gold-encrusted sabre hung at his side. And suddenly it was clear to her who this man really was.

She gulped wordlessly. Reaching out, he took her elbow and pulled her aboard. The doors slid closed. And finally she found her tongue.

"You…you're the prince."

He nodded, barely glancing at her. "Yes. Of course."

She raised a hand and covered her mouth for a moment. "I should have known."

"Of course you should have. I don't know why you didn't." He punched the ground-floor button to get the elevator moving again, then turned to look down at her. "A relatively bright five-year-old child would have tumbled to the truth right away."

Her shock faded as her indignation at his tone asserted itself. He might be the prince, but he was still just as annoying as he had been earlier that day.

"A relatively bright five-year-old child without a bump on the head from a badly thrown water polo ball, maybe," she said defensively. She wasn't feeling woozy any longer and she wasn't about to let him bully her, no matter how royal he was. "I was unconscious half the time."

"And just clueless the other half, I guess," he said, looking bemused.

The arrogance of the man was really galling.

"I suppose you think your 'royalness' is so obvious it sort of shimmers around you for all to see?" she challenged. "Or better yet, oozes from your pores like…like sweat on a hot day?"

"Something like that," he acknowledged calmly. "Most people tumble to it pretty quickly. In fact, it's hard to hide even when I want to avoid dealing with it."

"Poor baby," she said, still resenting his manner. "I guess that works better with injured people who are half asleep." Looking at him, she felt a strange emotion she couldn't identify. It was as though she wanted to prove something to him, but she wasn't sure what. "And anyway, you know you did your best to fool me," she added.

His brows knit together as though he really didn't know what she was talking about. "I didn't do a thing."

"You told me your name was Monty."

"It is." He shrugged. "I have a lot of names. Some of them are too rude to be spoken to my face, I'm sure." He glanced at her sideways, his hand on the hilt of his sabre. "Perhaps you're contemplating one of those right now."

*You bet I am.*

That was what she would like to say. But it suddenly occurred to her that she was supposed to be working for this man. If she wanted to keep the job of coronation chef, maybe she'd better keep her opinions to herself. So she clamped her mouth shut, took a deep breath and looked away, trying hard to calm down.

The elevator ground to a halt and the doors slid open laboriously. She moved to step forward, hoping to make her escape, but his hand shot out again and caught her elbow.

"Wait a minute. *You're* a woman," he said, as though that thought had just presented itself to him.

"That's a rare ability for insight you have there, Your Highness," she snapped before she could stop herself. And then she winced. She was going to have to do better than that if she was going to keep this relationship on an even keel.

But he was ignoring her dig. Nodding, he stared at her with a speculative gleam in his golden eyes. "I've been looking for a woman, but you'll do."

She blanched, stiffening. "I'll do for what?"

He made a head gesture in a direction she knew was opposite of where she was going and his grip tightened on her elbow.

"Come with me," he said abruptly, making it an order.

She dug in her heels, thinking fast. She didn't much like orders. "Wait! I can't. I have to get to the kitchen."

"Not yet. I need you."

"You what?" Her breathless gasp of surprise was soft, but she knew he'd heard it.

"I need you," he said firmly. "Oh, don't look so shocked. I'm not planning to throw you into the hay and have my way with you. I need you for something a bit more mundane than that."

She felt color rushing into her cheeks and she silently begged it to stop. Here she was, formless and stodgy in her chef's whites. No makeup, no stiletto heels. Hardly the picture of the femmes fatales he was undoubtedly used to. The likelihood that he would have any carnal interest in her was remote at best. To have him think she was hysterically defending her virtue was humiliating.

"Well, what if I don't want to go with you?" she said in hopes of deflecting his attention from her blush.

"Too bad."

"What?"

Amusement sparkled in his eyes. He was certainly enjoying this. And that only made her more determined to resist him.

"I'm the prince, remember? And we're in the castle. My orders take precedence. It's that old pesky divine rights thing."

Her jaw jutted out. Despite her embarrassment, she couldn't let that pass.

"Over my free will? Never!"

Exasperation filled his face.

"Hey, call out the historians. Someone will write a book about you and your courageous principles." His eyes glittered sardonically. "But in the meantime, Emma Valentine, you're coming with me."

If you enjoyed what you just read,
then we've got an offer you can't resist!

# Take 2 bestselling love stories FREE!

# Plus get a FREE surprise gift!

**Clip this page and mail it to Silhouette Reader Service™**

| | |
|---|---|
| **IN U.S.A.** | **IN CANADA** |
| 3010 Walden Ave. | P.O. Box 609 |
| P.O. Box 1867 | Fort Erie, Ontario |
| Buffalo, N.Y. 14240-1867 | L2A 5X3 |

**YES!** Please send me 2 free Silhouette Special Edition® novels and my free surprise gift. After receiving them, if I don't wish to receive anymore, I can return the shipping statement marked cancel. If I don't cancel, I will receive 6 brand-new novels every month, before they're available in stores! In the U.S.A., bill me at the bargain price of $4.24 plus 25¢ shipping and handling per book and applicable sales tax, if any*. In Canada, bill me at the bargain price of $4.99 plus 25¢ shipping and handling per book and applicable taxes**. That's the complete price and a savings of at least 10% off the cover prices—what a great deal! I understand that accepting the 2 free books and gift places me under no obligation ever to buy any books. I can always return a shipment and cancel at any time. Even if I never buy another book from Silhouette, the 2 free books and gift are mine to keep forever.

235 SDN DZ9D
335 SDN DZ9E

| Name | (PLEASE PRINT) | |
|---|---|---|
| Address | Apt.# | |
| City | State/Prov. | Zip/Postal Code |

*Not valid to current Silhouette Special Edition® subscribers.*

*Want to try two free books from another series?*
*Call 1-800-873-8635 or visit www.morefreebooks.com.*

\* Terms and prices subject to change without notice. Sales tax applicable in N.Y.
\*\* Canadian residents will be charged applicable provincial taxes and GST.
  All orders subject to approval. Offer limited to one per household.
  ® are registered trademarks owned and used by the trademark owner and or its licensee.

SPED04R                    ©2004 Harlequin Enterprises Limited